Make
ME
OVER
A NOVEL
JANAY HARDEN

For Ilia

CHAPTER 1

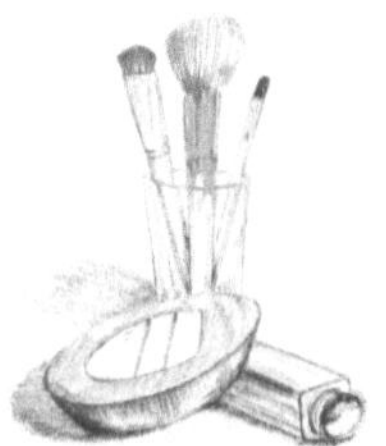

"Josephine, it's just not working out." Shelby leaned back in her old, rickety manager's chair. It groaned out the agony that churned in the pit of my stomach.

"What?" I sucked my teeth. "I've been getting to work on time ever since you put me on that . . . that improvement plan." The words vomited out of my mouth and didn't sound like anything I needed. But it wasn't up to me. *They* made all the decisions.

This was not happening. I was *not* being fired from yet again another job.

Shelby's voice squeaked through each word. Barely twenty-four herself—she was the manager at a yoga studio and in her fifth year of college. Only one year younger than me, confrontation was not her strong suit and she fired me with shifty eyes and bated breath.

"Your attendance has improved since we implemented the PIP, however, we received some . . . complaints. About your poor attitude."

Cheap plastic seats scraped across the floor as I scooted closer and cocked my head at Shelby. "Poor attitude?" Shelby and the crew won *best of the best* awards for the Center City Philadelphia location two years in a row now. Even though Shelby was hired as the manager *after* they won the award—she liked to tell people she was on the winning team.

And I was not.

"Have people been talking shit about me?" I stared Shelby dead in her eyes, only because I *knew* she was uncomfortable. If I had to be so should she.

A blind man could see I was the only Black employee here. And that was just the beginning of our differences. Everyone else went to college and worked at the yoga studio part-time for fun while it was my full-time gig. I was on the job for six months and by the second month, they had already put me on an improvement plan for time management concerns. I was the only one in the studio who didn't teach yoga. My job was solely confined to twiddling my thumbs at the front desk, getting people signed in and out for class, selling monthly member-ships, and offering water from paper cups.

They had weekly after-hours get togethers and huddled around the water cooler gossiping about nothing important to me. When I came around, the jokes and laughter died down and became tighter than the fake leather belts they wrapped around cardigan waistlines. They didn't purposely exclude me; but if she didn't know about it, she couldn't ask about it.

I knew. I saw. I heard.

They made jokes I didn't understand and went to parties that seemed like such a bore. They were Boathouse Row. Glitz, glamour, and everything Philadelphia represented in those tourist pamphlets they passed around in Center City. I was West Philadelphia, born and raised.

We were not the same.

Truth be told, I hated this fucking job anyway. It worked my nerves to no end sitting so still and watching people stretch all day to that slow ass music. I mean, yoga was great and all, and I loved the way it calmed my mind, but when I suggested we host an *R&B & Yoga* event, Shelby scoffed at me and said, *this is not the community center, Josephine.*

I wanted something with some substance, something that excited me and this place wasn't it. "You know what, it's fine." I waved my hands at Shelby. There was no use in making her job harder. They sent her in here to fire me and soften the blow.

"I'll clean out my locker and be gone within the hour." I stood and grabbed my work jacket. Or *their* work jacket. Shit.

Shelby's eyes fluttered closed and she softly exhaled a sigh of relief when I didn't bring the drama. "Thank you, Josephine. Really, this is for the best. You can find something . . . more your speed. You'll see."

The front office was a short walk to the breakroom and rows of employee lockers. I thumbed in my combination and prayed no tears would fall before I stepped my last foot out of this damn place. What a lousy job. It was my third job in one year, but who was counting.

I snatched everything out of my locker and left *their* jacket swinging on a rack. My best-friend, Amna, came through with the job posting. Amna and I met in high school. When we found out that we were both interested in history, art class, and fat cheesesteaks with the mayonnaise —I knew we would be a dynamic duo. She was also at a dead-end job outside of town at a diner and we desperately needed something different. Life couldn't be this boring, and I couldn't imagine working like a dog, sleeping, and going back every day to do it all over again. Is that why people were so grumpy and lived for beer and football?

Before my stint here at the yoga studio, I did hard time one steamy summer at the Philadelphia Zoo, and an even shorter appearance at a beauty supply store around the way.

The zoo was hot as hell; the kids were awful as they screamed and threw things at the animals. Their parents did nothing about their behavior and after a while, I couldn't tell the animals from the kids. They all looked like a pack of wild rabid— foaming at the mouth— mammals to me. I went home every day smelling like a camel's upper lip and my stress levels were through the roof. I dreamt of rhinos and every animal in the lion's kingdom. It was so bad that my boyfriend, Alonso, would make me strip my stinky clothes off at the door and had a steamy shower ready when I came home.

The beauty supply store . . . well . . . I don't know why I ever thought I could work *there*. Girls would trot in two and three at a time. They took turns distracting us, and while one employee was engaged in a heated conversation with one of their henchwomen, another would load up hollow bags with things they had no intention on paying for. It was like a game to them, to steal and get away with it. Gels, creams, packs of hair. They stuffed anything they could in their bags or under their shirts. It drove me crazy. One day, I caught one red-handed and I set her thieving ass straight, snatched the pack of hair back, and kicked her heisting ass out of the store. I yelled *and* cussed. Bet she wouldn't do that shit again.

They said they didn't want me arguing with the customers, though, and I lost that job, too.

I hated thieves. The customer was not always right. Besides, I was defending their place of business.

When I got this job, I raced home to tell Alonso and my dad. They had hired me on the spot. On the spot! I didn't know that was a thing. When I got there, I quickly learned the entire event was an "on the spot secure a job" deal. They didn't handpick me–technically I handpicked them.

I slammed the locker shut and stomped to the front, flinging the front door open. God himself must've wanted me to make a scene because a powerful gust of Philadelphia's December wind howled through and slammed the door into the side of the building. Rain was already threatening to spit, and the neon sign for the yoga studio sputtered and crackled when the force of the door hit. I shot my head around to Shelby and the other managers frowning at me, probably thinking they made the right decision.

I gave them the middle finger. Fuck all ya'll.

Marching to the Target on Broad St, I stopped inside to warm up for a second and ducked out of view in case the yoga studio tried to call the cops on me for vandalizing the door. I wiped my cold nose against the back of my gloves and pulled my beanie down on my head. A mirror in the women's section caught my eye, and I backed up to stare at myself.

Twenty-five-year-old Josephine Scott.

I was not a skinny girl, and I loved that about me. My kicks were clean, my booty was plump, and my North Face jacket sat right above my hips—just the way I liked it. That was another thing. They hated I wore Jordan's to the yoga studio. Shelby asked for something, *"a little more toned down."*

Humph. They wanted to tone *me* down.

I stared at my face in the mirror. Flawless chocolate skin without a blemish in sight. My face was beat down to the God's today, and truth be told—that's what made me late for work so often. My morning makeup routine was extensive, and I had to get better with applying lashes in fifteen minutes or less in case I wanted to keep a job. Doing my makeup was the only thing exciting about the day. Choosing colors and palettes to match my mood kept me sane in a way that no job could. Some people listened to music or books on their way to work, but I beat my face and let all the colors of the wind speak for me.

I strolled through Target for two hours; thumbing through clothes I couldn't afford, smelling perfume, and buying coffee with money I didn't have from a job I was just fired from. I checked the time on my phone a second, third, and fourth time. It took two trains to get downtown. I hated the commute, but yoga money from a *best of the best* establishment was deep and plentiful—until it wasn't. But it was more than I was making at the hair store. I could start walking to the station now, get on the train, and by the time I got home, maybe Dad or Alonso wouldn't notice that it's still only around noon— and I was home from work five hours too early.

How will they react this time? I shuffled my feet as a cold shiver slid down my back remembering Dad's anger. He damn near kicked me and Alonso out the house. Alonso didn't even do anything, but Dad was mad at me for getting fired from yet another shitty job, and so Alonso was in trouble, too.

I remembered Alonso's eyes that day I told him I was fired from the hair store. His shoulders fell like there was one second left on the buzzer and I missed the winning shot. I hated I put that look on his face and hated even more I couldn't do anything about it.

Dad never had trouble keeping a job. Not the great, Cannon Scott. Working as a production assistant at the chicken coop for the past twenty years, and a die-hard Eagles' fan for double that long. He was devoted to a job that gave him pizza parties for Christmas bonuses and left free stress-balls in the breakroom. But they paid him without fail, week after week, year after year and that was good enough for him.

I needed more. Wanted more. I was more.

I boarded the train and leaned my face against the glass. The windows stung my cheek cold. The city zipped past me. My city. Philadelphia was home and some days felt like a warm fleece straight out the dryer. It snuggled against my nose and felt safe and cozy, always ready to welcome me. Today it felt like a weighted blanket that had me trapped underneath, patching holes while new ones formed.

Dad was oh so Philadelphia and he could tell you where every important card game was played, where every crime boss still owned property from Chestnut Hill to Northern Liberties all the way to Germantown. He knew where to find the best fish platters in Kensington, and where to park so Philly parking authority didn't boot your car away, smirking while they did it. You needed guts, an insane work ethic, and a dash of luck to live in this city. He was crazy enough to do it and wanted me to believe that I was, too. Here I was, couldn't even keep a job. I was the bum of the family.

Getting on and off the first train, I sat at the station and people watched again. Maybe they were watching me, too. Had one of them gotten fired and was afraid to go home? It was possible. Where were they all going and rushing off to? Did they have careers they loved and couldn't wait to get clocked-in everyday? What did that feel like, and when would it kick in for me?

The last train came five hours too quick. With the slowest walk possible, I made my way to our row house and stood in front. My weak eyes raised up and searched for life inside. The door loomed in front of me— taller, wider, and so much meaner when you didn't have a job and a trigger finger dad.

My icy fingers grazed the doorknob, wondering if this was the last time I'd call it home.

Here we go.

CHAPTER 2

I crept into our house and eyed the walls in disgust. It was an older home and creaked and cried at every turn. Too many years of stomping and doors slammed made it sag in the middle, right in the center of the living room. Where the house was supposed to be the most lively and full of love and laughter; it was the weakest. Tip toeing to my room, I had to shake my head at my own luck. I *would* get fired on my dad's day off. He was in his bed, and I heard him watching *Family Feud,* screaming and cussing out answers from the hallway.

My bedroom was at the end of the hallway, and these depressed, repressed hardwood floors would have my dad grabbing his gun thinking someone was in the house. I held my breath and shimmied one foot at a time to my door until I was safely behind its protection, gasping for breath. I made it.

Alonso was laid on the bed, stupefied by my presence. He snatched his headphones off his ears and stared at me with wide eyes. "What are you doing here?"

"I got fired." I sat at my desk and crumpled my face in my now shaking hands.

"What the fuck, Josephine! What happened?" He sat up and searched my face for answers I didn't have.

"Keep your voice down!" I whispered and looked toward the door, hoping Dad wasn't eavesdropping. That man could hear a gunshot go off in South Philly at three a.m. in his sleep.

I explained to Alonso what Shelby said. Halfway through the story, my blood boiled and I jabbed my fists into my legs. Why did this always seem to happen to me?

Alonso kneeled in front of me and placed his hand over mine so I stopped hitting myself. "Hey, hey, it's okay." He sighed. "We'll figure something out."

"My dad is going to lose it," I sobbed.

"That he is." Alonso grabbed my hips and squeezed. "What do you need from me right now?" He looked into my eyes, running his thumb up and down my thigh.

"Just let me sit here for a minute by myself. I feel like the walls are closing in on me." I rubbed my eyes until I saw black spots. My chest rose and fell and my nose was wet.

"I'll go order lunch and make small talk with your dad so he won't come in here and bust you upside your head." Alonso tapped my shoulder. I swatted him away before his lips brushed against my forehead.

"Hey." He stood with clenched fists. A vein became visible in his neck. "We'll be okay. We'll figure it out. We always do."

A tired smile instinctively fell on my face. "We always figure it out. You're right," I agreed and blew him a kiss out the door. We would figure it out all right. Figuring it out was becoming exhausting.

My forehead was a little shiny from the day's events and the bronzer on my cheeks was dull. With my measly earnings, I could only afford drugstore makeup, and it faded faster than I lasted at a job. I combed through my small makeup collection until I found my favorite, Ruby Kiss bronzer. Grabbing a fan brush, I swept it across my cheekbones and thought about my predicament. Maybe Amna and I could take a course, a training or something. How did you find out your purpose? Was there a quiz I could take online? Something where I answered a few questions and it said *boom*, you are 75% most likely to be good at *this*. I thought the yoga gig was the perfect spot. I only had to interact with a few people and it was usually quiet. *Yeah, we see how well that worked out.* I reapplied the gloss to my lips and dabbed away the stress sheen sitting on my forehead. It was cold outside, and a light sliver of ice coated the grass. The sun peered through our West Philadelphia abode and sat on my cheekbones like it snuck out of the clouds and came looking only for my face. I closed my eyes for a second and let the sun warm me in the cold places. I loved the way my bronzer caught the light, and if I was on my deathbed tomorrow and they said *'Ms. Josephine, how you want us to do your makeup for your last day?'* I would say just get me a good bronzer and place it where my cheeks like to naturally shine. Where I shine.

Our room was the size of a semi large closet, and so Alonso and I had to be creative with space and storage. We had a full-sized bed; the same bed set I had all my life. It was pink and in the shape of a castle. Dad got it when I was a kid and in my princess phase. Now as an adult, it was a monstrosity eye sore. Every time we saved enough money to buy another one, Alonso and I had to pull the money to pay for something else that just came up. Things always just came up until a new bed wasn't a priority.

We got risers so we could store more stuff underneath the bed. Alonso liked calendars and writing things down. He had two dry-erase boards hung on the wall—one with his coaching schedule and another with different quotes he used to motivate himself. Every morning, he woke up and had a phrase or something he said to himself, and he made me say it, too. Alonso was also between jobs and spent most of his time coaching basketball to middle and high school kids. He sometimes secured a few high-paying weekly coaching sessions with the *Philadelphia 76er's* players kids, but it wasn't consistent.

Alonso and I met in high school. Some girls in the 11th grade said that I was looking at them funny. Like I said, I ain't never been no skinny chick and boys were always gawking at my booty. When the boys looked, so did the girls—but they were mad. Like I *wanted* boys looking at me. Shit, I wanted money, and *they* didn't have it. Next thing I knew—hair, arms, and fists would be flying. I can't say that it was always them— if I'm being honest. Once they rolled their eyes at me, I damn near dislocated my neck off my shoulders to give them shade right back.

During one particular school-fight in the cafeteria, Alonso came out of nowhere and scooped me up, just as I was about to land a full-face punch to the leader of their pack. She was humungous and looked like Rasputia. She tripped people in the hallway, and like a true bully, laughed and dared someone to challenge her.

I stopped swinging and my mouth fell open at Alonso whisking me away from the circle. High school, misunderstood, Black girl anger, seethed through me and if they wanted to fight, we could.

"Why you do that?" I demanded.

"They were about to fuck you up!" he replied.

"Were not! I was just fine!" I tried scrambling out of his arms, but he hoisted me out of the cafeteria just as school security rushed in to shut down the melee.

We didn't really know each other at the time; the school was huge and had so many students that we never crossed paths. After the fight, they suspended me for two weeks. Alonso found me on social media, and we talked every day I was suspended. He said he never met no one that got suspended from school for two whole weeks, and that I was a badass. By the time I returned to school, he was my man and I was his girl.

Years later, we shared a princess bed, love, and sometimes— my dad's wrath.

I turned around in my chair and stared at myself in my little vanity mirror. It, too, was princess themed and matched my bed set. I nervously slathered some edge control over my hairline and swooped it back into perfection. I took a few deep breaths, trying to calm and steady my hands.

I grabbed my phone and thumbed through my starred contacts until I reached Ms. Marta's face.

Ms. Marta lived in a row home directly behind us with the backs of our houses facing each other. I walked through a small alleyway every day to visit her. Ms. Marta and I had lived behind each other for over fifteen years, but it was one warm afternoon at the farmer's market in town when I was in middle school that we officially met. She was arguing with a vendor about the price of some fruit, and I came downtown to buy my favorite shea butter from the stand next to her. She was all of 5 foot 4 and she carried weight around her stomach, arms, and heavy legs like they were never meant to part. She was a light shade of butter pecan and huffed and puffed her way through cuss words that were never really directed at anyone in particular. She told the melon man that she was from Lancaster Avenue and she could tell by the small size of his melons he was a jack of all trades and a master of none.

I giggled. She was spicy—I liked spicy.

We started out conversing about the different foods at the market, but once we realized we were neighbors, she turned into one of my best-friends. She was the closest thing to a mom I ever had.

I pressed send and called her.

"Hell-lo dear! You on your lunch break?" she answered. My stomach danced. I wanted this to be a social call, but it wasn't.

"No, Ms. Marta. I got fired today," I hissed into my phone. From my room, I heard my dad's tv.

"Fired again? From that stretch arm strong place? Girl, you know you can't keep a job to save your life." She chuckled and coughed. I failed to see the humor in this.

"Ms. Marta, you know my dad charges us rent now! And I have to pay my cell phone bill, and you know Alonso's birthday is coming up. And I have . . ."

"Hush. Hush. You know you ain't have no business at that place, no way. It ain't what you love." She spoke each word through a crunch. She was eating potato chips.

"What am I going to do, Ms. Marta?"

"You are going to do what every girl in America does. Go out there, smile at them people, and get yourself a new job. You keep getting these dead-end jobs that you hate, and it don't make no damn sense to me."

I swallowed away a golf ball in my throat and tucked my feet behind my chair. I died a little inside. "But *most* people don't like what they do, Ms. Marta. It's not the job, it has to be me. I'm the problem."

"True. Before I retired, I had a few jobs that I hated. If we got new PTO in January, I guarantee you me, it was used and abused by at least March. Have you told the Cannon, yet?" Ms. Marta's tone was hushed like he could hear her.

"No," I whispered back. She knew like I *knew*. Cannon could be a cannon.

"You would get fired on the *one* day the Cannon is home." She coughed out another laugh.

"I know!!" I hissed into the phone.

"Make sure you go in there and talk to him. And be honest. Tell him you hate that fucking place and you don't want to go back. And that's that. And then when you're done, go to the Jamaican store over on 54th St and pick me up some beef patties and come over later so we can brainstorm finding you another job."

"I'm going to tell him." I nodded into the phone as nervous sweat made its way to my neck. I gazed toward the wall where Dad's lair lay on the other side.

Time for the real family feud.

CHAPTER 3

Tap tap tap. A quick, two second knock on his door and I immediately turned to walk away. Maybe he was asleep.

"What?" he barked.

Shit.

"Hey Dad, it's me."

"Josie? Why are you home? Come in here now."

Each painful step felt like I was walking the death planks.

Dad was lying on top of his bed with his latest girlfriend, Rose. They were watching tv and sharing a bowl of popcorn. He sat up in the middle of the bed and glared at me with suspicious eyes. His heavy belly, arms, and legs made the mattress creak with every move, and I wondered how Rose even enjoyed sleeping next to the meaty man, he took up so much space.

"What are you doing here?" He frowned.

Not even a hello.

"I um . . . Well . . . I was hoping uh . . ."

"Spit it out, girl. You got ants in your pants? This my one good day off and I don't want to waste time lollygagging with you. You know I hate all that stuttering." He muted the tv and cocked his head, waiting for me to speak.

Rose's head ping-ponged between us, popcorn lingering between her fingers.

"I was laid off today," I shot out. It tasted like nasty cough medicine sitting on my tongue, but there was nothing to wash it down with except the cold hard truth.

He stared at me. Didn't even blink. "Laid off? Don't be cute. Your ass got fired again, didn't you?" His top lip curled like he smelled something rotten.

Rose stiffened on the bed.

"Dad, it wasn't my fault this time, honestly! I was coming in on time and I did everything they asked me to do." I stood in the room's corner and waited for his word assaults that were sure to come.

"And I guess this was just like the time before that and the time before that, right?" Dad hopped off the bed and slid into his dogged slippers. Year of slipping into them after ten-hour work days had them flat as a pancake. He paced around the room. "Do you think I'm supposed to just take care of you and your boyfriend while you *find* yourself? We don't have that luxury, Josephine. The bills got to be paid today. Food has to be bought. Utilities kept on. What do you think this is, a soup kitchen?" He pulled a black Eagles sweater over his head and fumbled with the neck shirt collar.

I knew I should've waited to tell him, but the last time this happened and I waited—he went ballistic. "Alonso works, too. You're not taking care of us!" My nostrils flared. I was already beating myself up and down Allegheny Ave about this and here he was—nailing me in the coffin. Regret washed through me, and I was rolling on a river.

Rose seemed to wince smaller with each curse word and

the intensity at which it ripped from Dad's mouth. Bet she hadn't seen this side of him before. She slipped into her shoes. "This is a family thing. I'm gonna go," she mumbled. Her hair was short and sat at her nape. She grabbed her neck and nervously yanked.

Dad made everyone jumpy.

He stared at me with his arms folded across his chest. He didn't say goodbye to Rose or even acknowledge she was leaving. His disappointed face was glued to me and forever seared into my mind.

Damn, nothing was worse than *that* face.

I had been his disappointment ever since Mom died. Nine months pregnant with me with a perfectly, uneventful pregnancy. Yet, her heart seemed to give out during the delivery. She went into cardiac arrest, slipped into a brief coma, and died. After it was all said and done and a white sheet flitted over Mom's cold face, I was the only thing left.

What a terrible feeling it was as a child to think you had somehow killed your mom simply by being born. If you were capable of killing your mom, then surely Dad wouldn't know pure happiness because of you. From what I was told, Mom and Dad weren't seriously dating. They weren't married, and I wasn't even sure they loved each other. Dad wasn't the lovey dovey, recollecting about fond memories, type of man anyway. He was soft and hard at the same time, but his version of soft looked like obligation. I was the burden he was tied to—bound to. He was a girl-dad but didn't want to be. Didn't know how to be.

Bits and pieces of a phantom story about mom's death is what remained, repeated by Dad, but only when he was upset that he was the surviving parent. My mom's family says they fought for custody of me but that "no good judge" was soft on father's and awarded Dad custody. I wondered what type of life I would have if I lived with my mama's family? It wasn't like they were living the good life, either. They lived in Mount Airy, a suburb of Philly, and while they had more green grass and open space, would I be just another mouth to feed? Another reminder that a mama had lost a daughter, and every time they searched my face they would find hints of her.

A ghost parent haunted me every day. When I was in elementary school, they had a Mother's Day breakfast and another student said, '*but Josie ain't got no mommy.*' I hauled off and pushed that boy down to the ground and squished his cupcake between my no-mommy-having fingers.

I was kicked out of the Mother's Day event. My dad told the principal he was glad I wasn't scared to fight boys. He added, in real life, can't no girl beat up on no man, but at least his daughter could scare one really good.

When Ms. Marta entered my life, it was like she saw me. Me. Saw the anger, questions, and confusion. Saw it where I didn't see it, couldn't see it, was too young to see it. I needed a woman's touch—and she appeared.

When Rose finally slipped out of the room and the front door shut, Dad really roared to life without an audience. "I don't expect you to do nothing, Josephine. Nothing! You just can't do right, can you? All I ask is for you and your boyfriend to work and you can't even do that. And coaching ain't no real job no way." He paced the floor. Grabbing his cell phone on the nightstand, he flung the blackout curtains in his room back and used the sunlight to get a better view as he scrolled through his phone and huffed. "I know what to do." His fingers tip tapped across the screen, eyes furious.

I was scared to ask. "What?"

"They're hiring down at my job. I'm going to get you an interview."

"Dad, I don't want to work at your job." I collapsed into his lounge chair. Nothing could be worse than *that*.

"Are you too good for a chicken coop? It's an honest living, and it's stable. It's simple work and you can't mess it up. Even you." Dad nodded like he figured it all out and was silly for not thinking of it sooner.

Yes. Yes. Absolutely. I wanted to say. I *was* too good for a chicken coop and even though he was mean as shit—so was *he*. He came home from work every day with feathers attached to him from the rootie to the tootie. He permanently smelled like a three-piece leg and thigh platter with a side of mac. The only thing missing was ketchup and hot sauce. Who purposely went and signed up for that shit?

"In order for you and your man to live here, you gon' have to get you a job. And being as though here I am offering you one, I suggest you don't block your blessings." Dad sat beside me on the bed and folded his arms.

An angry tear made its way down my face. Dad patted my hand. "Listen. I know you hate boring work. But it's what we do. We work, pay bills, and maybe have some fun. Get serious about something, Josephine. You've had a couple years since you graduated high school and it's time you figure this out."

"By the way, I have something to tell you." He shifted his gaze.

"Oh?"

"I'm thinking about asking Rose to marry me." He looked out of the window, now avoiding eye contact.

"Huh? Marry? You don't even know that girl?" I gave him a dirty look. I saw her four times at the house, and that was just in the last month.

Women always thought Dad needed a wife because he was raising a daughter on his own. They came in trying to change everything from the furniture to the color of the toilet paper. If I was the princess, he was the king, and they thought we needed a queen.

Some girlfriends I hoped he would marry, he let them think he was serious but after years of watching him get close and then back away, I realized he didn't like to be tied down or attached to anything long term except the Eagles, the chicken coop, and his barber.

I didn't want to work at a chicken coop plant. Didn't want to talk about 401k's, sick time, and paystubs. Didn't want to think about dad getting married. I just wanted to make money and do something interesting. The thought alone made my stomach turn. But when Dad looked at me, I couldn't be a burden anymore. "Fine, Dad. You can set up an interview at the plant. I'll check it out." I pulled at a fuzz ball on his bed.

"You can think I'm being mean all you want. But I need you to be stronger. The world is tough and you have to be tougher. Start figuring shit out, Josie." Dad patted me on the head. "Now go make me something to eat. Please," he added a second later like it was an afterthought.

"Sure, Dad," I murmured and felt all the air suck out of my lungs.

CHAPTER 4

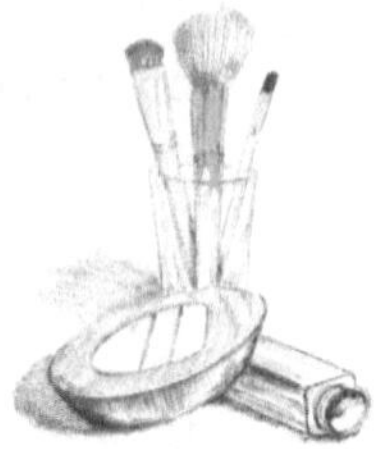

Two weeks later with my bottom lip poked down, I swept the black liner under my eye and sighed. My phone lit up on my bed and jiggled a soft hum. I popped the cap back onto the eyeliner stick and tossed it into my makeup kit.

"Interview Scheduled," the email said. I cringed and turned back to my princess mirror.

"What's wrong?" Alonso came up behind me and peered over my shoulder.

The chicken coop was a revolving door of on-the-spot interviews. I could have gone to one of their mega hiring fests weeks ago, but I told Dad it was *that time of the month*. He rebuked anything feminine, and *"lady"* related as he put it. That was the only thing that got him off my back and bought me some time. When I couldn't put it off any longer, Dad set up a personal interview at the chicken coop with one of his bosses.

A pink envelope stared at me from the electric company. The electric bill was my responsibility. They used to send yellow envelopes when the bill was due. The last few months, the envelope was pink. Pink meant past due.

"This damn interview my dad set up. They want me to come in this week." I spun around. The chair creaked under my weight and spreading hips. It was made for an adolescent, but it had me instead.

"What's the schedule?" Alonso furrowed his eyebrows and pulled his shirt over his head.

"The usual. Monday through Friday. You ever wonder why there are more weekdays than weekend days?" I stared at Alonso, dead serious.

"Josephine, don't start. Just go to the interview and see what they say. What do you have to lose?"

I faced Alonso and shimmied my jeans up past my hips. "Uh, I don't know. Maybe just my dignity." I flicked my tongue and frowned.

"Are you serious right now? Your dignity? What have you bought in the past three months besides makeup and food?"

These days my happiness lived in food and makeup. Alonso knew it, and if he knew it, that meant Dad knew it, too. Maybe there was a *reason* for him to be so hard on me. Maybe I needed direction.

"Electric. That's what I bought, smart ass. And don't turn this around on me. Mister, I coach kids' basketball during the week, but run with a gang on the weekends." I zipped my jacket and faced Alonso—ready for whatever.

Alonso glared at me. Hurt and shock rang over his face.

A bomb was dropped. A line crossed.

When you had a certain amount of money to spend, was it always right to spend it on bills or something responsible? How often were you allowed to buy things that made you happy?

Alonso moved in with me and Dad in our senior year of high school. It was a scandal when it first happened, and Dad cussed everyone who had something to say. They were getting ready to send Alonso to the alternative school for vandalizing school property. He wasn't the one who did it, but he ran with the crew who did, and in our school that was grounds for immediate expulsion. They were tough on crime in the high school zones, but I saw at least one burglary a month in our neighborhood and had to walk past and *act* like I didn't see at least two more. How was it that the high schools were constantly policed and patrolled, ready to pluck kids out for any infraction, but not our streets? How was it that little old ladies got knocked down as robbers fled past them and nothing happened, but they expelled students for toilet papering a school during mischief night? So many things seemed ass backward weird to me. More reason I was never a good student; the things I was taught in school never seemed to match my reality. And yet, my claim to fame should be a steady pension in thirty years, according to my dad and the world. How did people do the same job every day for years? Didn't they wake up one day and want something . . . different? I always wanted something different.

The princess wanted to see what was beyond the castle.

"Listen. I shouldn't have said that. I'm sorry. I'm just tired of this hard knock life." I cupped Alonso's face. His waves were shining and moisturized today. His face was bright, and I could smell the shea butter he lathered on his face this morning.

When the school was getting ready to do away with Alonso, his mom and her boyfriend were planning a move to Delaware to be closer to his older sisters. A *quieter life,* they called it. They wanted to *move out of the city and breathe,* they said. Philly was always hard to breathe in, and sometimes it made you hold every breath you had. Many people were existing just fine like this but the more I tried, the more I choked.

Alonso's mom told him he was seventeen and he could make the choice to move himself. They told him he was old enough to figure it out. Imagine that, leaving the option open for a teenager to decide where he was supposed to live. He could come with them to Delaware and finish his senior year at a new school or he could stay in Philly but he had to make his own way. They weren't supporting him and were cutting him off. Actual tears sat in Alonso's eyes when he told me that story, but he never let them fall. He seemed used to being let down by people, like he almost accepted it. I knew the feeling well, like you were a burden. I hated that for him. Delaware was light years away, as well as the life he grew up knowing.

I begged Dad. I told him all day and night the benefits of Alonso moving in. It would only be temporary. He would help pay some bills. Dinner would always be done. I lied as much as I pleaded. When Dad finally relented and said '*yes, your boyfriend can move into our home*,' it was the same day I found out about Alonso's *other* family.

Curtis was a member of the ruthless Young Lords of West Philly Gang. The gang started out as regular outcast Black boys. Parents working too much or not enough. Too focused on their own lives to pay attention and so they found a family in gangs. There was a recent rash of break-ins and car thefts in the neighborhood. You could unload groceries out of your car and come back to an empty space where your car sat seconds ago. They were smart and could use computers to program almost anything from anywhere.

Curtis was their gang leader, out of prison the past few years. I never met him, but Alonso described him as someone you didn't say no to. You couldn't say no. It was Curtis who helped Alonso fight when he was getting jumped. It was Curtis who said Alonso was untouchable when people tried to mess with him when they realized he was all alone and had no people. Curtis gave him a place to stay when Alonso and his mom fought. It was in gang life where he found a home. We didn't tell Dad that part, though. I mean, it could be a hard knock life with my dad too, but he wasn't into anything more illegal than stealing movies on his Firestick and buying burner CD's at the flea market. Dad would have my ass if he knew Alonso was gang-banging.

Alonso pulled me out of my thoughts when he wrapped his arms around my waist. I laid my head on his chest and listened to his heartbeat. Within seconds, our heartbeats matched, and I smiled to myself. We always fell into this familiar dance of being in sync, even if we weren't.

"Josephine, I'm sorry, too. I want us to get a place. Do our own thing. I know you don't like Curtis and them, but they're really not that bad. I'll introduce you soon, when the time is right. But everything we want right now we need money for. You get it your way, and I will get it mine." Alonso's voice was deep and I felt the intensity of his words. But his eyes . . . his eyes were full of sunsets and dreams that inched us further away from the city.

Just like mine.

"Get our own place? You think we're ready for that?" Numbers ran through my mind and the glare of a pink envelope stared back at me. I couldn't even hold down the electric bill, let alone an entire apartment? My bedroom housed me at every stage of my life, but it was time for something new. Could we do it, financially?

Alonso's lip curled into a weak smile. He was convincing

himself, just like me. "I think we can do anything we set our minds to. In the meantime, let's get you to this chicken coop interview, so we can use that as a launching pad to get closer to our dreams." He kissed my forehead and pointed to the wall where his dry-erase board hung. In his handwriting it said, *'the dream only works if you do.'*

I stood on my tippy toes and kissed his lips. Alonso towered over me by almost a foot, and I loved it. Most nights when we lie were in bed, he wrapped me in his arms and legs. He was so long I couldn't tell where I began and he ended.

"I love you," I whispered.

"Love you more. Now get to Ms. Marta, she's waiting." He slapped my butt.

I made the short trek down the back alleyway to Ms. Marta's row home behind ours. She gave me a key years ago, and I paced in place, trying to jiggle them into the door and stay warm at the same time on this cold, January afternoon.

"You ready, Ms. Marta?" I called out. I pulled my beanie down over my hair and cinched my jacket closer to my chest, searching for heat. I could see my breath when I spoke.

"I'm in here, Josie baby." Ms. Marta's Puerto Rican drawl beckoned me to her room.

I made my way down the hallway, and the putrid smell of her trashcan hit me square in the face. I scrunched my nose and covered my mouth. In her bedroom, she laid across the bed in her nightgown and empty Styrofoam cartons littered around her. She had on one sock.

"Ms. Marta? I thought we were going to the market today? We're meeting Amna there."

"I'm not in the mood for no market today. It's about to rain." Ms. Marta turned over in bed like it hurt to move. The mattress protector she insisted on having squeaked under her with every roll. She winced as she leaned on her side, and she turned over like a rotisserie chicken.

"I know you don't like to go out when it's raining. I checked the weather before I left, and it wasn't supposed to rain until later." I pulled out my phone to confirm.

"Well. I. Ain't. Going." She jerked her neck around. Her bronze cheeks were flushed red and sunspots kissed around her eyes.

"Are you feeling okay?" I stepped further into her room so I could get a better look at her.

"I feel fine. I'm an old lady, but I still got my brains about me," she insisted. She grabbed the remote on her bed and turned the tv up louder until I had to scream to hear.

I stared at Ms. Marta. She was the one who texted me and said she wanted to go to the market to get more fruit. The holiday season had already passed, and her family returned to their side of town in South Philly, where the vibe was drastically different. Our corner of West Philly was home to murals, fish-fries, and Korean hair stores. I guess for her family, it reminded them of harder times—and so they reserved their visits for only when they had to. Ms. Marta spoke highly of her sons, but I saw her daily and only saw them a handful of times. They were off living their own lives and "chasing tail" as Ms. Marta said. I wondered how it felt to have your mom a few minutes away and still never see her. Not care to see her outside of holidays. I didn't know what it was like to have a mom, so the feeling was a foreign one, but it seemed weird that Ms. Marta's children never really visited but she was always wanting them to.

"Fine." I took my jacket off. "We can stay in." I slipped off my shoes and shot Amna a quick text we wouldn't be making it today. I grabbed a few trash bags from her cabinets and began shoving trash into the bin, sweeping the floor, and cleaning off her counters.

"Give 'em some water, Josie baby." Ms. Marta pointed to a small dresser that housed candles and pictures of her ancestors.

"You been outside today, Ms. Marta?" I refilled the empty bowl with fresh water and sat it on the dresser as instructed.

"It's too cold out there." She waved her hand and scratched her forehead. "Now tell me again how you got fired and now you are about to work in the chicken coop with the Cannon?" She chuckled.

"Ms. Marta, I already told you this!" I stomped my foot. I didn't know what was going on with her memory, but I already told her twice what went down the day I got fired. She asked to hear the story again and fell out laughing each time.

Ms. Marta's room was small and filled with candles of various saints. She liked all her furniture extra-large, and for the life of me, I couldn't understand why she would want her dresser touching her bed and blocking her windows. Every piece was too big for the space, and I had to maneuver around every corner. She had the only house on the block that didn't have bars in the windows and instead of taking advantage of full sun, her massive bed blocked the sunlight. It was a sin.

I explained to Ms. Marta for the third time how Shelby was shaking in her boots behind her little makeshift desk when she fired me. I even added in some new choice words I should've said to her that I thought of while I was in the shower. Ms. Marta hooted and hollered. Her enormous stomach rippled with laughter.

"Girl, you is so funny. You know you can tell a story. Can you get me some water, Josie baby?" She coughed and laughed and laughed and coughed. She dabbed at her eyes and looked at me. "Josephine, you have to find something you like. Something you're good at. It's not working out at these jobs because it's stuff you don't care about and hate doing to begin with. Your work can't feel like work. At least not to you. Stop doing shit you hate so you can stop having an attitude."

"I don't have an attitude!"

"Well you ain't happy with you."

I climbed into Ms. Marta's bed and laid across the foot of it as I let her words stick. She pulled a pillow out from under her and plopped it under my head. "Ms. Marta, there is nothing I enjoy doing besides my makeup, and what am I supposed to do with that? Nothing really interests me. I have you, Dad, Amna, and Alonso. I don't have any secret talents and I don't have this magical singing voice that gets discovered at the gas station." The ceiling stared back at me as a tear slipped from the corner of my eye and down my neck. It wasn't a sad tear—it was an embarrassed tear. I was twenty-five-years-old and had no hobbies and no interests besides painting my face and my man.

"This is where your life gets interesting." Ms. Marta sat up in her bed and it looked like it took all her might. "You know, when I was your age, I worked at the toll booth. It was the loneliest, most boring job ever. Every day I collected money from people in these expensive, big body cars. I wondered, where were they going so early in the morning, all dressed up? Did they love that? Or did they hate it but felt obligated to do it to pay for those big cars? I hated the toll booth, but I loved them benefits. I did my twenty-five years for the State and I got out of there. And now I got me a good pension and health insurance. You deserve all of that, too, Josephine. And if you decide that's not what you want, that's fine, too. But you have to do *something*."

I wiped my eyes and sat up in bed. "I know, Ms. Marta, I know."

"And if you get that job with your dad at the chicken coop, don't mess it up. You know the Cannon will have your ass over that one."

She could read people like a book, and she wasn't wrong. If I got this position, I had to do the right thing for my dad. He was hand delivering me a steady and stable job on a silver platter, and the least I could do was be thankful. Did thankful feel like having to vomit?

"Maybe I'll stay at the chicken coop for a year. Just one year. And after that I will find something else. Something that I actually like."

Ms. Marta dipped her chin and chuckled. "You know you can't keep a job for no year. You give me one job, just one," she pointed. "That you've last at for that long." She didn't wait for my response and chuckled. "You keep coming in here with these jokes and making me laugh, girl. Talking about a year." She threw her head back and laughed until I saw all her teeth.

My cheeks were hot, and soon, I giggled with Ms. Marta. I took a pillow and bopped her on the arm. "Don't laugh!" I shrieked. "I'm going to make it one year. I have to. For Dad. For Alonso."

And I meant it. For them I would try. Millions of other people held down careers and didn't seem to hate it.

I took a deep breath, pulled my compact out of my purse, and dabbed some powder onto my cheeks so my makeup wouldn't shine.

I would try.

CHAPTER 5

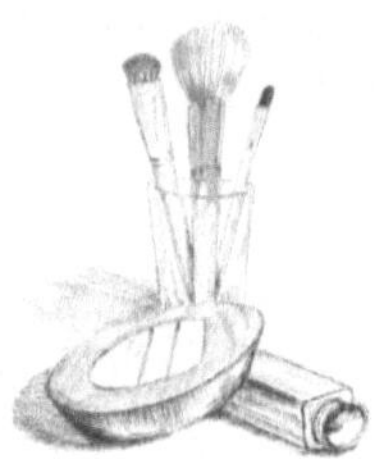

I rolled the fresh bottle of foundation between my thumb and pointer finger and gave it a good shake. I learned early, when you bought new makeup, you had to make sure everything was warm and mixed.

My chicken shit interview was at 2 p.m. today.

Dad got Amna an interview, too, and she was meeting me there. Her interview was at 2:30 p.m. They had us scheduled back-to-back like sitting ducks.

I laid out my makeup in front of me at my princess vanity. What kind of look was I going for today? I could tone it down with nudes and shades of light brown. That was my go-to color when I wanted a soft, natural, barely there look. Or maybe I could jazz it up with sweeping bright red blush and cotton candy pink gloss. Show them I wasn't like their other employees, and I could stand out among the pack.

Could I though? Did I even need to? And who would judge my makeup anyway, the chickens?

My hands went limp over my bright colors and settled for a little foundation, pink for my eyelids, and nude gloss for my lips. That would have to do. Today wasn't the day to shine. I put it off as long as I could, but today was the day I got myself a real job.

Yanking my closet open, we packed it to the gills. Alonso had thousands of dollars' worth of shoes. Every pair of sneakers known to man was right here—climbing the walls in our small, crouched closet. I pulled the light string hanging from the ceiling. Alonso insisted on keeping all the shoes in their original boxes, too.

Moving a few loose shoes around, I kneeled until I found them. A pair of black, flat, ugly ballerina shoes I only wore to things I halfway wanted to do. You know—funerals and interviews, like today. I squeezed my screaming toes inside of them and cringed the whole way as they clung to my feet like a noose around my neck.

I stared at myself in my small mirror. I had to crouch down to see my face and torso together in the frame. My black blazer was itchy and tight around my arms. I looked like one of those people rushing to work every day and nothing like me. What did *me* look like anyway? My perfectly flat ironed hair swooped to the side and light beauty marks that peppered my bronzed cheeks. Whoever she was, she wasn't staring back at me.

"Ouch." Dad jumped away from the stove. He was frying bacon when I walked into the kitchen, and a woman I had never seen before sat at the table with her head tucked in her hands. She was staring at Dad all googly eyed like she was in love.

"Who are you?" I opened the fridge and grabbed the orange juice.

"Don't talk to her like that," Dad snorted. "This here is Janet. And she is my number one lady." Dad trotted over to

Janet, slippers slapping against the back of his feet, spatula in hand, and kissed her on the mouth.

My eyebrows drew closer together. Number one lady, huh? And where was Rose, the same one he was allegedly proposing to? And Monica before that? And Yudy before that?

"Nice to meet you, Janet." I nodded in her direction, half paying attention. If she knew like I knew, she would keep her shoes on and coat close by.

"Your makeup is flawless." Janet searched my face and smiled. "Cannon, you didn't tell me you had such a beautiful daughter, my goodness." She sounded half surprised.

Dad grunted. "She can fight, too."

I sipped my orange juice a second longer and wondered where she came from. Dad had a type, and by the looks of it, she fit the bill. She looked young. I mean, she was way older than me, but she was definitely younger than Dad. Mid-thirties, heavyset, thick around the middle, and cocoa skin the same shade as chocolate chips in a cookie.

"Thanks." I couldn't help but blush. "I didn't have time for a full face, so this will have to do."

"Josie has an interview today at the plant." Dad thrust his chest out and grinned.

I hoped the bacon popped him again.

"Ain't she a little young for the plant, Cannon?" Janet stiffened.

Dad spun around and stared at Janet, utterly confused. "Young? The girl is twenty-five! It's about time she get herself a big girl job. She already got her big girl shoes on, so she knows what comes next. Besides, we talked about this." Dad leaned over and loaded dishes into the dishwasher. "I thought you weren't never coming out of there. You take hours doing all that makeup stuff." He eyed me up and down. "But you look nice. They like when you're not too flashy. This ain't the Oscars, you know." He washed his hands and transferred bacon to a plate and started whisking eggs. "Do you want cheese in your eggs, Josie?" Dad talked a mile a minute. Everything he said was pressured, like it had to be said immediately. He changed the subject like my future was in danger and he had to save me. A byproduct of being under his roof and subjected to his rules.

"I'm skipping breakfast today. I want to get there early and get situated."

"Good girl." He nodded with a soft smile. "You'll see this is the best thing for you. You need some stability. You're twenty-five and can't even keep your phone on half the time."

Janet chuckled at Dad's half assed attempt at a joke, but I saw nothing funny.

Dad's big belly jiggled as he padded back and forth in the kitchen, setting the table for him and Janet. "What time will Alonso be back? Me and Janet need some alone time." He flashed his eyes at her the same way he did at Rose when she laid across his lap in his bedroom.

"He left early. Went to Jersey for a private coaching client." I grabbed a banana and stuffed it in my bag. I didn't mention that the private client was referred by Curtis. Curtis used his connections to promote Alonso as a basketball trainer for the teen kids of some B-list celebrities. I wasn't sure what it meant for Alonso long-term. One thing I knew about the gang: once you owed them, you owed them for life. Alonso loved me and basketball. Those two things I was sure of. When he couldn't stay awake in class or they kicked him out for talking too much, basketball seemed to be the only thing that calmed him down. He promoted his coaching services on social media and got some customers, but it wasn't enough to pay all the bills and appease my dad.

It seemed like no matter how much we got ahead, there was always something that needed to be paid for, paid down, or paid off. There was never anything left over for something fun. Fun had to be planned and even then, we had to find a cheap deal. Some people we went to high school with were on social media catching flights. They were on islands, out at fancy restaurants, clinking their glasses together and toasting to the good life. Maybe I was exaggerating but when it was something that you longed for through the looking glass and never really experienced yourself—it hit different.

"Good. Tell him don't rush home. Actually, ya'll don't come home until tonight. I got a meeting in my bedroom, and I can't be late." Dad winked at Janet, took her hand, and kissed it. He slathered syrup on his pancakes and wolfed them down, not waiting for Janet to pick up her fork.

Disgusting.

I shook my head and grabbed my coat. The short walk to Ms. Marta's house was a cold one as the wind whipped between the row homes and created a wind tunnel.

"I'm here, Ms. Marta," I said, shutting the door behind me and shaking off the even chillier words of my father.

"I'm sitting down!" Ms. Marta shouted from the living room. The space was a disaster. I blinked rapidly, trying to adjust to what I was seeing. I was just here yesterday, and it wasn't the cleanest, but it wasn't *this* either. There were clothes strewn all over the floor and her lamp shade was flung in a corner. She had empty McDonald's bags littering the carpet, which was surprising because Ms. Marta hated McDonald's. Her bedroom was directly at the end of the hallway, and from here I could see she pulled all the blankets off her bed and put them in a pile in the middle of the living room floor.

"What's going on?" I shivered. My body shook and my ears perked. It was an ice box in here.

"It got cold in here last night. I don't think the thermostat is working." Ms. Marta was bundled up. A cord spilled from under her heated blanket she was using to keep warm.

"Why didn't you call me?"

"I don't know. I didn't want to make it a fuss. I figured you would come over first thing this morning to harass me. And here you are." She looked me up and down with a small smirk.

"Did you call the landlord?" I bit my lip.

"I did. He said he would be here this Friday."

"Friday? It's Tuesday!"

"I am just fine, chile! Ain't no Jack Frost got me worried. This heated blanket is doing me just fine," Ms. Marta exclaimed.

Over the years, I worried more and more about Ms. Marta. Her home used to be her walking museum. She had pictures of all her family members and different trinkets she collected over the years. And it was spotless. She made it a point to clean everything, every day, with a dab of bleach.

"I'm going to talk to my dad. Maybe he can get someone in here earlier than Friday." I grabbed some loose blankets, folded them, and placed them on the open couch. I gathered trash off the floor and stuffed it into her bin. Already filled to the brim, I took out the overflowing bag and replaced it with a new one.

"Come in here and let me get a look at you on your big day," Ms. Marta called out.

I sauntered into the living room with my best version of a slow, sexy walk. Two painted fingers unbuttoned my coat and I placed my hands on my hips. I tripped over a pillow laying in the middle of the floor and almost tumbled face first into the coffee table showing Ms. Marta my best interview day strut.

"Are you okay?" Ms. Marta was sipping from a large cup and a deep laugh bubbled up from her belly and her boisterous chuckles lit up the room.

"I'm fine," I stammered and pulled at my collar. My cheeks flushed red, but I laughed with Ms. Marta.

She glimpsed me again and gave me a thumbs up. "You look great. Not too much makeup for an interview. You don't look like one of those streetwalker girls with the lashes from here up to the heavens."

"Thanks." I curled my toes in my ugly shoes and fidgeted.

"Now let's make this your last interview for a while. I feel good about this one." She wiped the funny tears from her face and held her stomach.

"How are you feeling?" I frowned.

"My stomach is a little upset. Go on in the bathroom and grab me my Alka-Seltzer."

When I brought the bottle back to her, she took a whole swig of the thick white liquid and swallowed it with one gulp. She wiped her mouth with the back of her hand and said, "now let's practice what you're gonna say to those people when they ask you questions."

"Okay." I stood in front of her and ran down the usual spiel. "I'm Josephine Scott, twenty-five-years-old, and looking for work. I am competent, dedicated, and hard-working . . ." All those things described me, but not for this job. It sounded like an unbelievable lie sitting on my lips and I wondered if they would smell bitch on me.

"Good. Good." Ms. Marta coached. "And see what time they want you there. Lord knows you'd be late for your own funeral!" Ms. Marta shook her head.

"Well, I'm off. Wish me luck." I blew out a nervous breath.

"You got this." Ms. Marta gave me two thumbs up and grinned. "On your way home, can you stop and get me some Pork Rinds?"

"Sure thing, Ms. Marta." I chuckled.

When I made it outside, the wind was still whipping. "Dad!" I shouted into the phone. A fire truck was passing, and I couldn't hear a thing. "We have the same landlord as Ms. Marta, right?"

"Yeah, why?"

I explained to Dad that Ms. Marta didn't have any heat, and the landlord wasn't planning to fix it until Friday. "Can you please have someone look into it?" I begged.

"You need to stop spending so much time over there, anyway. Ms. Marta ain't your Thelma and you ain't her Louise. Focus on yourself and getting this job. But I'll take care of it. Tell her I'll be by in about an hour. Me and Janet got a meeting." He hung up.

CHAPTER 6

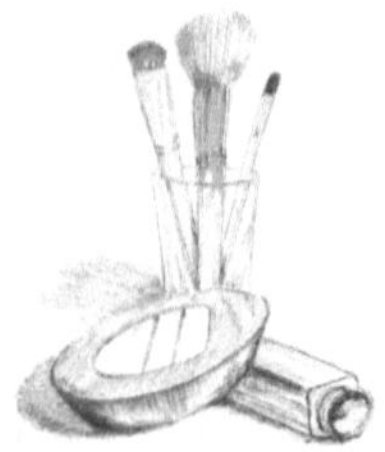

"What are you wearing?" I tilted my head at Amna trying to figure out her get up.

She scrunched her face and smoothed down her dress with blacked out coffin nails. "What?"

Amna wore a long black and white polka dot, flannel dress, combat boots, two pigtails on either side of her head—and a scowl seen from a mile away. She looked like a Black, Wednesday Addams.

"You couldn't find something regular to wear?" I stared incredulously. We hustled to the building as the January wind tugged underneath my coat and crept up my back. The commute to this job was even worse than the yoga studio, and I knew I would hate it. They couldn't plop a chicken coop in Center City, Philadelphia. No, they needed land and lots of it. Philly had lots of land all right; two bus rides out of town worth. I cursed myself for not packing my sneakers in my bag.

"If I'm going to do this, I have to be me." Amna pushed her shoulders back and jutted out her chest.

Is this what made Dad so surly every day? Work was the

worst in the winter. When you woke in the morning and by the time you headed home for the day— it was dark. I stared at the sky and imagined the blackness that would paint the sky as I sledged home, back hunched over like Dad.

I didn't press Amna further. She didn't need to explain anymore as I squashed my toes in my ugly shoes. "Come on, let's go in."

Amna and I sat on plastic benches with a stack of paperwork. They wanted to know my date of birth, social security number, and everything except the date of my first period. *Where did I go to school? References? Personal statement? Emergency contacts? Allergies?*

The questions were never ending. I looked over at Amna and nudged her shoulder. She had one leg crossed over top of the other and her pen was barely moving. She answered one question at a time and went back and forth between giggling at her social media page and checking off boxes on the form. I zoomed down the sheet, circling things, and scribbling *N/A* when necessary. It was all the same blah blah mumbo jumbo.

Amna and I met in middle school. She was adopted as a kid to white parents and the family moved from Seattle to Philadelphia, where Amna's adoptive dad was from. She was forever in trouble for challenging the teachers, which I never understood because she really just questioned everything. Adults don't like when you question them. When we learned about George Washington and Abe Lincoln, she argued with the teacher about Malcolm X and Nat Turner. When we went outside for recess, she got in trouble for staying behind in the library and reading books. Her dad's friendship with the mayor saved her from being expelled time after time. Amna made her life colorful, and she drew out of the lines in every way. This chicken coop was her rock bottom–just like it was mine.

"Josephine Scott," a round man called out, pulling me out of my wallowing stupor.

"Here goes nothing," I hissed to Amna and turned in my clipboards and paperwork.

"Break a leg." She fist pumped me in the air. She was still scribbling away on page two of ten.

"Ms. Scott. Take a seat. I'm the Plant Manager, Mr. Fields." An older gentleman smiled. His salt and pepper hair was more salt than pepper. His round belly cinched his tight belt and I was sure if he breathed too hard it would snap in half. Stale pastry sat on his desk like it was the breakfast of champs.

"Nice to meet you, Mr. Fields." I shook his hand and sat down.

"Your dad thinks you'd be a good fit for us. Says you're not afraid of hard work." Mr. Fields smiled, real Steve Harvey style, and his teeth gleamed. A stale pot of coffee sat warming behind him, along with a stack of employee files. So much for privacy, I could see names from here.

I licked my lips. "Yes. I need something stable. I'm a good worker and I always try my best." There. That was the truth.

"And is that your friend that you arrived with? Is she. . ." Mr. Fields shuffled through a stack of papers on his desk. "Ms. Amna Lavender?"

"Yes, that's my friend."

"Is that her *real* name?" Mr. Fields chuckled and waited for me to laugh.

"Uhhh . . . yes it is." I squirmed in my seat, looking away. I was no good at the fake small talk shit. The plastic clock on the coffee pot clicked. Two minutes had passed.

"Very good. Well Ms. Scott, I am here to tell you I hire just about anyone. I try to give everyone a chance and let them prove themselves. The first month working in a chicken processing plant isn't hard work, but it is tedious and some-times messy. If you can make it through that, I think you will have a very rewarding job here. Complete with all the perks of a stable job, as you say." Mr. Fields waved his hands around like he was on a game show.

"So, I got the job?" I sat up in the chair and gripped the sides.

"Yes, Ms. Scott. You got the job." Mr. Fields turned and poured a cup of coffee. He poured so much powder creamer into his scrawny cup I wasn't sure if he emptied the bottle.

"Thank you so much! My dad will be happy." I shook his hand and grinned.

"No problem, Ms. Scott. Let's say next Monday will be your first day of work. 9 a.m. start time." Mr. Fields signed his name at the bottom of a form and placed it on top of the growing pile of new hires.

"9 to 5?" I confirmed.

"Yes, this is a 9 to 5 position with some swing shifts."

"Swing shifts? What does that mean?" I frowned. My dad swung nowhere and didn't mention it to me.

"It means one weekend out of the month you may have to work 2nd or 3rd shift instead of your regular work hours."

"My dad doesn't work swing shift?" I rubbed my chin in confusion. My feet were sweating in these ugly shoes.

Mr. Fields stopped scribbling, lifted his head, and looked me up and down. "Your dad has been working with the company for over twenty years. He doesn't have to work swing shift anymore. Don't worry, you'll get there soon, too." He leaned back in his chair like he told that story to all the new hires.

"Got it. Thanks again." I pursed my lips and closed the door softly behind me. Twenty years.

When I returned to the hallway, a deep, soul sigh rattled its way up. Tension had lived at my temples the past few weeks. Even though it wasn't my dream job, I let relief wash over me like water in the desert. Seeing dozens of young people crouched over clipboards, I understood it better. This *was* the game. Hire all the newbies and make them work the horrible shifts.

Twenty years my ass. But I would swallow my pride. I wouldn't complain.

"Amna Lavender," the receptionist called out.

Amna stared at me with wide eyes. "How was it?"

"Not bad at all. I got hired on the spot and I think you might, too," I whispered. "Just go in and be confident."

A few minutes later, Amna returned to the waiting room with a smile. "I got it!" She jumped in the air and clicked her heels together like she was in a movie. Her combat boots made a loud squeaking noise when she danced over the linoleum floor.

I covered my mouth and giggled. Her parents were on her too about figuring out life; they would be happy.

Amna and I rushed out into the January chill. "Ahhh!!" Amna yelled once we got down the street. We jumped up and down, sharing questions.

"He was so weird! He asked me if your name was really your name!" I babbled.

"He saw my crystals and asked me if I was one of those praying to the sun and moon girls!" Amna squealed.

We laughed and boarded the bus to take the long journey back home.

I shot Alonso a text message:

I got the job!

> Alonso: I knew you would. Fortune favors the brave, my love!

> Me: Wya? Want to catch a movie and celebrate?

> Alonso: Your dad told me not to come home for a while, so I have some time to kill. Sure! Check the times and I'll meet you there.

I smiled.

The city whizzed by and we whipped past murals. Philly was famous for its artistry and many times when I was bored, I'd people watch. I would see a mural and come up with a story about who drew it and why. It was interesting, *you know?* The things people find beauty in, and the colors and flavors they use to bring their vision to life.

The chicken coop was going to work. *It had to.*

Dad would be thrilled and maybe it wouldn't be so bad. The alternative was having nothing and being assed out. Besides, Alonso and I could really start saving for our own apartment now instead of just talking about it. The thought of our own space and a non-princess bed would have me up early Monday morning, ready for work. *Grin and bear it, Josephine, grin and bear it,* I whispered to myself.

"Your makeup looks lovely. I love how you young girls paint up your faces." An older woman's eyes sparkled as she held onto the safety bar on the bus. The doors opened and she got off. She turned back, right before the doors closed and smiled. "Real art," she said.

My cheeks reddened and my stomach jumped. People told me all the time how beautiful my makeup was. Knowing people were staring and making judgments about my face was scary, but it made me feel damn good to know they were staring at something that came easy to me. Honey, I could *do* me some makeup, and no matter how small and insignificant my dad thought it was, I was good at it.

My face *was* lovely. My life was lovely, and I was off to meet my man at the movies and officially as a working woman—again.

CHAPTER 7

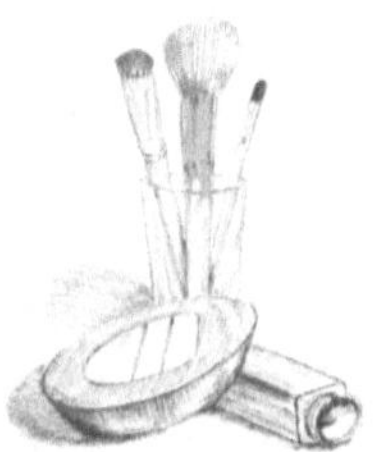

A few hours later, I scrolled through my phone, squinting at my bank account balance.

"How much do you have?" There seemed to be so many withdrawals, quite a few overdraft fees, but never enough deposits. I toggled between the calculator app on my phone and running the numbers in my brain. I scoured each entry, waiting to find something wrong and figure out why my balance was so low, but there was no reason. It was me—it was all me.

I was never the best at saving money. I mean, the concept made sense. Save your money and your money will save you. Rainy days always come and when they do, you'll be prepared for them with your savings. But it rained cats and dogs for me and Alonso. If I made more money, would I manage it better? Or did I have a weird relationship with money because I didn't have enough of it?

Alonso snapped me out of my thoughts as he held up his fingers and counted. "I paid the electric bill, I had to spot

Curtis some bread, and then you know; just food and stuff."
He held the door for me. "So I can pay for the tickets."

"Spot Curtis some bread?" I frowned and flung around so
fast, Alonso fell back into the people behind him.

"Watch where you're going!" The guy pushed Alonso and
huffed off toward the exit. He yanked the theater's door open
and screamed when he got outside. Everyone watched him
throw a tantrum and his hot breath steamed in the snowy
January afternoon.

Annoyance sat on Alonso's face as he clenched his fist
watching the man outside. He took one step in the direction of
the door. Never backing down from a fight, fear rippled
through my body playing out in my head all the scenarios in
which this could go. My hand flung to Alonso's chest, and I
pushed back. *Don't go outside Alonso,* my eyes willed to him.

Alonso sighed in my direction and brushed off his jacket
from where he was pushed. He cleared his throat. "You know
how to keep things exciting. I will give you that."

"Well, why did Curtis need money?" I asked more in a
hushed voice this time. "I thought he was some Gang Lord or
some shit." My fingers grabbed Alonso's, wanting to tangle
them.

He flinched, not wanting to be held.

Alonso shoved his hand in his pocket as the line moved
forward. "Will you chill? We're supposed to be here celebrating
your new job. Your dad told us not to come how for the entire
night and I'm trying to treat my lady." He batted his eyes. His
lashes were so long and full. I wanted to run my lips across his
face and rain down butterfly kisses and melt his anger away.

I got lost in them—but not for too long. "So, you're really
not going to tell me?" I questioned as my stomach rumbled for
movie theater popcorn.

Alonso tutted. "He didn't have cash on him while we were at the carwash so I spotted him. Damn!" His neck veins popped. I had at least three more questions, but I choked them down. *Why didn't big shot Curtis have cash? Did Alonso offer to give him money that we didn't have to spare, or did Curtis ask him to borrow the money, knowing we didn't have money to spare?*

Did he know we didn't have money to spare?

"I'll take a large popcorn, large soda, and two candy bags, please." I leaned over the counter.

The young worker pressed a few buttons. "That'll be \$35." She smacked her gum.

I only had \$20. I chewed the inside of my cheek. The line was growing behind us and people were crossing their arms and getting restless.

"Uhhh. Can you take off the candy, please," my voice cracked.

"And take off the popcorn. We don't need a large soda. Give us a kid's size, please." Alonso grabbed my hand and finally squeezed his fingers into mine.

Someone snickered from behind us in line.

I stared into his eyes and got lost again. "You don't want any popcorn? You love popcorn?" My eyes fell. This was supposed to be a happy day, but we were constantly reminded of what we didn't have enough of and all the ways we had to sacrifice.

"Babe. I don't need any popcorn today. Besides, we have some at home." He stroked the back of my finger.

"Can ya'll hurry up!" someone behind us shouted.

I stared at Alonso, not meaning to turn this into a moment, but popcorn was his favorite.

"Josie. It's okay. Seriously."

I licked my dry lips and nodded to the worker. "Just a soda then."

Alonso liked to get to the movies early and see all the previews. Sometimes we would even be there before the previews while they were still cleaning up from the show prior and they gave us dirty looks for being in their way.

The newest Marvel movie was out, and that would kill at least three hours so Dad could do whatever he was doing and with whom. We sat down and I put the soda in the cup holders between us as I stole a few sips.

"I want to tell you something. But the way you acted up in line, I don't know." Alonso smirked.

"I didn't act up," I hissed, trying to keep my voice low in the dimly lit room.

"It's about Curtis."

My toes scrunched in my ugly black shoes I *still* had on. "What?"

Alonso rubbed his hands over his eyes and leaned back in the seat. "There's an important client I could land. It could mean consistent coaching for the next year. Real money, too. It could be good for us. I think I'm going to do it."

My stomach grumbled. I wasn't sure if it was from hunger or fear about what Alonso had to say that had him fidgeting in the movie theater in the middle of the day. "Well, what's the problem? That's great for you. You don't sound excited?"

"The kid. it's a big-time hustler's kid. He wants him to have the best, and Curtis connected us and he thinks that's me. I would have to be at their house a few days a week." Alonso tucked his chin and smiled. He took out his phone and scrolled. The bright light illuminated the dark space, and I stared at him. He was low-key honored and trying to hide his excitement from me by playing it cool.

"Lonz . . ." I reached over and touched his cheek. "I want you to have big-time clients. I want you to be excited about this. Coaching and mentoring youth is your dream and you're so good at it. I just don't think we should get into bed with drug-dealers and gang members to do it."

"They're not as bad as you make them out. And the money will help us save up for our own place. By the way, we're going to an event with Curtis next week."

"Next week?" I rose my voice. Someone in front of us looked back and gave us a stank face.

"Keep your voice down," Alonso muttered. "I told you I would set something up so we could all meet. Curtis has been in my life for years, and it's time you guys met face to face."

"Well, where are we going? Will we need money? What if I have to work? You know I can't take off from the chicken coop, I just started . . ." I racked my brain with all the reasons I couldn't go.

"It's some sort of fashion show."

"A fashion show?" I contorted my face and raised my voice again.

"Yeah, Curtis' girl does hair, and they got free tickets to some fashion show. He says it's dope."

I sat back in my chair and pretended to watch the movie. *A fashion show?* I had never been to a fashion show before. The closest I came to a show was when my grandmom took me to the Philadelphia Flower Show at the convention center when I was in the fifth grade. I saw a few fashion shows on tv, and I remember their makeup being flawless and carefully laid. Would this show be like that? With women walking the runway in full glam faces? The thought intrigued me.

All I needed was Alonso, Ms. Marta, and Amna. They were my too live crew, but Alonso seemed to *need* people. Their approval. Acceptance. When we first started dating, I loved that about him. He was loyal and defended everyone. If he felt like someone was being wronged, he stepped in, even if it meant having to get his own hands dirty and do the fighting. He was a real social worker at heart. I hoped the things I accepted in the beginning wouldn't be the things I regretted years later. I didn't understand the power Curtis seemed to have over Alonso, but perhaps getting to know Curtis would help me understand Alonso's needs.

A sharp pressure shot to my temples, and I exhaled. "Okay, Alonso. A fashion show it is." I gulped the soda.

"Save something for me to drink." Alonso stood up. He unzipped his coat and I caught a waft of something delicious. He looked around and carefully pulled out a long cheesesteak sub from the inside of his coat pocket and a bag of chips.

"What's all this?" My eyes shot open in surprise.

"We didn't need all that expensive food at the counter because I stopped at Max's and got us this." He laid the cheesesteak on his lap, unrolled the aluminum foil, and carefully split it into two pieces. "Just shut up sometimes. I got you, babe."

My stomach rumbled with happiness as he handed me my piece. "Alonso, you snuck an entire cheesesteak into the movies?" I eyed the people around. "You are crazy!" The bag of chips crackled open, and we dove into our food and sucked down the soda, passing it between us.

Alonso's cheeks were full of meat and cheese, and I could see it rumbling around in his mouth. "It's dark as shit in here, but your face looks beautiful. You really did your thang today with the makeup." A messy mixture of mayonnaise and ketchup shot out of the corner of his mouth.

"That's the nicest thing you've ever said to me." I leaned over and licked the mayonnaise off his cheek.

A Marvel movie and my man.

This was not enough for either of us, but we had plans. And today, it was okay.

CHAPTER 8

"The entire first floor is where we do all the deboning." Mr. Childress, the floor manager, swept his arms around giving us the tour. The other new hires and I donned white hard hats and bright yellow hazmat jump-suits. The room was so cold my teeth chattered. Even though the hazmat suits were thin, I was grateful they covered all of my skin and kept out some of the chill.

"As some of you may notice, it is very cold in here, so we advise you to layer up. This room has to be kept at a steady fifty-five degrees in order to keep everything sanitary and the health department off our backs." He chuckled. No one laughed.

Clearing his throat, Mr. Childress said, "Moving on. Working in a poultry plant is a dangerous job and has some of the highest amputation and laceration rates of any plant. You have to be careful here," he warned. They filled the room with equipment and conveyor belts. A long line of poor poultry converged on different belts around the room heading off to their final destinations. Catching me eying the belts, Mr. Childress explained. "Check out the sprayers above the belts. They continuously spray anti-microbial agents to keep the pathogens at bay. Keep your mask on so you don't inhale the mist from that spray." He motioned with his hand for someone in the front to pull up their mask. They gassed us daily with a spray that was so strong we had to wear masks.

Got it.

Amna trailed at the end of the line of new workers. She had her mask pulled up to her eyes and even though people couldn't see her face, I could tell by the way her brows were knitted that she wore a scowl. I adjusted my mask over my face. I woke up even earlier than normal today. The commute getting out here was wicked, and I spent an entire hour doing my makeup. It wasn't supposed to take that long, but I got lost in choosing the best makeup look for my official first day. It was a waste, anyway. Even though light pink bronzer grazed my cheeks and my eye shadow blended perfectly with my indigo nails, the inside of my mask was a gross brown color as my foundation rubbed off inside the fabric.

Even though I walked around and tried to adjust to my new place of employment, my body hung limp like a deflated balloon. When you were somewhere doing something you really didn't want to do, heaviness weighed you down at every turn. I wanted to rub my eyes and close them just for a second, but it didn't seem smart to rub my eyes in a poultry processing plant where everything was slippery and greasy. I spied everything around the room, and it was worse than I imagined, not that I had quite imagined this.

Before I left this morning, Dad was up before me. His favorite meal of the day was breakfast, and it was the one thing he could cook with no help. Greasy bacon dripping onto a paper towel, two scrambled eggs with cheese, and two silver dollar pancakes. He even added in chocolate chips. I inhaled my pancakes and let the sweetness of the syrup settle into my heart where sourness was sure to grow. He said this type of work would be a change for me; having to follow a precise order and schedule. I had a feeling it was going to be an adjustment, but my heart sank when I watched workers with sharp knives slice into chicken, hacking away at their parts and tossing them down the conveyor belt. I shuffled in place and leaned against a massive piece of equipment and watched people around me quietly work with their heads down.

"I see you have found our disinfectant," Mr. Childress pointed as I leaned against the massive silver drum. "The lacerations are not just from the cutting tools but from sharp chicken bones. We keep a vat of disinfectant and soak the chicken carcasses to lower the number of pathogens," he explained.

I didn't care to know the details and the word *carcass* made me shudder.

"You must process all the live chickens by the end of each day. If someone doesn't show up for work, we still process them all. Nothing gets left behind. Not a wing, drum, or thigh." Mr. Childress giggled at his own makeshift joke. "If you have to use the bathroom, raise your hand and a floater will come and relieve your spot. You cannot just walk off your position. This is an assembly line and if one missing link clogs up the pipes, it messes up the entire production. Work efficiently and work together," Mr. Childress explained.

"You haven't mentioned lunch?" Amna appeared from the back of the line and stood beside me. Her mask was pulled down and tucked under her chin. Her lips were blue. Mr. Childress looked Amna up and down and raised an eyebrow before responding.

"Please pull up your mask. We have to do our part and keep each other safe."

Amna pursed her lips and sighed. She pulled up her mask and folded her arms.

"Lunch is thirty minutes. The entire plant closes down for lunch, so no one will have to relieve you. You might want to wear something heavy under your hazmat suit." He eyed the outline of Amna's short sleeves through her hazmat suit.

"Last but not least," he continued. "As you can see and feel under you, everything here is slippery. A lot of chicken fat falls off the machines and onto the floor. Everything's greasy. We must keep things clean and dry as possible. Be careful walking next to the equipment and no horseplaying. There's a disk cutter with a rotating blade, your fingers are always in danger," he warned.

Mr. Childress looked around the room. "Oh! Mr. Mike Friedland!" Mr. Childress called out. "Please show the new hires your hand."

Mr. Mike Friedland stepped away from his assigned location, removed his thick glove, and wiggled a knub where his pointer finger used to be. "I wasn't paying attention and got caught in the grinder about ten years back."

A few of the new hires, including myself, let out an audible gasp.

"And you're still here?" Amna questioned with wide eyes.

"That is why we value safety, cleanliness, and tidiness in here. We don't want anyone else to get hurt," Mr. Childress explained.

Lost fingers or not, the moral of this story for me was that he was there ten years. And my dad—twenty.

I checked out the scene around me. The conveyer belts were about waist height, and from what I could see, the taller workers had to stoop down and shorter workers had to stand on stools on their tippy toes to reach the belt. Everyone had one specific task, and the workers repeated it over and over and over again. Lift wing, cut, toss down the belt, repeat. Dad mentioned all of this but to see the assembly line in action was a different story.

Amna brushed up next to me and I shivered, feeling her cold arm even through our hazmat suits. "Hey, girl. You okay?" I whispered.

Amna shook her head. "This is a terrible place," she said with sad eyes.

I nodded without a word.

"Okay team, that's the basics. This is a very simple job. You just have to be extremely careful. We take being late and calling out serious business around here, especially when you are on probation."

"How long is probation?" Amna interrupted. She stuffed her arms inside of her hazmat suit and her open sleeves flapped in the cool air where her arms should have been.

Mr. Childress cleared his throat and cut his eyes at Amna for interrupting him. "Probation is ninety days. To ensure everything runs smoothly, we like to approve all time off beforehand. It's not that you can't call out, but again, if we have over five call outs in a day, it affects the assembly line, and no one goes home until all chickens are cut and packaged. We have a system around here and like I said, if one person clogs up the pipes, well, it slows down production. Is it fun and exciting? It is not. But it's honest work, and the plant is doing extremely well for our region. The Philadelphia community can depend on us for jobs, and we are here to stay. After your ninety days are up, we even have an intra-mural softball team in the spring, and we have a Sunshine

Club to celebrate holidays and everyone's birthday." Mr. Childress gave a proud smile and pumped his fist. "I started here eons ago when I was a young man and I've worked my way up. If you work hard, you can, too." He looked out of place in his gray suit and shiny shoes. I guess he was the mouthpiece for the workers but never really did the work himself. Figures.

I heard about said Sunshine Club years ago from my dad and rolled my eyes, knowing it was really a glorified pizza party and donuts in the breakroom.

"We can't play softball or celebrate our birthdays until after ninety days?" Amna frowned and leaned against a large vat.

"Uhh Ms . . ." Mr. Childress couldn't remember Amna's name, but he sensed her sowing the seeds of descent.

"Just call me, Amna."

"Ms. Amna, we have a work culture here. A way we do things. Sometimes you young kids don't understand that, but please trust me. This is a good job."

An hour later, Amna and I were side by side, slicing into chicken pieces and tossing them down the belt ourselves. I had to stand on a stool and a searing pain was already shooting through my lower back from being hunched over. My fingers were stiff from the room being so cold and I stared at the large digital clock hanging high on the wall at least a hundred times, wishing it was lunchtime. I constantly pulled my mask up over my nose, and the inside was an even darker shade of brown from my makeup.

This place didn't deserve a pretty face. I couldn't believe my dad did this for so many years. No wonder he acted the way he did.

A bell rang, and the workers began shuffling from their stations and in a single file line out of the room. Everyone in their hazmat suits looked the same, until we arrived at the cafeteria and took off the masks.

There were people from all walks of life. Older women and men who walked hunched in constant pain from years of bending to cut chicken. My dad had the same walk.

Young people around my age were there, too, and while they moved a lot faster than the more seasoned folks, they wore tell-tale songs of their impulsive injuries. Small cuts and scars on their knuckles and fingers told me they had met the sharp end of a blade a time or two.

I washed my hands in the large basin in the corner, and my stomach growled. Amna motioned me over to her table and I plopped down across from her, exhausted. She pulled two sandwiches, chips, and two bottles of water out her lunch bag and laid them out on the table.

"I didn't even think to bring lunch. Thank you for this." I pulled my mask off my face and scowled. Most of my makeup had transferred and was inside my mask. I smacked the sandwich between my lips and it was pasty in my dry mouth. I took a swig of water. I guess I would have to invest in a good makeup setting spray for this place. Or not wear makeup at all. The sandwich stuck to the roof of my mouth.

Amna said nothing. She didn't eat her food—she people watched.

"What's wrong?" I scoured her face.

She shook her head. Her curly braids were squished under her suit. "I don't think I can stay here. This is barbaric. And boring. And . . . I just can't." She leaned over and whispered. She checked behind my back to make sure no one was listening.

This *was* barbaric.

"So, what are you going to do?"

Amna shrugged, and I had seen that shrug before. It was the shrug she gave when she was figuring something out in her mind. A way to get out of something barbaric.

"Did I tell you I found my birth brother?" Amna changed the subject and munched on her chips.

My eyes shot out, and I almost choked. "Uh, no! You just casually drop that bomb. That's great, Amna! How do you feel? What's he like? Do you look like him?" I badgered her with questions. My eyes shot between her and the digital clock behind her, counting down how much time we had left for lunch. Twenty-one minutes.

Amna blushed. "I found him on Facebook. I was checking through the old adoption paperwork my mom gave me and I found a random name. I did some detective work. . . . Oh my God, Josie, he looks just like me. Like me!" Amna grinned. She pulled out her phone, scrolled for a second, and then held up a picture of a man with her same toffee baked features and build. I had to blink to make sure I wasn't looking at a picture of Amna as the same fiery eyes stared back at me.

"Damn, girl, he looks just like you." My hand shot to my mouth and I giggled. "Did you talk to him?"

"Shut up!" Amna chuckled. "He lives in Hawaii with his wife and daughter. My niece. I have a niece." Her eyes sparkled. Amna and I shared one half of the same heart. She longed for a birth family and demanded answers about why she was the child given away, while I adapted to life with a dad who I wasn't sure even liked me.

"Hawaii is halfway across the world, though. Hopefully, you guys can meet in person soon." I wiped my hands with a napkin.

Amna sighed and began scrolling through her phone. She stole a disgusted glance around the room, remembering where she was. "Hopefully. Hawaii for sure has to be better than this."

Every few minutes, we took turns looking up at the clock. How many times would I stare at this clock in my lifetime? How many times had Dad stared at this clock? He worked here just about his whole life, so he had to be okay with it—that was the scary part.

"Hi. Josephine, is it?" a female said behind me.

I shot around, my eyes starting at her feet and following her curvy torso all the way up her body until I met her beautiful cat eyes. She was brown-skinned and even through her mask resting right underneath her chin and her large, oversize hazmat suit—she was striking. A trail of men, young and old, nibbled their lunches and watched her stand in front of me.

"Yes, that's me." My forehead wrinkled and shoulders rounded. What was this?

"This is super weird, but. Your makeup is absolutely flaw-less. I've been staring at it since we sat down for lunch. This is really the only time we get to see each other's faces, so yours stood out."

Heat washed across my forehead and I pulled my knees together under the table. *I stood out.* Did I want to stand out?

"Oh okay . . . well thank you, I guess," I stammered, still not used to people complimenting me on my makeup even though it happened a few times a week. What was I supposed to say? Dad didn't care, he thought it was a waste of money, and Ms. Marta thought anything besides a little eyeshadow was hoe activities.

"Listen, my birthday is in two weeks, and I've been looking for a makeup artist. I want a soft glam look. Are you available?" She peered down at me and tilted her head.

"Available to do, what?" I gawked at her, unsure what she

was asking me. Deep in my belly past *Fear Street*, taking a left at *Shocked Drive*, and heading down *I'm a Fraud Lane*, I knew what she was asking. What no one had ever asked me before, and I had never done. Never ever ever.

"My makeup." She chuckled. "Do you do makeup professionally? Can you do mine for my birthday? I'll pay you, of course."

Ohhhh.... She *was* asking.

"Oh . . .Uh . . . I don't do that." I fumbled through the words.

Amna kicked my shin under the table, and I jumped in my seat. "Ouch!" I glared.

"What she meant to say was she stopped for a while since starting *this* new job. You know, the bills have to be paid." Amna took charge. "But she's back in business and accepting new makeup appointments." Amna hopped up from the table and gently placed her hands on the girl's back and invited her to sit down.

"Great." The girl beamed. "I'm Christeen. Let's exchange numbers." She whipped out her phone and started scrolling.

I sat cottonmouth, unsure what to say. Amna sat next to Christeen, and she raised her eyebrows and motioned for me to grab my phone. I blacked out of my daze and grabbed my phone. After we exchanged numbers, she said. "So, what are your rates?"

"Uhhh . . ." I rubbed my chin, trying to come up with a number.

"It's been a while, she doesn't remember her rates," Amna interrupted with a light chuckle. "I think the last time I saw your price list it was $100 for a soft glam look." She winked at me and gave a slick 'okay' sign with her fingers.

"Works for me." Christeen smiled. "We have to get back to

work, but we'll talk more later. Thanks so much, I'm looking forward to it."

I gulped.

"Excuse me, I have to use the bathroom before we head back to work." My legs swung from under the table as I rushed to stand. The cold shivers disappeared from my body. I had to call Alonso to tell him the news.

Someone wanted to pay me one hundred fucking dollars to do their makeup.

CHAPTER 9

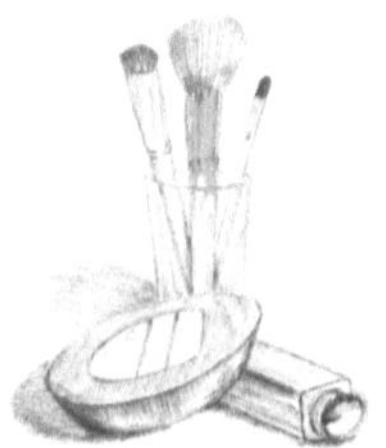

My leg was slung over Alonso's on our day off. His chest grew and fell as a light snore blew from his lips. I shimmied out of bed, tripping over clothes and Jordan's, and crept to the overstuffed closet. A small box seemed to glow under piles of socks and tote boxes. Our window had bars and when the Saturday sun peeked through, it created lined strips of light in my room. One week of getting up early for work had me waking up with the chickens— no pun intended. It was okay, though, I welcomed the quiet lull of the city.

I yanked the box out from under the junk and dusted it off. The box held more questions than answers and my fingers melted over the light pink embroidery that was as old as me.

Josephine Scott, it said on the front lid.

My mother. Named after a woman I had never met. Technically. Why did my mom have to die in childbirth with me? Not that I wished it on anyone else, but out of all the moms in the world, why did it have to be mine? Was this karma? In today's day and age, women were still passing away from childbirth. Having a baby was dangerous business, and it was a business I wanted nothing to do with right now. I wondered what her and my dad's relationship was like. When I asked my grandmom about it, she always said, "oh baby hush. That's water under the bridge now. Your mom is living in glory with the Lord. She ain't wanna live with no Cannon no way."

I hated that answer. I lived with the Cannon. I wanted her to live in glory with me.

When I was about twelve years old, I visited my grandmom one day. When she fell asleep in her chair, my Aunt Deedee, grandmom's youngest baby and biggest troublemaker in the family, made a psst sound at me, and motioned with her eyes to follow her into the back bedroom. I tip-toed past a snoring grandmom and when we got into the room, she rummaged through her closet and pulled out a box with my name on it. She said, "Your mom was a beautiful soul. She helped people. She was fiery, just like you. She would put on her makeup and do herself up all real pretty like. All the boys in the neighborhood liked her. She only had eyes for your dad, though."

My eyes bugged out of my head. "What was my dad like?" My skin held goosebumps to all the family secrets that were getting ready to literally spill out of the closet. Dad never talked about Mom and when he did, it was usually a disappointed soliloquy about how he was a single parent and didn't want to be. I couldn't imagine anyone voluntarily loving him.

Aunt Deedee licked her lips and clasped her hands. "Your dad wasn't always like this. I think life made him hard, you know? It happens sometimes when people experience grief. They don't always know how to process things. Grief sits on your heart like a weight that sets up shop and doesn't move. Sometimes you become friends with the darkness; it's easier than letting the light in. Your dad has lived in darkness ever since your mom. He didn't plan to be a single dad, and frankly, he's not much good at it." She patted my hand and stole glances at my weeks old braids like she felt sorry for me. "But there's grief in love, and there's love in grief. It just looks different for all of us."

"How did they meet?" My throat lurched with a hard swallow. My adolescent mind needed answers.

Aunt Deedee scratched her head and snorted. "They worked together at some call center. I think he always liked her but wasn't until Christmas time when things really kicked off. Their job had one of those gift exchanges for the holidays. She said he switched names with someone else to get your mom's name. Then he went and bought her every damn thing he could think of for Christmas. It was a gamble, but he got the girl."

"Forreal?" I whispered. The only thing my dad happily bought was bacon.

I held on to every word Aunt Deedee spilled in a hushed tone. Anything about my mom was secretive and Dad clammed up and turned cold. Now he spent his days with different women who occupied his time and bed, but had he found anyone who made him feel like Mom did?

"Here. Take this." She pushed the box toward me. When I opened it, the sweet smell of Plumeria tickled my nostrils. All different shades of lipsticks, eyeshadows, and blush palettes stared back at me. "This was all your mom's. Some of this stuff is really old; I wouldn't recommend using it. But I thought you might like to have it. Your mom did herself up real pretty with the best of them and could go outside and pull anyone's man."

"Thank you." I nestled the box in my hands. It felt warm sitting in my lap, knowing my mom used this same box and stored her favorite makeup and beauty items. Did she smell like Plumeria? Was her lingering scent still all over her things years later?

When I popped the top today, I pulled the caps off all the lipstick tubes. I studied the lip indents and creases. Mom seemed to like nude colors. Hues of browns, oranges, light red. Why did she like those colors? I wondered if she had red undertones or hints of yellow. Where did she get all of this stuff, and how did she afford it?

Sitting cross-legged in the closet, I leaned against the wall and cursed away the panic that was creeping into my mind. My entire collection was from the drugstore. Christeen hired me as her makeup artist, but I only had the regular degular stuff I used on myself, not the fancy makeup from Sephora or like my mom had. My shoulders slumped and my eyes hung low. Was I in over my head? I would surely have to pick up more stuff from the drugstore. That was even more money that me and Alonso simply didn't have to spend.

Just then, the room darkened and I saw his shadow before seeing him.

"Hey," Alonso murmured. Morning gruffness sat in his voice.

"Hey," I sighed. Gathering the lipstick caps, I put them back together.

Alonso eyed the makeup around me on the floor and the dejected look on my face. Like a doctor searching for answers, he already knew where it hurt. Kneeling down he said, "We got this. Don't let imposter syndrome beat up on you. You got this. Josie, you *do* this shit."

"Imposter syndrome?" I giggled. "What are you, a motivational speaker now?"

Alonso chuckled. He pulled me to my feet and pressed me against the wall.

"Did I wake you? I'm sorry." I nestled into his neck.

"No, I was getting up anyway. Hey, look at me." He held

my chin until I was facing him. "There is no one more ready for this."

"But I don't have—" I started to say.

Alonso shook his head no. "That girl hired you and she ain't know what you did or didn't have. She hired you on fucking faith. She just saw your face, and that was enough for her. You're ready. Have faith."

My body went limp under his words and warmth. He was right. Everyone around me seemed to know *but* me.

Later today, we were going to the fashion show. My mind was consumed with thoughts of Christeen and what the hell I had agreed to. Worry danced across my forehead as we inched closer to the day I did her makeup.

I pulled my robe around my waist and tip-toed down the hallway.

"Morning, Dad." I shuffled into the kitchen.

"How was work yesterday? Mr. Childress said you're making good progress with deboning?" Dad stood at the counter washing dishes. His belly pressed against the sink, and he was barefoot.

"Hi, Mr. Cannon," Alonso greeted Dad. He paddled into the kitchen and grabbed the cereal off the fridge.

Dad nodded in Alonso's direction and grunted a good morning. He turned his attention back to me.

I shrugged and pulled a frying pan from the cabinet. "It's okay, I guess. Work is work. Nothing really to write home about." It was Saturday, and I didn't want to talk about no chicken on a Saturday.

"Well, I heard Amna is having some problems." Dad eyed me as I pulled out eggs to scramble.

Amna got into an argument with Mr. Childress about

taking a too long bathroom break. She told him he could pluck and fuck the chickens himself.

She got sent home for the day.

"I don't think she's having problems. It's not the most fun work in the world," I admitted. The frying pan sizzled in front of me and as soon as the words escaped me—I knew Dad would be hot on my heels.

"That's what's wrong with your generation now, anyway. Don't nobody want to work for nothing. I bet Amna thinks she can just smile and land herself one of those ballplayers, huh? She better do the right thing. I had to call in some favors to get you girls those interviews."

"I know, Dad, and we are grateful. Thank you." I flicked my gaze upward. How long would I be thanking him for something I didn't want?

"And you and your boyfriend don't be eating up all my bacon and eggs. I went to the market and bought the thick cut this time. I'm making some bumping BLT's this week." Dad grinned.

"Well, I have news." I changed the subject. Dad didn't know about my makeup gig, but he seemed in a decent mood today. I peeled a few strips of bacon out of the pack and let them sizzle in the cast-iron skillet. "There's a girl on the job, Christeen. She saw my face during lunch last week, and she asked me to do her makeup. Said she'll pay me!" I gave a big, toothy grin.

Dad's lip curled into a snarl. "Do her makeup?"

"Yes." I cleared my throat. "For her birthday party."

Dad rolled his eyes at Alonso. "Was this nonsense your idea, Mr. Everything is Terrific?"

"Mr. Cannon, she's really good, and if you—"

"Oh, Josie, you don't know nothing about that stuff!" Dad

cut off Alonso. "You shouldn't be wasting your time on it anyway, it's a waste of money. Who ever heard of such a thing? Paying for makeup?"

"Mom liked makeup," I said in a soft tone.

"And your mama ain't here to tell you to focus on what can make you some real money and not be playing with lipstick and shit. You go to that job to work, not play makeup counter. What? Are you going to be an old Avon lady? Tuh!" He smirked and shook his head like he just heard the most ridiculous thing. "And Alonso, I know you had something to do with this. Always telling that girl to dream. I'm glad to see ya'll up and out that damn room, though, I was wondering if ya'll were going to sleep all damn day."

"Mr. Cannon, it's 8 a.m.?" Alonso squinted in confusion.

"Humph," Dad scoffed. "All of Philly already up."

My heart sank and I wanted to vomit. Dad shot out insults and changed the conversation just as quick. The bacon looked extra oily in the pan, and I wanted to sling it across the wall, walk out, and never come back. I would get my first paycheck from the chicken coop in another week, and I vowed to save every penny. Alonso was right. We had to get out of here; me and Dad were not the same.

"Somebody gonna pay her to do makeup. This girl is crazy as a bedbug." Dad paddled to the living room and turned on the tv. I could hear him still talking from the other room as he flicked channels. "I don't understand you women. You get a good job, and yet you make another job for yourself. Ain't never happy."

"Mr. Cannon, with all due respect. Why you gotta be mean about it? If someone will pay her, what's the big deal?" Alonso chewed his cereal so hard a vein appeared on his forehead. He kept his eyes focused on Dad.

I held my breath.

"What's the big deal? What's the big deal?" Dad shouted from the living room. "I'm forty-one-years-old, my birthday is next month! I ain't never let no pipe dreams take me away from the real deal. From the here and now. Josephine needs to focus on figuring out why she can't stay somewhere for more than a few months, not what colors to slather on someone's lips."

Dad hopped to his feet and shouted in Alonso's direction. "And I know you got to defend your woman. I like that and I'll allow it. But you can do better, too."

"You know Alonso coaches! He works, too! Don't do that, Dad!" I yelled right back from the kitchen.

"*Humph.* It ain't the Sixers and he *ain't* Allen Iverson."

Alonso frowned and shoved a big scoop of cereal into his mouth. The *you need to do better* lecture came every day and he was tired of it too.

"And I'm not mean. I'm making her strong. The world is a cruel place, and it's even crueler and meaner for a Black girl with no direction. If she wants to paint people's faces—then fine. But you also have a job you need to focus on. Do you understand?" Dad's eyes bored into my soul, and I wondered if he spoke to Mom with the same intensity that he did me.

"Yes, I understand," I sighed and whipped together the eggs. I grabbed my phone and texted Ms. Marta to see if she was up yet so I could bring her some breakfast and a fresh plate of drama after I complained about Dad.

He was wrong. I *was* strong. Even if the world was cruel.

CHAPTER 10

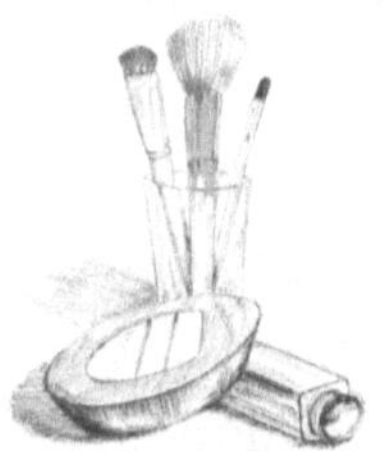

Alonso wore a **Temple U** hat and pulled it down over his eyes. He grabbed my hand and spun me to face him. "You look good, girl." He sucked his teeth and looked me up and down. "I should take you right here."

"Shut up!" I giggled and swiped his shoulder. We stood in front of the VIP entrance. Alonso nodded at a big, burly bouncer wearing sunglasses and he pulled the curtains back as we ducked through them. My eyes adjusted to the dimly lit hallway.

Dark and smoky.

My eyeshadow *and* this room.

I tugged at the bottom of my plaid skirt and eyed my black stockings for runs. I didn't see any. My hands nervously smoothed my backside even though everything was perfectly in place. Further into the room I spotted a floor length mirror, and I stole a glance at myself, Josephine Scott.

My calf muscles poked out and were strong from lots of walking to and from the train station. I wore six-inch block heels with a peep toe exposing white painted toenails and my sheer, lace black blouse tucked perfectly into my skirt. My lips were bright and bold blood red tonight. Ms. Marta had a floor length beige fur coat that was bad ass. She said she bought almost fifteen years ago when she used to go dancing. I tried it on one day and she gave it to me; said her dancing days were over. The coat cascaded down my curves and hugged my waist like it was made for just two special people. Ms. Marta and me. My makeup only took about an hour today from start to finish. Amna said if I was going to be a makeup artist I had to be quicker and my standard two hours wouldn't cut it.

She was right, I chuckled to myself as my eyes danced back at me in the mirror. My makeup was still flawless, set in all the right places.

I looked good.

They housed the fashion show in a building that looked like shit from the outside. It was run down and had drooping **for sale** signs plastered all over the front. Most of the small, square windows had bars blocking the glass and they were boarded up. It was a warehouse that I wouldn't give a second look any other day. When Alonso and I strolled inside behind the long line of people, I did a double take.

The lights were low apart from a few floor strobe dimmers pointing to the ceiling. They bounced and danced around the room as I eyed everything it illuminated and tried to hide. A DJ booth stood next to the front stage, and he already had the crowd on their feet with a few hits from Power 99. The music thumped in my chest, but it wasn't assaulting my ears; low enough so I didn't have to scream.

A few short steps down a hallway behind a sheer curtain, scores of female models, hairdressers, makeup artists, and designers raced around preparing for the show. Some of them were barely clothed and didn't seem to care who saw them partially naked as they hurled themselves into teeny tiny clothes or fussed with their hair.

I stood next to a long table filled with fruits, cheeses, meat assortments, small sandwiches, chicken wings, and salads. My stomach growled. I hadn't had cheese and pepperoni in months, not since me and Ms. Marta went to the market and tried a sample. It was our favorite, and she said it was the one thing people shouldn't skimp on.

"Cheap ass cheese will always break a dish. It's a sin," she said.

"A sin, though?" I chuckled.

"You heard me. God himself wouldn't eat no packaged cheese and pepperoni."

They weren't eating the packaged stuff back here. Back here the pepperoni was thick cut.

"Hey, my man." A large, light-skinned man dapped up Alonso and pulled him in for a big hug.

"Hey, Curtis." Alonso grinned.

Curtis.

Alonso and Curtis embraced and banged on each other's backs. A tall, slim woman with a massive ass that looked like it was expensive sitting so high, slid next to Curtis and nuzzled his ear.

"Is this the woman?" Curtis asked, gazing me up and down. He opened his arms for a hug, just like he did with Alonso.

"This is Josephine, my woman." Alonso showed all his teeth, smiling between me and Curtis like a proud parent.

I cringed at being called *woman.*

Curtis was thick. His arms were thick, legs were thick, neck, fingers. He wasn't tall, but he was stocky. He wore a crisp, hunter green t-shirt and his shoulders and arms jutted from his shirt struggling to contain his large body. He wore tons of jewelry, and it covered every stitch of his brown skin with a chain, bracelet, or ring. A cigar hung out the side of his mouth and his hand was cradling the woman's behind, nuzzling his ear.

"Nice to meet you, Josephine. I've heard a lot about you." Curtis stepped forward and extended a hand when he didn't see me move an inch to him wanting a hug.

I wanted to say, *what's your intentions with Alonso? And who is this big booty skinny girl hanging off your arm?*

I cleared my throat. "Thanks for the invite. I've never been to a fashion show." I looked around and stared at everyone working.

"My main lady here is a model. She's sitting this one out, though, but normally she would be up there showing out with the rest of them." He swung his arms around like he owned the place. "I actually own the place." He finished my thought for me.

He spoke to me, but his eyes were everywhere but on mine. People tapped on his shoulders and whispered in his ear every few minutes. They demanded his attention and he seemed to enjoy it. I peered over his shoulder and was shocked when I saw Rose. She was standing behind a seated model in front of a mirror, flat ironing her hair.

"Excuse me," I said, scootching past Alonso, Curtis, and his booty girl.

"Rose?" I raised an eyebrow.

She turned and smiled. "Josephine! What are you doing here, girl?" She clamped the model's hair between the flat iron plates and it sizzled under the heat.

"I'm with Alonso and his friend, Curtis. He invited us to the show. I didn't know you did hair." I watched her shuffle around her model, fixing wisps of hair with edge control. She moved fast like this was just a regular day and she knew what she was doing.

"Curtis, huh?" Her face fell flat. "You be careful with that one. He can be a mess," Rose's voice trailed off as she looked around to see if anyone heard her.

I inched in closer. "Why should we be careful?"

"Oh, never mind, we can talk more later." Her eyes darted around like someone was listening. "But anyway, yes! I do hair for Philly Fashion Week."

"Is that this week?" I shifted in place.

Rose chuckled. "Where have you been, girl? Yes, it's this week. It's actually more like a ten-day, two-week span. This isn't an official Philly Fashion Week event. It's a smaller show that the radio station put together. With the help of Curtis, of course. Since he does technically own the place . . ." She drifted off. "The bigger one they are holding next week at the convention center."

"So, there's a bigger one next week? When?" I questioned, trying to make sense of the fashion show life.

"The same day as your dad's birthday party, girl. Don't even think about it. That's why I'm working this one, so I can be home for him that night."

I could care less about Curtis or Dad right now, I wanted to know more about the glamourous life and what was happening here. Rose's hair model scrolled on her phone and popped gum in her mouth, paying no attention to me and Rose.

"Fashion Week is big business," Rose continued. "People throw a lot of events all over the city to make money. Curtis threw this one. Word on the street is he's friends with a few ball players and this is a good way to throw an event and call it charity. But chile, Curtis don't do *nothing* for no charity, that's for sure. I would bet his books are *overcooked,* you hear me? I thought with the way you can beat down a makeup look, you would already know that."

My face flushed and cheeks tingled. Someone wanted to pay me to do their makeup, and I didn't even know about Fashion Week and where all the makeup artists frequented.

"Have you seen the makeup room?"

"There's a makeup room?" My neck craned around so fast I had whiplash. "A whole room?"

Rose sat her flat iron down. "I'll be right back." She patted her model on the shoulders.

She winked at me. "Follow me."

We walked past models wearing lots of clothes and some wearing very little. She pulled back a small black curtain, and I instantly died. I died and went to fucking heaven.

In the large room I counted eight makeup artists— all Black women. They wore small waist aprons with pockets that held their makeup brushes, cotton balls, Q-Tips, and containers of lashes. They wore black, and their own makeup was flawless. Dark hued eyeshadows, expensive foundation, strip lashes, golden baked bronzers, lipstick in every color of the rainbow. Setting powder, setting spray, finishing powder. The models went from drab to fab in a matter of minutes, all with the help of makeup. They painted the models to perfection, but when I studied their own faces, I saw freckles and moles. They didn't hide things that made them unique and different. In fact, they were highlighted and makeup was a tool to do that. There was so much artistry in each nuance. Each crack and crevice.

Was this that faith Alonso was talking about? Whatever I was looking for, it was looking for me, too. I clenched at my chest, feeling faint. This was beautiful. The women had models leaned back in makeup chairs and large ring lights around them to magnify their work. They held onto large palettes of eyeshadow and blush colors in their hands. I bounced from foot to foot. "Look! She's using magnetic lashes! Magnetic! And look at her. She has the new YSL foundation!" I shot out my words fast and pressured as I took in the sights of women doing what I loved. What was I thinking? I could do this and *I knew it.* My hands itched to pick up a brush and attack someone's face right beside the other makeup artists, but I stood back and watched.

Rose giggled. "These girls are the real deal. Professionals. They do makeup for a living. That's why I wanted you to see it."

"Why?" I scrunched my face.

"Because you can do it, too, Josephine. I've seen your skills. I scoped out your Instagram page. You got it, girl. Stop sleeping on yourself."

"I have to get better with Instagram. I just post pictures every now and then to my personal page." My cheeks flushed from embarrassment. My mind rolled back to my most recent posts and if they were good enough.

"Your dad told me someone wants to pay you for your makeup. He's against it. But he's an asshole. You're the real deal just like these women and you can do this. It's almost fate that you're even here right now. I didn't know you were coming!"

Dad was quick to run and tell my business. I bit my tongue down in instant disgust. "I don't know if I can do this. Look at all of their equipment and products. I only have a few things that I picked up at the drugstore." My voice was low.

"Is that it? You need stuff?" Rose smiled and placed her hand on my shoulder. "Come with me." Rose led me down another dark hallway and we stepped into a smaller room that was filled with . . . stuff.

"What's all this?" I squinted around.

"This is the gift lounge. They give out free gift bags to some of the big names that come to the event. The bags are really nice and filled with high-end merch," Rose said over her shoulder. She was reaching under a table and pulling out square crates, her back facing me. "Come on, we have to be quick," she whispered.

"Why would they give out free stuff to people who already have stuff?" I inched closer, confused.

"Just hush up and come help me!" Rose exclaimed.

Rose opened the crates and my heart stopped. The box seemed to glow like it was waiting for me to be there, peeled open by me and me only. Dozens of high-end eyeshadow palettes, long, thick strip lashes, bright metallic blushes, golden bronzers, and juicy lipsticks greeted me. Rose grinned like a proud parent on Christmas morning.

"They give all this stuff away?" I gasped.

"Yep," Rose said, moving boxes around. "And the sad part is if no one takes it, they throw it away."

"Why would they do that?" Anger welled in my chest. Throwing away perfectly fine makeup. Now *that* was a sin.

"Who knows why rich people do what they do." She shrugged.

"Ten minutes' til showtime, everyone!" someone shouted into the room and ran off.

"Ahhh!" Rose and I jumped in surprise. My heart raced and I didn't realize we had been clasping hands.

Rose clutched her chest. "Girl, we gotta hurry up!" She grabbed a large trash bag and filled it with three of everything in the room. I watched her place all kinds of makeup into the bag, and she even threw in various lotions and perfumes. Everything was high-end. The bag grew heavier as she grunted and hoisted it over her shoulder. She raced around the room, filling it with anything she saw.

"Here. Put this under your coat." She shoved the bag toward me.

Without a second question, I stuffed it under the massive fur, thanking God for Ms. Marta giving it to me.

"Five minutes people! Let's get lined up!" someone shouted again. It sent everyone into overdrive, and people zipped around at warp speed, fretting about costumes and hair.

"I have to go, but just think about it. I work at the factory with your dad during the week, and I do this on the weekends. Life doesn't have to be hard, Josephine. It's what you decide to make it. This is how you make lemonade."

Alonso and I vibed to the music and checked out everything in the room from our front row seats. Curtis and his booty girl were sitting next to Alonso on the left.

A super long runway stretched in front of us and dozens of flashing lights made my eyes blurry. A deep rumble rippled through my chest when the music screamed. One by one, each model came out and they were long, leggy, and fierce.

I geeked over their faces, though. The beauty. Each model more illuminating than the one before. The way the light bounced off their highlighted cheeks and glossed lips looked straight out of a magazine. Some models wore toned down, natural glam, barely there looks with light notes of pink, pouty demure features.

Others were glammed up in high fashion, deep reds and shades of smoky, dark, cat eye looks. When their hair, makeup, and outfits all came together, they catapulted down the catwalk ready to take the world by storm.

They were all subtle and different in their own way.

Just like me.

They wore clothes, too, but I just glanced those over. The fits were different and colorful, but the makeup tied it all together and took it from a ghetto ass mall walk to a *fashion show*.

It was the makeup for me — it always was.

As model after model stormed past me, my eyes locked in on something different. Alonso and the rest of the crowd craned their necks to the left of the stage watching the models walk, but mine drifted to the right. I could see some of the hair and makeup team standing together, peeking from behind the curtain. They were grinning and giddy watching their work. Their *work*. Their creations demanding to be seen. Demanding a place in the world. Not letting someone tell them what to do. Were they living life in a strait jacket? Didn't look like it. We all had things that held us down and stopped us in some way. Was it always tied to money, a job, or a person?

For a moment, my heart sank. Music pounded around me and a lump the size of regret formed in my throat, and I used anger to swallow it away.

I never met Josephine Scott, technically. But in this moment, I wanted my mom and I wanted to cry. Comfort wasn't something that found me easily and green jealousy ripped through me. I wondered if any of them didn't have a mom or someone to sit and teach them makeup. I was probably light years behind them. I forced back the tears as loneliness found me in a room full of people like the Grim Reaper. When you looked good, it made you walk differently. The models strutted down the walkway, and their makeup accentuated their features and who they were in that moment. Who could I be—in a moment's notice? Who did I want to be?

Christeen wanted me. I was self-taught, but I was still good. She was going to pay me. She found me in a crowded room, waltzed over, and *chose* me. That meant something. Makeup was my art, and she wanted me to share my art. Even if my nerves felt otherwise, I was getting my ass ready. I wanted a different life, one that didn't involve hiding my makeup under a mask every day. Hiding my art.

Rose was so sure of herself. She worked with Dad and on the weekends did what her soul loved. She seemed like she was happy, sans my dad. What was it like to have blind faith like that? To just know you had a thing, and you could be so good at that thing and no one could do that *thing* like you could?

I had never even been out of Pennsylvania. Never had thoughts about moving or saw myself as one of those kids who went away for college. My entire life was right here—in this city.

The music abruptly stopped and out of the corner of my eye, I saw a few bodies moving, and then a chair behind me shattered.

"Get up!" Alonso shook my shoulder and shouted me out of my stupor.

"What-wha?" My eyes shot around. The room was so dim; I squinted to adjust.

Curtis and his humungous body were uppercutting some man. His big, burly arms were hulk smashing this dude's shoulder blades. The man was holding his own through a few of Curtis' ferocious blows, taking the uppercuts. He threw a few of his own hits, but they landed everywhere but on Curtis and that wouldn't last long. Curtis was waiting like a panther with a fury in his eyes that was missing earlier when he pulled me in for a fake hug.

Curtis wanted to kill the guy.

They were both tugging at their waists and something shiny and thick gleaned against Curtis.

"Run!" Alonso shouted in my face. His head shot between me and Curtis fighting with himself. He squeezed my hand and pushed away.

I instinctively pulled him back. "Come with me!" I shouted.

A hairdresser I saw backstage fell at my feet and tucked herself into a ball underneath an overturned table next to us. Her eyes were squeezed shut and she was crying as people continued fighting and trampling each other to get out of the room.

"I . . . I can't." Alonso snatched away from me and ran to Curtis.

My heart dropped into my pants and my beautiful, painted up face fell flat.

Alonso ran around to the man fighting Curtis, punched him in the ribs, and began pummeling him in the head. Alonso raged with an intensity I hadn't seen since he defended my honor in a high school cafeteria years ago. The man's friends jumped in to help their guy, and a few more of the Young Lords jumped in to help Alonso and Curtis. They began stomping each other out.

I gasped watching everything unfold in front of me.

"Let's go!" Rose yelled and tucked me under her arm.

I took one last look at Alonso over my shoulder as someone clocked him in the head.

"Let's go, Josephine!" Rose pushed me forward. I was already being shoved into a hoard of people trying to get out of the building from one small exit. Those few seconds without Alonso felt like hours. My legs felt like weights. My super cute heels felt like cement blocks.

When we burst through the double doors outside, I panted for air. Makeup jostled under my coat threatening to spill. A blast of February chill slammed me in the face and in seconds, I was shivering and crying.

Where was Alonso? *I should've stayed.*

Rose pushed me down the street, her adrenaline kicking in while mine ached for my man. I pulled my coat around my waist and tried to see through my blinding tears. Rose directed us to the nearest train, and I was so grateful, so grateful, so grateful for her because Alonso ruled my mind, my brain, my body. My mind was not my own right now, something reserved it just for thoughts of him.

With shaky hands, I called his phone over and over. Thirty minutes passed. No answer. I checked his social media accounts. He wasn't active for hours, but he was never big on social media, anyway.

When we got to our stop two blocks up from our house, I whipped around the corner and stomped to Ms. Marta's house.

"Are you coming?" Rose panted. Her chest was rising and falling, and hot air blew into the dark night.

"I'll be up in a minute. I'm going to see Ms. Marta."

"Okay. I'll tell your dad what happened. Take your time." Rose rubbed my back.

"No, don't tell him!" I cried. The tears whipped down my

face even faster now. My body shook and whimpered in the cold. I was ablaze inside.

"Hey, hey, calm down. It'll be okay." Rose pulled me in. Her heartbeat was fast and furious close to mine. I realized she was scared, too. "Let me talk to him. I promise you; it will be fine. You go up to Ms. Marta," she instructed and gave a weak smile.

It was after 1 a.m. when I used my key to let myself in. She went to sleep every night like clockwork at 11 p.m. Taking the steps two at a time, I heard her cackling from her bedroom. She was up.

"Ms. Marta, Ms. Marta." I burst into her room. I tripped over pizza boxes and empty water gallon jugs.

"Who say that? Who there?" Ms. Marta jumped in her bed. She wore an oversized moo-moo dress and her breasts hung limp and long.

I burst into the room, tears streaming down my face. I kneeled and fell into her lap at her bedside.

I choked out bits and pieces of what happened, but I really wasn't sure. I gulped out words, but they didn't make sense. A fight. Terrified people. Terrified me. Makeup.

One minute I was fantasizing about makeup on stage, and then Alonso was screaming run. He probably had two dozen phone calls from me at this point.

"Let it out. Let it out." Ms. Marta held me as tight as her weak little body could allow. She rubbed my back and squeezed and squeezed and squeezed. "Devil let go of her! She got on that red lipstick, but I say let her loose this minute! Let her loose!" Ms. Marta shouted and prayed over me. She cupped my face and wiped my snotted hand with her St. Anthony handkerchief. "You know Alonso loves you. He strong, he will make it out of anything. Best believe he coming home to you."

"But what if—"

"No. . . No. You *can't* think about that other stuff." Ms. Marta slapped her hands together. She squared her shoulders. "We must pray." Ms. Marta hopped up from her bed, shuffled to her ancestor altar, and grabbed her rosary beads.

"Ms. Marta, I don't want to pray." I wiped my face and leaned back on my elbows. I checked my phone to see if Alonso called.

He didn't.

"You cry. I pray."

For the next two hours, we cried and prayed. And prayed and cried. Then we got hungry.

"I took out some chicken earlier," Ms. Marta said. Next thing I knew, the kitchen was filled with sizzles of late-night grief, strewn flour, and fried chicken.

I called Alonso over and over. No answer.

I posted a picture of my makeup today to my social media page, too.

I was terrified—all for different reasons.

"Here. Smell this. You would love this one." I pulled a perfume out of my bag of goodies from Rose and pushed it toward Ms. Marta. None of it was broken in the melee.

I leaned back on the couch and rolled a joint. Somewhere after fried chicken and later, homemade strawberry short-cakes, hours had slipped by. We lit up and shared one between us. Ms. Marta was old-school and only liked to smoke weed with white EZ Widers.

She smelled the perfume and between that and the joint, she coughed and hacked and choked her way through it. After a few what looked like painful coughing spells, she relaxed and forgot about what hurt on her body.

"What else you got in that bag?" she croaked.

My eyes sparkled, pulling out all my treasures. I felt like The Little Mermaid.

"What's all this, a hoe kit?" Ms. Marta eyed my lipsticks.

We cracked up laughing.

"How old were you when you fell in love, Ms. Marta?"

My phone lit up, and Dad's name and face popped across the screen. The Cannon. I let it ring all the way through. Me and common sense weren't friends right now. I wasn't in the mood and was high as a kite.

Besides, this is where Ms. Marta's best storytelling began.

"I loved my Papa. He was an okay man. Not a good man, but he was okay. He was born in Ponce, back in the old country and he liked to pounce. He always had his hands wrapped around some woman's neck, mi madre included. He seemed to like the control of it, you know. Being able to tell someone what to do. Mi madre hid it well for a while." She puffed and puffed and passed, remembering the things she thought were buried.

"One day we were sitting at the dinner table. She had dinner done every day at three p.m. And every day that was okay with Papa. Until one day he came home and Madre had made us great, big, fresh salads for dinner. She had all the good stuff in there, too— avocados, eggs, chicken. Even made the dressing from scratch. Papa was a meat and potatoes kind of guy. When he saw the salad, he said, *'You know this is not dinner, right? We need a snack or something. This can't be it.'*"

"Mama laughed it off and said he was loca and he needed to watch what he was eating. To support him, she said we would all eat healthier —and once a week that would include no meat. He turned to me and said, *"in 20 minutes I'm gonna smack your madre."*

"Why?" I asked.

"Because she don't believe in me."

"And don't you know, my papa got up, and he sure enough smacked mi madre across the mouth. That was the first time he did it right in front of me. I think that was the first man I loved, and I also knew I didn't want one like that. When I got older, young Marta kept finding little, tiny pieces of Papa in everyone. Can you imagine, finding your daddy in every smile—every place you thought was your new home?"

I couldn't.

"Not til I met my husband. Even then when he came into my life, I was a whistling hen, and you know they come to no good ends, if you're not careful." She chuckled. Ms. Marta puffed and wiped a lone tear from the corner of her eye.

"Anger and disappointment in men was sitting on my heart and wouldn't let go. But I had to make it, Josephine." She stared at me. Long pillar candles she lit hours ago danced and jumped in orange conjure over her shoulder. "Everybody got a pattern in they life. Some lesson that keeps popping up until you learn it. Some people spend a lifetime learning their lesson the hard way. I learned my lesson. My family and my daddy ain't my family and my daddy today. I wasn't them and my family wouldn't look or feel like them."

I puffed on Ms. Marta's words and was quiet for a few minutes. Her heater hummed behind us, listening to our night-time secrets. "I lived with Dad my whole life, aside from a few summers with my grandmom," I started. "But I always feel like a burden to him." I puffed on the joint and handed it to Ms. Marta. "One time he had this girlfriend. She was the new flavor of the week, and Dad worked this crazy ass schedule at the plant and she watched me a lot. Nakiya was her name. We had a lot of fun, at least I thought we did. But every time I misbe-haved, or did something she didn't agree with, she called my dad at work and screamed into the phone complaining about *'Your daughter,' 'Your child,' 'Your kid.'*

"Dad was saddled with me after Mom died. Where do I fit in? Where do I belong? I'm a kid with no mom."

"Who is she, though? NUH-KEY-WHO?" Ms. Marta flung her neck around and rolled her eyes. Her left eye drooped lower than the right. "Who is she? She wasn't nobody then and she ain't nobody now that got you still thinking about this. You can't let people get ahold of you like this, Josephine. People gon' say things that turn your stomach to pieces. To pieces, you hear me? You are going to overhear some stuff that'll make you question how some folks sleep at night. People will only see you as big as you see yourself. So you better start to see yourself real big." She poked me in the shoulder with the joint and handed it to me.

Tears had dried on my face hours ago and salty lines now painted my cheeks.

"The sun is coming up. Do you want some eggs?" She looked out the window and yawned.

Peeking behind her the sun was rising over her shoulder. "Ms. Marta! We stayed up all night. Look at this view you have." I stared out the window. "The sun looks amazing from your house!" Shades of burnt-orange, red, and yellow were slowly rising in the sky, painting her slice of Philadelphia wine red, cherry, and coral hues. Her pillar candles burned low and slow, now down to little nubs on her table. No yelling, horns, or trains barreled through the silence. The city was quiet, everyone asleep except for me and Ms. Marta.

Ms. Marta smiled and hobbled her way to the kitchen. "It is a nice view. I love how blessed we are. Now, about those eggs?" She rose an eyebrow.

"Sure. And did I tell you they had fresh cheese and

pepperoni at the show last night? You have pancakes? I'll whip up a few."

Ms. Marta spun around in the kitchen and clasped her hands like she just won the lottery.

"The good cheeses?! And I bet you they got it from that new Italian market in South Philly!" she exclaimed.

I chuckled, knowing her tricks. That was her way of saying she wanted us to try out the new market.

"Matter fact." She rummaged around in the bottom of her pantry until she found what she was looking for. "Member when we went to the market last? Use some of this fresh vanilla in the pancakes. Make it smell real good in here. And we'll wait for Alonso."

"And we'll wait for Alonso," I uncapped the vanilla and repeated.

CHAPTER 11

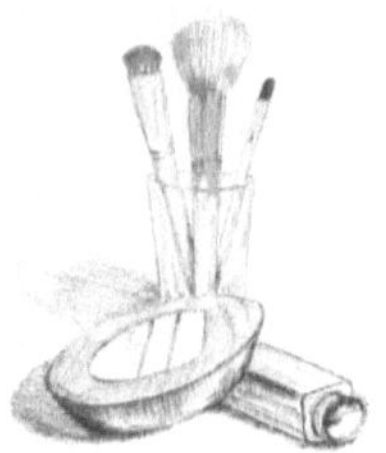

Stumbling back to my house in the dawn glow, I carried my heels in my hands and slid around in Ms. Marta's house slippers on left-over ice from a storm.

"Oh my God!" I shouted. Alonso leaned against the back door, his battered face screaming for attention. His left eye swelled shut and his cheeks were covered in a dark shade of black. The collar of his sweater was torn and his beloved sneakers were scuffed and covered in grass stains.

"What happened? Where were you? I called you over and over? Why didn't you call me?" I shot out questions and pressed my hands to his body searching for wounds or blood.

Alonso crawled to a standing position and winced in pain. Anger was still present in his eyes and with every grimace from his injuries, he grit his teeth and clamped down on his tongue. He covered his face in his hands and didn't speak.

"Why were you sitting out *here*? It's freezing." My voice lowered and hand brushed his face.

Silence.

"I don't think my dad is home. His car was gone when I walked over, and he said yesterday he was going out to get stuff for his birthday party. Come on, let's go inside."

Silence.

My keys jiggled softly as we pushed open the back door and peeked around. *God, please don't let my dad be home.*

Rose jumped to her feet in the kitchen, her eyes wide and alert. She looked like she, too, had slept little. Her hands shot to her mouth in shock and her cheeks turned a pale pink as she took in Alonso's face. Without a word, Rose turned to the refrigerator, pulled out bacon and eggs—and did what every Black woman in America did when trouble rang out, she started cooking.

I walked and half-carried Alonso to the bathroom and turned on the shower. My fingers danced under the water testing it to make sure it wasn't too hot. He liked the water lukewarm, never scorching like me. Alonso was spaced out. His eyes were glassed, and one eye was growing larger and blacker and bluer by the minute.

A knock at the door interrupted my thoughts. Rose was on the other end.

I stepped into the hallway and softly closed the door behind me. "Breakfast is ready. I sent your dad to the store so it'll be awhile," she whispered. "He was pissed about you not coming home after I told him about the fight."

I groaned. "You told him about the fight?"

Rose's back stiffened. "He's my man. We don't keep secrets like that. And besides, he wanted to know how the fashion show went and I didn't want to lie to him. But he's calmed down. He's just worried about you. Talk to him," Rose pressed.

My body weakened at the thought of Dad knowing what happened. Funny he could support Rose and inquire about her part-time job but it was out of the question for me. I didn't know what was worse. Worrying about the Young Lords and what Alonso's involvement in all of this meant or if Dad would make good on his promise and kick us out.

"Thanks." I mouthed to Rose and shut the door behind us. Alonso needed me.

Pulling his sweater over his head, he sat mute leaned against the sink in a stupor. Fluffy steam engulfed us and tried to hide his spirit, but I saw him. My hands scratched his scalp, and my hands rubbed his face hard. Alonso always liked a little pain with his pleasure. He closed his eye and a tear slipped down his cheek. *Let him loose . . . let him loose . . .* I prayed and banged on his back.

Unbuckling his jeans and helping him step out of them, they fell to the floor. Bright red blood splatter interrupted his crisp, white kicks and I recoiled, knowing dirty kicks would hurt him just as much as any physical trauma on his body. We slid those off to the side.

Alonso stared blankly at the bathroom wall; his shoulders slumped. What was he thinking? What did he need from me right now? Sweat was pouring from my fully clothed body and drenched hair clung to my forehead. It was times like this I realized how much my mom's absence was seared into me like a tattoo. I never saw a woman comfort a man. Never saw a man let his guard down and take comfort from a woman. Wasn't sure I knew how. But showing up for him was like showing up for myself. And I would always show up for myself.

After pulling the rest of his clothes off, Alonso stood before me in the nude. Cuts and scratches littered his chest, some old and new. Some told tales of fights and disagreements long before I came along, and some fresh from last night. My man was a warrior—in every sense of the word. He defended his tribe even when the fight wasn't his own.

I loved and hated him for it.

I slipped out of Ms. Marta's house slippers, removed my stockings, and blouse. My bare nipples grazed against Alonso's chest and grew instantly. My makeup still looked good, even lasting through a long night at Ms. Marta's. I grasped Alonso's hand and pressed our fingers together and squeezed and squeezed for dear life. We stood before each other naked. Steam enveloped us and I could barely see through our essence. My hands roamed his body, praying over him and sending him love in all the places he couldn't find the words for just yet. Even with a busted lip, I ached to kiss him. Even in his worst moments, he started my body up like a car. As light as my shivering body could muster, I brushed my lips against his so he felt me. I was there and wasn't going anywhere. Where would I go, anyway?

We stepped inside the shower with him in the front. Once the water hit his chest and burned his fresh wounds, he grimaced in pain. *"I got you. I got you,"* I whispered.

Wringing a washcloth down his back, I let the warm water trickle over his body. He leaned his head back onto my shoulder, and his weight was crushing. I held him up from behind, praying I didn't fall. *God, please don't let us fall.*

A wail the size of a whale escaped him. His whole body shuddered and he cried in my neck. I wrapped my arms around his waist as tight as I could. My breasts and flesh pressed up against his back. Alonso cried and cried. He banged his hands on the tiled walls inside the shower. "Fuckkkkk!" he screamed.

I held on for dear life. *God, please don't let us fall.*

After the shower, Rose finished cooking breakfast and laid everything on the table. Alonso plopped down, and Rose had a fat icepack waiting for his shiner, now even more red and inflamed from the shower. He carefully held it to his lip and eye while taking bites of food. He looked more like himself now cleaned up.

The three of us ate in silence.

"Thanks," Alonso mumbled and slid from the table and retreated back to our bedroom.

Rose watched him walk away and made sure he was out of ear shot before she spoke. "I didn't tell your dad why the fight started. I'm not even sure myself. So, you guys will have to come up with why Alonso looks like that. You know he has the guys coming over in a couple days for the party. Let Alonso get some rest. And talk to your dad," Rose warned. She put her arm around my shoulder, and a tear slipped down my cheek. I was glad Alonso was home and glad Rose was here, too.

Not a minute too soon, the familiar jingle of Dad's keys met me at the door.

Rose's eyes widened, and she put distance between us faster than I could blink. She smoothed out her shirt and pulled her hair behind her ear and cleared her throat. When she pulled the heavy door open, she grinned at Dad. "Hey baby. I got breakfast all ready for you. Alonso is sleeping and Josie and I just finished eating. Here, let me take those." Rose grabbed the shopping bags out of Dad's hand. She scuddled to the kitchen and cut her eyes at me. *"Talk,"* she whispered.

Fortunately for her, Dad never wasted time or breath.

"So, what's this I hear about a fight last night? You can't call nobody back? So, you and your knucklehead boyfriend are in bar fights now, Josie?" Dad popped shelled peanuts into his mouth and chewed as he spoke. He kept sunflower seeds, peanuts, and other things on him at all times. His phone buzzed at his hip where he still wore a phone clip and a Bluetooth earpiece. He didn't answer, but continued to shoot questions, comments, and beef at me. "You know, this really don't make no damn sense. I know what Alonso and those young boys be doing. Ya'll really think I'm stupid. Alonso mixed up with them gangs, ain't he? I don't say nothing because you and your boyfriend are grown, but you really ain't grown. How ya'll fussing and fighting but live in somebody else damn house?"

Like Alonso, Dad could also start me up like a car but for different reasons.

"It wasn't even his fault!" I shouted. "We don't know why the fight started, and Alonso was trying to break it up. Can you at least try to understand for one second? Just listen for a second before talking!"

Rose stood in the doorframe from the living room and kitchen, wiping her hands with a dish towel. "Come on ya'll. Listen to each other."

I swallowed, trying to even out my breath. I had been up at least twenty hours by this point and the worry and frustration were wearing on my mind and body. I licked my lips. "Dad," I started. "It wasn't our fault. Before you just accuse and blame Alonso, can you calm down for a second and hear me out? You're not always right."

"Mr. Cannon. I apologize," Alonso's voice cut through the tension in the room like a boat slicing through water.

All eyes turned to him, and Dad gasped, witnessing the full display of Alonso's injuries.

"My God, son! Look at your face. Did you even fight back?

How many of 'em was it? Had to be at least ten! You need to go to the hospital!"

"It's not as bad as it looks. I'll be okay." Alonso tried to stand upright. "The truth is, yes, I am a member of the Young Lords. They came into my life long before I knew Josie." Alonso's eyes roamed the floor before taking a breath and looking Dad square in the eye. He could come up with a lot of words to try and explain his way out of this one, but nothing but the truth would suffice in this moment.

"For the most part, it's been about protection, family for those who didn't have any. But lately, it's turned into something different." Alonso frowned and shook his head like he was trying to figure out where it all went wrong and how he missed it. "To be honest, I don't know what happened last night. There could've been some beef I knew nothing about beforehand, or something new that brewed up that night. Mr. Cannon, just know that regardless of if I knew it was going to happen or not, my reaction would've been the same. I ride for family—whether I know why or not. But either way, I hear you, Mr. Cannon. I hear you and I see your concerns. I hear you." His eye pleaded with Dad. "Please know that I would never do nothing to put you or Josie in jeopardy. I'm sorry."

Cannon, the Cannon, always weakened when someone waved the white flag. He wasn't the type to keep things going and when someone apologized, it calmed him. I stared at Alonso, too, wondering if this fight was a bitter taste of truth serum. The Young Lords were his *family*.

The permanent scowl that created deep worry lines across Dad's forehead flattened. He stared at Alonso for seconds. Black man to Black man.

"And don't be bringing this drama up in my house again.

You untangle yourself from this leash, okay, Lonz? It's either us or them. You hear me? This house. Or them."

"I understand, Mr. Cannon."

"Now let's sit down and talk about how this whole thing unfolded. Again. Tell me about these Little Lions. Josie, make some more eggs and pour some orange juice. Start it from the top."

CHAPTER 12

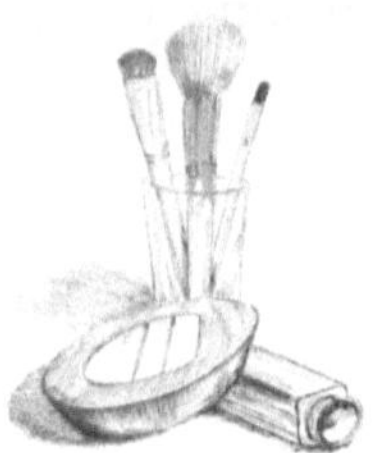

Days passed and Alonso's bruises lightened, and with time a piece of him returned. After the dust settled, his eye was the only major injury, and he poked his chest out and claimed he took it like a champ.

Dad's birthday party was in a few hours, and he would only eat cake from one bakery way across town in Center City. It drizzled this morning, and it was already a pain to get out there. Alonso's cap covered my hair and had my eyes low and in-cog-negro today.

Two busses later, I added to my travels and purposely took the long way home. The long way led me past the convention center. The long way led me past the *fashion show.*

Balancing Dad's cake in my hands, my free hand peered up to the dark, two-way glass. Couldn't see a thing inside. A ferocious Philly wind whiplashed me when I scurried around the corner toward the entrance. Dozens of people were making their way inside the warm, beckoning building. I closely followed some of the ticket holders like I was going in with them. With my face concealed under the cap, I held up Dad's cake and said, *"delivery for makeup."*

"Do you have a ticket?" an employee asked.

"No, just dropping this off." I shrugged in what felt like the most unconvincing way.

"Hold on." The older man eyed me, turned to his colleague, and whispered.

I held my breath.

"You can head on. Hang a left at the bathrooms and head down the tunnel. You'll run into the dressing rooms," he instructed.

Ahhhhh!!

"Hey, one minute!" the guy shouted.

My feet froze like quicksand. I was caught.

"Is that cake from the shop down on Market Street?"

"Yes." I cleared my throat and tried to connect my feet back with my brain. "It is."

"Man, I told you it was! They get all the good stuff downstairs!" the employee yelled over his shoulder to his colleagues as he scanned tickets.

"Look like you belong. Stand tall," I whispered to myself through my heartbeat screaming in my ears. Hanging a left and heading down the tunnel as I was instructed ran me right into heaven. Heaven.

An even bigger room than Rose's event, this open space was dimly lit and lined with rows of tables filled with every food you could think of and fresh roses. Soft music played from hidden speakers, and there seemed to be more photographers recording and taking pictures of all the behind-the-scenes action. Dad's cake felt like a rock in my arms as I gawked at everything around me. In the center of the room sat two rows of five, back-to-back makeup workstations. At each station, a model and a makeup artist dove into palettes, lookbooks, and sample jewelry. One thing remained the same—everyone rushed around and there was a buzz of activity that said what they were doing was important. *They* were important and people were coming to see their art.

This is a world I was already a part of. I knew how to craft a look and beat a face with the best of them. Heartache could spread like wildfire if I chose to let it and that's not what I wanted to choose anymore.

"Is that cake for us?" someone with a clipboard stepped in front of me and asked.

My fingers tingled wanting to push the box forward. Wanting to do an even trade and say, *'hey, you take this cake if you let me sit in for one of your makeup artists.'*

"Oh, uh . . . no . . . sorry. I'm in the wrong room. Took a wrong turn." I rushed out in search of the nearest exit. I had to get home and let the men eat cake.

When I stumbled into the back door, Alonso was getting down in the kitchen. He had a mean BBQ recipe and volunteered to cook all the meats for Dad's birthday. He braved the late February winter for my moody, February Pisces of a Dad, Alonso donned a trench coat as he flipped slabs of ribs on the smoker out back.

I shot Ms. Marta a quick text message inviting her over for the party, but I knew she wouldn't come, and I wouldn't want her here, anyway. This night was for my dad and his meat-head friends. They liked to drink, play cards, and complain about work and women.

Rose was in the house blowing up balloons and refilling the plug-ins from the wall. I wondered if she remembered paradise was just a few steps away at the convention center or just didn't care? Or maybe she liked shucking and jiving for Dad? Alonso never made me choose.

I pulled my coat on and stood next to Alonso at the smoker, staring him square in his fat eye. My body jiggled from the cold, but I needed Alonso alone. We calmed my dad about the fight last week and he was in a good mood today for his birthday party, but I needed my own questions answered and Alonso had been ducking them. Enough was enough.

I got right to it. "What am I missing, Alonso? Something about this fight still don't sit right with me."

Alonso pursed his lips in disgust, tired of the questions. "Don't start, Josephine, I'm not in the mood for your investigation discovery bullshit!" His back stiffened, and a readymade, fabricated lie ran down the length of his spine. The truth sat right on his lips, waiting to be spoken out loud.

He shook his head and frowned. "They were some dudes out North Philly Curtis had beef with. I told you that already!"

"And?" I snatched a pack of hotdog buns and slammed them onto the grill's hood.

"Curtis. . . he . . . he told some Young Bloods to grab a few of their cars and chop them down."

"Grab? Don't be cute."

"Stole, Josephine. They stole it. Broke it down for parts." Alonso opened the smoker and flipped the meat. The heat from the open flames and the smell wafting from the smoked ribs made my mouth water.

I touched Alonso's shoulder. He kept this part from Dad. "Alonso, did you . . ."

He shrugged me off him. "No, I didn't. I'm not that dumb." He tightened and untightened his fists as he dabbed BBQ sauce onto the meat.

"So, you jump into a fight with him, then go knock off a few cars? Alonso, you're a basketball coach. You bring it up all the time. This is what you say you want. So why would you do something like this to jeopardize that?"

Alonso slammed the smoker shut and the entire barrel shook. "Don't you think I know that? Curtis and the guys have been there for me when I had no one. You have your dad, you have Ms. Marta, but who do I have? My family up and left me to figure it out. And even before they left—they were already gone."

"Well, that's stupid, Lonz. You have me. You've always had me," I said, my voice cracking. *Did he think he didn't have me?*

"You don't get it. It's easier for girls. Men have to tough it out and man up. We have to know we're protected. It's not always about gang life and the shit you see on tv, Josephine. That's family. Curtis is family."

"*That's* family?" I snorted. "It's never something simple with them. You can't help them change a tire or something? You have to help fight in a brawl and steal cars?"

"Run the Chop Shop." Alonso looked around, making sure no one heard him.

"What?" I searched his eyes.

"Run the Chop Shop," he repeated. "Curtis wants me to run the Chop Shop after they bust down the cars."

Air escaped my body, and for a second, I forgot to breathe. "And you're considering this? And you weren't even going to tell me? I had to corner you like this at a damn hot dog stand for the truth?"

Alonso smacked the lid down for the second time and shot around. "I don't really have a choice in the matter. Since he got me that big coaching client and all. I owe him."

"You haven't even started with the client yet! You can still back out."

He shook his head. "That's not how this works, Josephine. I can't just back out of an opportunity like this. I could get in good with the players, really make a name for myself."

I glared at Alonso; my hands itched to wring his neck. "Do you think I've had it easy? Do you think I've never felt alone? I go to a fucking job where I process dead chickens. I have to ask to use the bathroom and I eat lunch in front of a clock counting down my every moment. I'm sorry, I didn't know you were the only one who had it tough." Waves of anger shot through me, and I scrunched my shoulders to my chin. Each shallow exhale reminded me I was no longer cold. I was hot and furious. He made it sound like he was the only one sacrificing. He was letting Curtis concoct scheme after scheme and pull his strings like a puppet, and I was plucking chickens for a living. I lived, loved, cried, and—when I was in trouble—felt like I almost died in the same apartment. Same princess bedroom, same everything. But *he* was suffering.

My furious eyes shot around to the folding table next to the smoker, and, I don't know why, but I grabbed a packet of uncooked hotdogs and hurled one at Alonzo's head.

Alonzo ducked as a raw hotdog whizzed by his ear. "What the fuck are you doing?" He dropped his spatula to the ground.

One, two, three... I grabbed more hotdogs in the pack, and I chucked them at his fat head, blinded by rage. Me and Ms.

Marta had waited up for him all night until my eyes were burning and red. Hell, even Rose. And he was seriously standing in front of me spouting off some *'it's a secret society. All we ask is trust'* bullshit.

Alonso stepped forward and snatched the remaining package from my hands. He squeezed the rest of the processed meat until hotdog guts seeped through his fingers. His face was contorted. "Don't you ever, ever hit me with no fucking hotdogs again. Do you hear me?"

"Hit you with the hotdogs? What is going on out here? Is the meat done?" Rose pulled the sliding door open and shut it behind her before shooting a questioning glance at me and Alonso. There were at least six squashed hotdogs on the ground in front of Rose's feet. "You two better get it together. Your dad just got home with the guys!" Rose had on light makeup and her hair was up in a bun. She fidgeted with her purple dress, Dad's favorite color, and checked over the food.

I turned on my heels and stomped inside the house. Our small apartment was filled with grumpy, old men. Dad's friends: Thomas, Gordon, Martin, and Reggie. Reggie was the oldest out of the group, and he was my godfather. I never understood the role of godparents. When I was in school, my Hispanic friends talked about their godparents like they truly were second parents. If Reggie was my godfather and supposed to be an extension of my real father, then he knew my father didn't have a loving bone in his body. So why would he allow me to stay where there was no love?

"Hey, Uncle Reggie. Hey Mr. Thomas, Mr. Frank, Mr. Martin." I nodded and waved at everyone around the table.

"Heyyy, Ms. Josie!" they called out back to me. Even though they had watched me grow up from a child, their hungry eyes still roamed over my body and in a flash flicked back to their cards.

"Yeah, she ready." Mr. Martin scratched his head and eyed my chest. "I give credit where credit is 'due and it's looking like an 850! Whose turn is it?"

"Excuse me." Alonso brushed by me, placing his hand on the small of my back and scooting by me. I shivered under his fingers.

"Lonz! What happened to you, man?" Uncle Reggie stood up from the table and stared at Alonso's face.

"Josie, did you do this!? You better keep your hands to ya self, girl!" Uncle Reggie huffed. He tried to scoot around the table to assess Alonzo's injuries, but Rose guided him back to his seat.

"Don't worry about the kids, they're fine. Enjoy the party. Here. Try a few ribs Alonso just pulled off the grill."

"I'm okay, Mr. Reggie. Just had to set some people straight." Alonso flexed his knuckles next to me.

Dad puffed his cigar and stared at me and Alonso for a long time. Rose's worried eyes darted between the three of us while she rubbed Dad's shoulders.

"And did you? Set some people straight?" Dad squinted at Alonso.

Alonso nodded. "Indeed, I did." He turned and began making two plates; one for me and one for himself.

Rose and I locked eyes.

The guys at the table shuffled cards and nibbled at food from their plates while trying *not* to steal glances at Alonso's face. If awkwardness lived anywhere, it set up shop and changed its address to our place.

"These damn ribs *is* good. What did you use?" Mr. Martin wiped his mouth as BBQ sauce sat in his mustache.

"It's an old family recipe." Alonso grinned. Happy the questions were off his eye, he added. "My mom uses a recipe she got from her mom and her mom. The secret is in the dry rub."

Our little living room was swelling with people, food, and noise. Two long tables were next to each other that had Spades games running at both ends. People were in the kitchen making plates. Dad had the 65-inch tv blasting on the wall and was hell bent on screaming at everyone over the noise. I grabbed the remote and turned it down a few notches.

"Turn that back up, Josie. I can't hear a thing!" Dad fussed, a cigar hanging out the side of his mouth. Every time he laughed, so did his belly, and it made the table jump. He was peering down at a stack of cards in his hand and squinting like he couldn't see them. Rose stood behind him stroking his head.

Mr. Thomas had his lips wrapped around a beer when he casually tossed a card on the table and said, "My new lady said her and her old man ain't dating anymore, so I asked if he spent the night and she said no; but then in the next breath she was talking about what they had for breakfast." The guys at the table collectively cracked up laughing, and like Ms. Marta, this was where their storytelling began.

"You can't trust them." Dad picked up. "That's why I got my one, and she knows a good thing when she sees it." Dad pinched at Rose's butt. She blushed, pushing his hands away.

"My old lady got cats. Like three of 'em." Mr. Martin snorted in his seat and slapped a card down on the table.

"I hates me a cat." Dad frowned and turned up his beer bottle.

"I will never understand Black people's beef with cats. What is it? Does anyone know?" Mr. Frank waved his hands around in confusion as the men grumbled in agreement at the table.

"They sneakkyyy." Mr. Martin curled his lip and hissed, as strong Jack Daniels hit his taste buds.

The guys snorted out their laughs and I giggled in my seat, watching my dad's friends talk shit and eat. Not one of them was married and I could see why.

"Cannon, you remember Big Josephine loved cats." Uncle Reggie chuckled.

I perked up, hearing my mom's name.

"Yeah, she did. She used to sit food out. There was always this one, completely chocolate cat that came to the back step. I had never seen a chocolate cat before. We went to the library and looked it up; said it was a rare species. That made Josephine happy, she said out of everyone in the world, the rarest of rare cat chose us. She said the cat came around when good things happened. It was her good luck charm."

I tucked my leg underneath a couch pillow and folded my hand under my head. Alonso sat down next to me and handed me a plate and napkin.

"Mmmmm . . ." The guys at the table murmured, taking in Dad's words.

Rose gave me a weak smile, and I wondered if she was choosing Dad and if he was choosing her.

"What ya'll think about that new center down on Mount Airy Ave? I heard they got some talent down there." Mr. Martin raised his eyebrows and winked.

"So that's why you brought up the cats. You thinking about some cat, huh?" Dad joked and shook the table when he slapped his card down.

The guys chuckled, and Uncle Reggie laughed the loudest. "You know that used to be the old post office. Remember—it had that lot in the back with that small shed, and we used to come back at night after everything closed down with the womens?"

Before anyone could respond, Uncle Reggie turned to Dad and grinned. "You see how I be remembering some shit, Cannon? And those doctors say I got a head injury."

That about did it for me I covered my mouth and burst out laughing.

"Ya'll know Josie got herself a job down at the factory with me," Dad announced.

"Awww shucks, Ms. Josie. You'll be henpecked and tired of that shit soon enough." Mr. Frank shook his head. "That was one job I couldn't do."

"Why?" I sat up on the couch.

"All that bending and twisting. You have to do the same thing over and over again. I like jobs where I can think for myself. If you didn't go in crazy, you sure come out crazy. Look at ol' loose cannon over here. Ain't got a bit of sense and mean as an Ox. Shiiittt, I'm running a risk even talking to you, Ms. Josie!" Mr. Frank's shoulders jumped as he poked fun at Dad.

"Don't be putting all that free-spirit nonsense in her head." Dad put out his cigar and smacked his lips. "She already want to charge people to paint their faces. Ain't nobody got time for that. We work in this house."

"But Cannon." Mr. Frank shifted in his seat. He passed a joint between his hands to Mr. Martin. "You ain't never wanted to live nowhere else? Get out of Philly and do something different? My daughter and her husband got a place down in Houston. They say it's nice. I'm thinking about going out there for a visit for myself."

Dad tutted and turned his face up at Mr. Frank. "Houston!? What's in Houston that Philly ain't got? Ain't no use going somewhere and starting all over again. Home is right here. Besides, Houston got tornadoes, and I don't do tornadoes."

"Aww this old fool talking about tornadoes, now." Mr. Martin waved away Dad. "You can tell he sat in one class all his life. Home is where you make it. Home is where the heart is." Mr. Martin nodded, agreeing with Mr. Frank.

"Home is where the heart is," Dad mocked in a baby voice. "I see ya'll on that coo-coo, you gotta practice positive thinking shit, too."

"It's not positive thinking, Dad." I cleared my throat and stood. I grabbed a few empty plates from around the table and emptied them into the trashcan. "If you found something you really loved, and it made you money, wouldn't you want to do it full-time?" I leaned against the wall beside Rose.

"Oh, hush, girl. Don't nobody *want* to work. Even if it was something you liked, do any of your old asses *want* to work?" Dad looked around the table.

"No, not me," the guys grumbled and shook their heads.

"Exactly. You do what you have to do. I didn't have no choice when Big Josephine passed. I had a mouth to feed. What I wanted to do? Ha. I don't even know what that looks like. Besides, all the things you *want* to do are either bad for your health or they'll get you arrested. You lay low and do what you have to do."

"I'm gonna go lay down for a few minutes. You want anything more to eat?" Alonso leaned over and whispered.

I shook my head. My stomach suddenly turned listening to how my dad really felt. How did I tell him I was tired of doing what I *had* to do? When did I ever get the option to do what I *wanted* to do? Dad talked about Mom like she was a saint and she was to be worshipped. His idea of perfection was tucked away in a box in my closet filled with pictures and faint scents of a life they almost had. Mom fed the cats—and that told me she had a heart. But did Dad feed her soul? Did they balance each other out? Was she the calm to his storm? If Dad constantly badgered her about his expectations and what he saw for her life—would she have stayed?

Tears sprung to my eyes. I ducked into the kitchen and leaned over the sink, taking deep, even breaths.

"You okay?" Rose stepped into the kitchen and blocked the guys from seeing me.

I nodded. "I'm going to check on Alonso."

While the men laughed and screamed back and forth at each other, I crept into our cramped bedroom and gently shut the door behind me. Alonso's clothes were neatly folded and stacked on his side of the bed and mine were strewn all over the floor. He was laying down over top of the covers with his arms tucked behind his head, his eyes closed, and earbuds in.

I took off my shoes and climbed into bed next to him.

Alonso.

He fed my soul.

He balanced me out.

He was the calm to my storm.

"I'm sorry," I whispered, pulling out one of his earbuds.

"I'm sorry, too." He snaked his hand around my neck and pulled me in for a kiss.

"I don't want us to live like this anymore, Alonso. Something has to change."

Alonso nodded. "I agree. Let's not fight anymore. I hate it; we're so much better than this."

Home is where the heart is.

CHAPTER 13

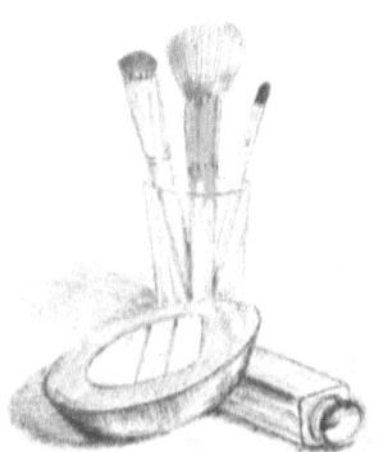

The big day was here.

Dozens of different foundation shades and palettes stared back at me. Boring store music played from the speakers and I wanted to scream, *shut uppp so I could focus.*

In a few short hours, Amna was coming with me to the hotel and we were meeting Christeen, where she was getting ready for her birthday party.

Biting down on my lip, the choices were overwhelming. Christeen had warm undertones, I did a patch test on her last week at work and when I checked the inside of her wrists, she had bright, yellow veins. A nagging suspicion told me we needed a different shade of foundation for her complexion to match perfectly. I needed to be sure.

I had to be, *sure.*

Alone in the aisle, I leaned in and ran my finger across the tabs until I got to *Tawny* and I stopped.

The foundation I *might* need was $40. Shit.

Nervous feet had me pacing in place. I was so used to not

having money and having to make tough calls. Did being poor make you more impulsive? Well, it wouldn't anymore. I was crossing all T's and dotting all I's going forward. I was robbing Peter to pay Paul. *This had to work.*

When I started at the chicken coop it was between pay periods and when I got my first check, it was fatter from three weeks of work instead of two. The extra money was split right down the middle; half went to a savings account with Alonso, and the other half went to stocking my kit and paying Dad.

Why did I wait until today to get the foundation? If I had checked before, I would've seen how expensive it was. I might need it. *But then again, I might not.* My heart beat out of my chest as I fake smiled at a woman breezing behind me. My phone buzzed—Amna was calling. I squeezed my eyes shut, trying to calm myself before I lost my shit right there in aisle 6.

Think, Josephine. Think.

With no other options coming to mind, only one solution made sense for the moment.

Dad could never know, and I wouldn't ever tell Alonso. "I will pay it back," I whispered and unzipped my coat. My head shot around looking for people looking for me. Up and down the aisles my eyes quickly roamed for cameras or anyone watching. Seeing no one, I swiftly tucked the bottle inside coat pocket, zipped it back up, and walked out of the store.

Ah hour later, me and Amna loaded her dad's car in front of the house.

"Is all of this your personal stuff?" Amna tugged some of the plastic containers.

"The shadows and colors, yes. Everything else is brand new from the fashion show!" I exclaimed.

"Holy shit. There's so much of it. Rose really hooked you up." Amna grunted and lifted a plastic tote into the trunk.

My cheeks reddened as I watched Amna scope out my set-up. I didn't have fancy personalized aprons or a massive kit with everything you could think of, but thanks to Rose, a little luck, and some uncomfortable thievery—it was more than I had last month. And if Christeen saw something in me—then shit, it was time I opened my eyes and saw it, too. With Alonso's cap on over my hair and below my eyes, I was ready for war.

"Any more news from your brother?" I clicked my seatbelt across my shoulders.

Amna started the car and smiled. "They want me to come out for a visit. We've been talking every single day. It's been cool getting to know my niece. Adoption is weird like that, you know? I mean, I had a great life with my parents, but I always wonder about these other people. Do I look like anyone? Talk like anyone?"

I nodded. Those same questions lived rent free in my head about my mom, too. Did I have her sugar or her spice? Was she all fire or more grounded? Was she a church girl on Sunday or did she fill her days praying to the moon and stars? Grandma filled in a few of those questions for me now and then. But her memory was hazy and she didn't recall as good. I held onto ghost stories of Josephine Scott. I learned early on it was better to tuck those feelings away and forget I was one part orphan.

We pulled up to the hotel and Christeen was waiting outside with a cart and a big grin.

Amna and I locked eyes and we nodded at each other, knowing what we needed to do.

We were going in.

Christeen gave me a full three hours to do her makeup and that was a glorious amount of time. I loved working without being rushed. Going slow, painting my face, and trying out new shades and colors without being hampered by the clock kept me in a good mood. When Christeen's friends turned on their Bluetooth speakers, Ari Lennox's music filled the room with warm energy so contagious, I couldn't help but smile and sing along to the music.

I'm really doing this.

I pulled a shiny black sheet from my bag we bought from Walmart the day before and laid all my makeup out in small sections. Eyes, lips, skin. Each section had three to four different items. My heart swelled seeing it all laid out and if Rose was here—I'd kiss her!

Christeen sat down in the chair and leaned back so I could study her face. She had exquisite bone structure and cat-like eyes. I wanted to accentuate both. When asked what type of look she was going for, she used words like *'soft glam,' 'natural,'* and *'fresh.'*

I could do *that* with my eyes closed.

Pulling the stolen foundation from my coat pocket, it was warm in my hands. I shook the bottle and dabbed a little onto the back of my hand and did a patch test on Christeen's face.

Fuggin A. It was a perfect match like a lock to a key.

A layer of foundation primer went on first and sat on her skin for a few seconds. While that dried down, I studied Christeen's hair, dress, and jewelry all laid out on the bed next to us. Sexy, black lace lined the boddice of her gown, and her hair was curled neat and pinned back with a rose gold blush diamond studded hair fasten. I saw the look she was going for and where she needed me. Next came a light layer of foundation to her entire face, making sure not to cover her freckles. You never covered freckles on a Black girl—that was a sin.

Amna worked the room and talked to Christeen's friends. Every few minutes she looked up and checked my progress, giving me a thumbs up sign. Every thumbs up she gave sent punctures through my dark worries and sunlight to my confidence. It pulled the blanket out from under my fears and made room for hope. Hope stood in the light. Fear stood in the dark, and according to my dad, I was born in late August when the sun blazed and sat high in the sky.

I swept shadow over Christeen's cat eyes. We chose a blushing pink color to match her soft pink brooch and heels. A big, fluffy brush was used to dust nude powder over her cheeks and a fat lip crayon did its job to make them full and pouty. Standing upright, I stepped back to see my work from a different angle. Every piece made up the puzzle.

Dad said I had to do back-breaking work to make a living. Somewhere in our conjoined life—I believed him. We create these false stories in our lives that say in order for us to be good at our jobs—it had to stress us out. In order for us to feel worthy—it had to be tied to our work. In order for us to perform under pressure—we had to give even more of ourselves.

I squeezed glue out of a tube and placed it on an eyelash. The edges folded perfectly around the top of Christeen's eyelid, and I used a small handheld fan to dry it down.

Amna insisted we get the fan, and I was grateful. We fussed because I didn't want to waste money we didn't have when I could just blow on their eyes, but Amna sucked her teeth and said it was ghetto to be blowing in people's faces. She must've felt me thinking about her because when I turned around, she winked and raised her eyebrows at the fan.

"Okay. You can open your eyes," I whispered.

Christeen blinked and her eyes sparkled open with a longer, fuller lash. I grabbed my setting spray and misted Christeen's face so everything would stay in place for her party.

Stepping back, Amna and I carefully studied Christeen.

A grin crept to my face where nerves once were. Amna placed a small mirror in Christeen's hands and when she saw what we saw—she gasped and her eyes flung open even wider.

She was a *BAD* girl, and I meant that in the best way possible.

She looked like new money to a Sunday morning preacher. Like a Saturday afternoon in Fairmount Park. Like the Roots Picnic on a balmy, June night. Spruce Street in the summertime. She had me rooting for everybody Black.

"It's beautiful, Josephine. I knew it would be," she exclaimed. She tilted her head from side to side to see every angle. The bronzer highlighted her cheeks just right and every time she smiled—it framed her face.

"Do you have an Instagram page?"

"How can we follow you?"

"I have an event coming up and I want this same look!"

"If your man ain't chasing you like the cameraman on Maury after he sees that face, get you another one, Christeen!" Amna chuckled.

"Do you have any cards I can take, Josephine?" Her friends circled me.

"I'm just getting started, I don't have—"

"She doesn't have a professional Instagram page up yet, but she will soon. We're getting some of her most popular looks together," Amna lied. She smiled between me and the girls asking. She was already in her phone feverishly typing, creating a social media account for me—I'm sure.

I beamed at Christeen and admired my work. Not bad for a self-taught girl from West Philly. I pulled out my phone and took pictures of her at every angle and sent them all to Alonso. When I left this morning, he had written a quote on his board. It struck me somewhere deep that didn't make sense at the time, but I took a picture of it anyway. It read:

"Every day we have a conversation with the universe through our actions. If we ask the universe for happiness but won't take a moment to do small things that makes us happy, the universe won't believe that we want happiness. Instead, the universe will keep sending the things we respond to, like other people's demands on us."

This. This right here made me happy—and I was going to do it my way.

CHAPTER 14

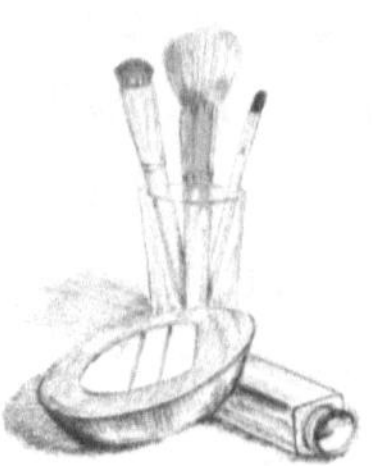

mna lunged toward me and giggled. She scooted closer, gliding over chicken guts on the floor and slid all over the place. "You rang?" She smirked.

We looked around at our coworkers—too uptight to stop and smell the roses—or chicken.

With a snort, I said, "I did *not* call you over here! And you better get back to your workstation before you get in trouble again!" I winked and repositioned the Band-Aid on my finger under my gloves.

"Your fingers all sliced up, too?" The playfulness disappeared and her face fell flat. The machines roughed us up and a few bruises now lived on the sides of my hips from leaning over the machinery for hours. My lower back was hurting, too.

"It's getting better, I'm learning how to use the butt of the knife instead of the blade." I removed my hand from the glove and flexed my fingers to show her.

"That's what I'm about to do. Bump this job."

"Do what?"

"Use my butt." Amna shimmied in place and shook her

breasts in front of the conveyor belt. I choked back a laugh behind my mask but Amna threw her head back and laughed out loud until people stopped and stared.

Mr. Childress stepped out of his office and glared an icy stare down at us from his glass tower.

Amna and I turned our backs to him and got back to work.

"Did you see your page?" Amna whispered. She kept her head low so no one noticed she was out of line and bullshitting next to me. I sliced into the chicken pieces and made them into drums and flats.

I blushed. Of course I had seen it. It was all I thought about.

"What the fuck, Josephine, you weren't going to say anything?" she shrieked, her voice giving a high-pitched school-girl. "I knew you fucking saw it!" She pumped her fist with the knife in her hand.

Tired yawns and burnt-out coworkers rolled their eyes at us. Some were curious and others annoyed. *How dare those young kids laugh*, I'm sure they thought. With me and Amna being the youngest, we seemed to bring the noise even when we tried to lay low.

"I took all the pictures you sent me from Christeen's party. And I threw some filters on them and made some cool reels. I even added in one of those **Book Now** buttons like the big influencers be doing. Josephine, you're at 500 followers in like four days!!" Amna whooped and danced.

"Can you believe it!" I hopped in place, knife in hand. Five hundred followers, following me! Me!

"Oh shit!" My gloves grabbed Amna's arms, and she held onto my elbows as we almost slid and fell from the slippery floor.

"I hate this place!" Amna stewed and leaned against the belt for support. "Listen, I've been thinking, Josephine." Amna shadowed over me once we were upright. "Makeup is your gift. Did you see the way Christeen and her friends were ogling over you? You have to take yourself seriously."

"How can makeup be a gift?" I scoffed and wiped my forehead with the back of my hand. The lunch clock ticked away and was never too far from my sightlines. Thirty-three minutes to go. Ms. Marta made me soup for lunch and my mouth watered for it. I was planning to call and check on her during my break, she was feeling sick the past few days.

Amna's eyes narrowed above her mask. "Be serious! Makeup is a skill, and you got skills, baby! This is your lane, girl."

"So, what happens now?" I dropped my hands to my side. This *was* my thing, but Amna had all these great ideas. How did I pull it all together? Something needed to happen here but what? I felt something; *something*. I couldn't put my finger on it—but gawking at everyone else in their duplicated hazmat suits working quietly with their heads down, it became more apparent what I didn't want. Working on my own face and then Christeen's put me into a trance. It was like . . . meditation. It took me to a place where I felt expansive. Seen. I was ready to be seen more and, in the process—see more of myself. Each color, each mood, was a feeling. I dreamt in hues of rose gold palettes draped in metallic shimmers, bronzy highlights, and long lashes.

You could go to the same place day in and day out, but you could dress up and be someone different every day. That's what I wanted. The option to be something different every day. My life? Freeing—not confining.

"Post more pictures. When you're doing your makeup,

make Alonso record it. Get a ring light. Tell social media you're accepting clients. Start talking about what you have to offer. It's a lot. You have a lot to offer, but you have to see it," Amna said the last part like she was gently sitting down fine china in front of someone who just discovered they were royalty.

Maybe Amna was right. I could put myself out there more. And Alonso *would* record me if I asked him—I just never had asked before. Every day I was coming home smelling more and more like Popeye's and less and less like me. Alonso sniffed me and mentioned it a few times, but after a while, I got used to the smell and so did he, just like Dad had gotten used to it years ago. But that didn't make me feel better.

I refused to get used to any of this.

"Amna, up here, now!" Mr. Childress shouted from the second floor. He leaned over the railing and his face was filled with red rage directed at Amna.

Amna and all her personality, giggles, and random dance moves stood out like a sore thumb in a room full of robots. And some places tried to break her spirit for it.

"Oh shit!" Amna clumsily paced back to her cutting station.

It was too late. She was out of her assignment location, and therefore according to Mr. Childress—out of protocol.

Again.

"In my office!" Mr. Childress fumed. He stared down at Amna before turning on his ugly shoes and slammed his door behind him.

Amna and her bright blue Converses chucked it upstairs.

Eight minutes until lunch.

Seconds later, loud voices were flowing from Mr. Childress' office, and I heard him say, "You can't speak to me that way. You're fired!"

I gasped and covered my mouth.

Amna snatched the door open and stared down at the workers from the second-floor glass offices. We all gaped up at her. "And that's all folks, I am out of here!" She stepped out of her hazmat suit and threw it over the railing to the conveyor belts below. It crumped on the floor. She took a bow, swung around, stuck up both middle fingers at Mr. Childress, and then she stomped out.

Grinning, I turned back to my belt and restarted the emergency shut-off button while shaking my head and smiling to myself.

Amna was crazy.

CHAPTER 15

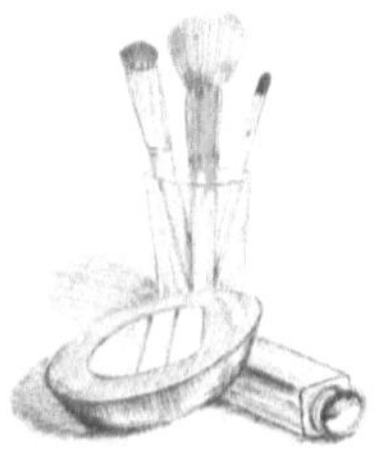

Buttery steam wafted from the hot bread and fogged the glass.

Ms. Marta hobbled behind me and pressed her fingers to the glass. "Mmmmm." She closed her eyes.

Some Saturday mornings were spent wrapped around Alonso—refueling from a tough week—and others with Ms. Marta at the Reading Terminal Market ogling fresh bread, homemade chocolate, and rows of fresh fruits and vegetables. Ms. Marta and I hadn't perused there in a while as today was the first day in a few weeks she felt well enough to make the trip and do the walking. We took the bus all the way into Center City and Ms. Marta had pep in her step on this brisk, early spring morning.

"Did you still want to get some fudge?" Ms. Marta asked. Every time we came, she bought the same things: cheese and pepperoni, tomatoes, fresh vanilla, fudge, popcorn for Alonso, and cookies. She hobbled across the aisle to the candy store and lusted after warm cookies coming out of the oven. I twisted my left-over bag of food around my wrist and looked down at my hands. I couldn't carry another thing, but Alonso loved fudge.

"Darn. I should've brought a cart," I fussed. "Can I get two dozen pieces?" I pulled a crisp twenty-dollar bill from my purse and handed it to the worker.

It felt good to have money. *Damn good.*

Before Ms. Marta and I hit the market, it was Amna and I who watched the sunrise this morning on the phone. She had a few ideas about business cards and using QR codes. She also babbled on and on about the chicken coop cutting her check short for being fired before the pay period ended. I chuckled through the whole thing and gazed out the kitchen window. My face was bare and my skin supple and smooth. The sun slowly woke up and in the distance, I could see the Ben Franklin Bridge, its amber lights twinkling their way toward a different world. Amna didn't believe there was a connection between her not following any of the rules and getting fired. In some ways I envied her. She always believed that things would work out. She genuinely believed in herself and her ability to change her life.

With Amna now running my Instagram page, Alonso and Ms. Marta's blessings—I was stepping into an energy and a storyline that felt more like me.

Christeen's friend asked me to do her makeup for her graduation pictures. My social media page was growing. It seemed like every time I posted about my creative process from beginning to end, people had questions and wanted to know more. *Which shade should I use for my skin tone? What eyeliner do you recommend? What's your go-to setting spray?* And even more strange—was the fact that I actually had answers and recommendations for them. *Me.*

"Hurry, I think the bus comes in about thirty minutes. You

know it'll take me that long to hit the ladies room, get my compression stockings down, and then back up again. Don't get old, Josephine." Ms. Marta waved a hand in my face and trotted toward the bathroom.

She wasn't lying.

Minutes later, we barely made it to the bus stop in time before it came rolling around the corner.

"Wait!" I shouted in a full sprint with Ms. Marta trailing behind me flailing her arms.

"Tell 'em to hold on!" she huffed.

I banged on the side of the bus and it screeched to a halt, its center doors popped open.

"Come on!" I shouted and positioned myself between the door so it couldn't close on Ms. Marta. She half-jogged half-limped her round body to the bus, and with one last grunt—hurled herself inside before it pulled off and tried to leave us in the dust.

"That was a close one," she said, breathless and sweat forming at her hair. Her cheeks were red from the cold and her eyes watering.

"Who you telling?" I huffed, my chest rising. Alonso's fresh fudge sat in my lap a little jostled, but intact.

One of her large tomatoes she bought at the market fell to the floor with a heavy thud and we both shrieked at the noise. People on the bus frowned at us. *What an odd pair,* I'm sure they thought. This old, Puerto Rican lady with thigh-high compression socks and a moo-moo; and this young, Black girl with the movie star makeup.

I didn't care. We cackled at our shenanigans on the bus. When we came to, I noticed we were going a different route home.

"All of this construction downtown makes everything

twice as long." I shook my head and surveyed the new route we were taking. Streets, stores, and faces we rarely saw lived on this side of town. We rode past Temple University and I people watched. Students always looked so busy; like they had things they absolutely *had* to do. Everything about their lives was interesting to me. The way people stopped, thought about something, and hesitated. The unspoken feeling of nervousness. The fear of *I'm not good enough, am I on the right path*, lurking right beneath the surface. Everyone was afraid of something, and I was getting good at pretending not to be afraid. When I thought about makeup, a calmness found its way that wrapped its arms around me and said don't be afraid. When something is for you, it will be easy. I couldn't afford to be afraid, and I wouldn't.

"Josephine . . . Ain't that Alonso?"

"Huh?" I jerked out of my thoughts.

"Over there. Ain't that Alonso?" Ms. Marta pointed out the window and frowned. We were at a red light and when I turned my head right, Alonso and Curtis were standing out front of an auto-body shop, talking.

He and Curtis seemed to be in a heated conversation. They were using their hands to point and I could make out a vein in Alonso's head popping from where I sat. When Alonso frowned, tilted his head, and looked away—his eyes landed on mine and widened.

I jumped from my seat and pulled the signal cord to stop the bus. The driver gave me an angry look as he slammed on the brakes and turned the large steering wheel to the left. He screeched to a stop and pulled the center doors open.

"Ms. Marta, I'll see you back at home, okay?"

"You gon' and handle your business, baby. I'll be fine." She nodded at me and shot a worried glance out the window at Alonso and Curtis.

I jumped off the bus, clutching fudge with a sinking feeling. He watched me walk off the bus and take large steps toward him. I smelled his nervousness and damn sure wouldn't pretend to not see what I saw and felt.

I knew what this was—*and so did he.*

"Josephine, what are you-"

"No! What are you doing here? Mr. *'I'm coaching a client in Jersey'* today? So you're lying now? And for what? Him?" I gave a disgusted face to Curtis. He leaned against a car scratching his chin watching everything unfold. A small smirk sat behind his blank stare, and I wanted to take the fudge and smash it right into his face. I clutched the small box of chocolate and squeezed.

"Calm down!" Alonso barked.

I gripped the box and threw it to the ground at his feet, twenty-dollar chocolate spilling to the pavement. "What are you doing here?" I grit my teeth.

Alonso shot a glance between me and Curtis. He rolled up his sleeves and loosened his collar. "Inside. Now."

"I'm not going anywhere!" I shouted. More workers from the auto-body shop came outside to see what the noise was about.

All Young Lords members.

I saw red.

I dove in and punched, slapped, and clawed at Alonso's chest. "Why are you here? Why are you here?" I screamed, already knowing the answer. Curtis and the other guys were smiling and watching the theatrics.

"Yo, handle your girl, Lonz," one guy said.

"Don't say shit to her!" Alonso's tone was sharp and meant business as he dodged slaps from me.

"I think you should take your lady home and handle all this domestic stuff privately, Lonz. We'll get up tomorrow." Curtis eyed me up and down before strolling away. He and the rest of the members trotted back into the auto-body shop like I was nothing to see and nothing to do.

"What the fuck is your problem? You're always tripping!" Alonso hissed. He grabbed my hand and pulled me down the street. We stepped over melted fudge that now looked like trampled shit.

"My problem? So that's it? You decided you're going to run an illegal chop shop for Curtis?" I sulked. My shoulders dropped and tears sprang to my eyes. It was already cold outside, and the tears made my face and heart extra frozen. Car horns blared and streetlights shone around us as we sank into something I wasn't sure we could get out of.

"Josephine, we need money—like now," Alonso huffed.

"But I'm making more money. And we have a savings account!" I shouted.

We shuffled across the street, now directly in front of the shop. "This isn't a bad thing and I'm not going to do it for long. I already told Curtis that I'm not in the game long. He's cool with that."

"But we have steady money coming in. That's an excuse and you know it. You can't get in bed with Curtis," I sobbed. "Anyway, you know if my dad finds out he will kick both of us out of the house. You're okay with jeopardizing that?" I stiffened. For the first time in our relationship, I wasn't sure if he would choose me.

Alonso cocked his head and rolled his eyes. "That's bull-shit, Josephine. You hate that fucking job, and you know it.

But I don't blame you." He shifted his weight, threw his head back, and rubbed his eyes. "No, I'm not okay with that. But I'm trying to build something for us now, so we don't have to worry about being kicked out of anyone's house ever again. You think I want to do this? I want to coach full-time. I want to do things, too. But we need money to make that happen. You know how it is, pay to play. Sometimes you have to do things you're not proud of to get where you want to go. It's like an investment." Alonso stared at me, wishing I understood.

I rubbed the back of my neck, thinking about my five-finger discount at the drugstore.

"Alonso, we have to do things the right way baby," I said, my voice even.

Alonso furrowed his brows, his frustration leaking through. "What is the right way, Josephine? All I know is the money is funny. We had to scrounge around and put money together just to catch a movie. You think I want that for my girl? For us?"

"But Alonso, the movies *is* expensive. That's just life."

"No, that's not life. It ain't life if we say it ain't life. and I say it ain't."

"So, what is it then?" I paced. I pulled my coat around my waist. My mind, body, and heart was getting colder by the second.

"I don't know." Alonso lowered his eyes. "Just give me some time to figure this out. But this is where I'll be for a while, and I need you to understand that."

I didn't understand it at all, but I swallowed those knowing feelings away.

"Okay, Alonso. I'm not okay with this. But okay." I frowned at him.

"Can I have a hug? And I hope you're getting me more fudge, woman."

"Too soon, Alonso! Too soon!" I shoved him away as my cell phone rang with a number I didn't recognize.

"Hello?" I raised one finger to shush Alonso. I could barely hear over the noisy street-sweepers.

"Hello? Josephine?" a woman said in a hurried tone. She was shouting over beeping noises.

"Yes. Who is this?"

"Yalitza; Marta's daughter. Listen, I got your number from her phone. The hospital called. They said she fell out when she got off the bus. They rushed her to the hospital. I'm about an hour away, can you get there?"

Ice ran through my veins.

CHAPTER 16

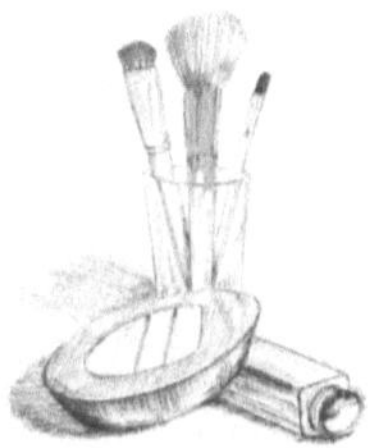

Alonso and I burst through the double hospital doors and they slammed against the wall so hard I felt the ricochet in my chest. The woman at the nurse's station jumped from the noise.

"Excuse me! May I help you?"

"Marta Ruiz? Where is she?" I blurted.

"Are you family?" The nurse frowned at me from behind her desk. A group of nurses looked startled behind her.

"I'm her neighbor, but we're—"

"I'm sorry, if you are not family, you're not permitted to see her." The nurse turned back to the women and resumed their conversation.

"What room is Marta Ruiz in?" My voice was louder. "I'm not family, but I'm family, so where is she?" I slapped my hands on the counter and leaned over. They could play with me today if they wanted.

Not Ms. Marta.

"Ms. Lady. I say this with as much respect as I can. Please let her see Marta. She's like a mother to her. And she'll act up in here if she has to—and I won't stop her." Alonso's eyes were wide with concern.

The older woman eyed me up and down before turning behind to the other nurses. They whispered together for a few seconds before she said, "Room 206. Here's a family pass. Don't make me regret it."

"Thank you." I grabbed the pass and clipped it to my coat with shaky hands.

Room 206 was all the way at the end of the hallway, and we ran as fast as we could, our sneakers squeaking along the way. I peeked into each room we passed and with every new patient, they looked sicker and frailer than the room before. Ms. Marta didn't belong here. She wasn't like those people. They were *sick, sick*. She had some health issues, but nothing like those people.

Ms. Marta laid in a hospital bed tucked in tight under white blankets and beeping sounds. Her eyes were closed, and her skin, usually golden, was taunt and ashen. Her breathing was ragged and it sounded like something rattled in her chest.

"Ms. Marta," I breathed and fell onto her bed, stroking her cheek with the back of my hand. She looked nothing like the woman I saw an hour ago. Did I not notice it then?

My hands roamed her forehead, hair, and arms. I needed to touch her, make sure she was here and real. I needed to restore our connection. When I was a kid and didn't feel well, my grandmom would touch my forehead and tell me to lie down. Maybe she just wasn't feeling well and needed to lie down. Maybe she just needed to rest.

"Give her some space." Alonso gently tugged at my shoulders.

"Are you family?" The nurse barged into the room, disturbing the peace. She pressed the hand sanitizer on the wall and shot some into her hands before coming closer to Ms. Marta.

"Yes, she's my godmother." My head was pounding. "What's happening? Is she okay?"

The nurse sighed and shared a glance between me and Alonso. Alonso towered over the woman, and we stared at her, waiting for war—but praying for a white flag.

"We're not sure yet. We'll be running tests way into the night. What we do know is her hemoglobin, magnesium, and potassium levels are dangerously low and that could have caused her to pass out the way she did."

My body collapsed into anger, and it padlocked me into the chair next to Ms. Marta's hospital bed. My gel manicure was a neutral pink color. They had to be short enough to still fit into my gloves at the chicken coop. Ten perfectly crafted, medium coffin digits stared back at me— caked in nasty brown fudge under my nails. Alonso walked behind me and I could see fudge had danced all over his sneakers, too.

I cringed and tucked my hands behind my knees. If I wasn't arguing with Alonso's ass this wouldn't have happened. I would have been there when she fell and been able to do . . . do something.

"Do you think she'll be discharged soon?" Alonso ran a hand across my back.

"We can hope for the best, but right now we just don't know how things will go. Only time will tell. But she's strong. Her heart sounds clear." She checked Ms. Marta's vital signs before pulling off her gloves and leaving the room.

About thirty minutes later, Yalitza burst into the room. "Mom!" she shouted and ran to her bedside. Tears spilled down her cheeks and in seconds, they spilled down mine, too, as I watched Yalitza see her mom so different than how she looked during the holidays. There was something about the thought of not having a mother that didn't feel right. Didn't feel natural. I hoped it was a feeling Yalitza would know later rather than sooner.

There was no benefit to knowing it sooner.

Alonso stood from his chair so Yalitza could sit down, but she burned a hole in the floor, pacing back and forth.

"She's strong," I cried as Yalitza and I embraced. It was only the third or fourth time we had met in person, but we talked on the phone a few times. Her body heaved and wept into mine. She grabbed the back of my head for support. I did my best to hold her until it felt like I would fall down from mental exhaustion. *I was so tired.* When I felt my hands slipping and gravity calling, Alonso slid in and scooped me up from behind before I hit the floor.

When the nurse returned and saw the three of us embraced in a three-way hug, she cleared her throat. "Umm . . . we have some tests back. The doctor will come in soon to talk to you. It's shift change and things have been a little crazy."

Yalitza grabbed the nurse's hand. "We have to wait? You can't tell us what's going on? Please?"

The nurse shook her head and gave a weak smile. "I'm sorry. Only the doctor can read the oncology reports."

Oncology.

The next hour felt like torture while we watched a constant stream of nurses poking and prodding Ms. Marta while she laid motionless in her bed. No one with any more information than the last one.

"You should go ask them what's going on," I whispered to Yalitza. I stiffened, hearing the nurses laugh down the hallway. Ms. Marta was here, between worlds, as they discussed their front lawns and weekly grocery lists.

Yalitza's eyes were beet red, and she seemed to be in a trance when she shook her head no. "We have to wait for them. They said they'll let us know," she muttered. She had crawled into a ball and laid in the bed next to Ms. Marta cradling her hair.

Alonso was sprawled out in the chair directly across from Ms. Marta lightly sleeping. Hours slipped by into the evening, and I stared at the clock, biting my nails, and shaking my leg. Remembering and trying to forget I signed up to work overtime the next day. Amna and I were also planning to hit Fairmount Park and take headshots of my makeup.

The nurses were kei-kei-keing at the nurse's station. I ran my nervous fingers across the windowsill and stared outside at Philly. A SEPTA train zoomed by at top speed, and a group of teens were playing basketball under a mural of another young, Black boy and his parents. The family gazed at each other with so much love in their eyes. Was it possible for me to feel jealous over a mural? My family—or at least part of it—was right here, in this room, but she needed something even I couldn't give. She was in a world I couldn't reach. The city moved forward; not caring my world was crashing. Chickens needed to be slaughtered.

The chicken had come to roost.

The silence from the so-called doctor, and giggles of bored nurses was more than I could take. Jumping to my feet from the hard hospital chair, I stomped across the room and flung the door open.

"Josephine!" Alonso hissed behind me.

I stomped to the desk with my eyes narrowed. "We've been here for hours! Hours! Can someone please tell us what's going on?" My breathing was noisy and my nostrils flared. My feet hurt and stomach grumbled. They took her out for an EKG, CAT scan, PET scan, and all the other letters in the alphabet.

But what did it say? What did it all mean? I didn't understand. Just a few hours ago, we were traipsing through the market and laughing, buying the ingredients for her homemade flan she was famous for.

The same nurse who told me to lie low was giving me death stares. "You have to calm down. We are short staffed tonight, and that means everything is running a tad behind schedule. The doctor will get to your loved one, but you have to stay calm."

Another nurse came up next to me and she looked young. "I just got a few tests back from the lab. I do have some news. Follow me, I'll walk with you down to Ms. Ruiz's room."

I sucked my teeth and pushed away from the counter, stomping back to 206, the new nurse in tow.

"Hey." I crept to Yalitza. She was still tangled in Ms. Marta's bed. "They said they're short staffed. But this lady has some news." I sighed and folded into the chair.

"It's not much." The nurse lifted her mask over her face as she talked to us. "But her white blood cell count is extremely low. There's an infection somewhere and her body is trying hard to fight it. We will need to give her a blood transfusion by tonight. That's all I am permitted to say so far, but I wanted to give you something."

"Thank you for the information," Alonso cut in. Yalitza seemed to crumple into a withering ball of fear, and no words found their way to me as I processed what I was hearing. *Transfusion? White blood cells?*

Yalitza and I collapsed onto the hospital couch as exhaustion took over both of our bodies. It was late, but I sent Mr. Childress an email letting him know tomorrow would be my first sick day due to a family emergency. It was only overtime; I shouldn't be in trouble.

Hours later, the sun peeked its way through Ms. Marta's hospital room. Yalitza sat up in the bed and yawned with tired eyes. "You and Alonso go home. You've been here all day and night. I'll call you with any updates."

"No. We're staying." I pouted and crossed my arms.

"Josephine, it's okay. I'm with her. She's not alone. You guys go get some sleep. I'll call you with any updates."

I glanced over at Alonso. He was awake now and resting his head on the cold chair. His body hung heavy, fatigued from the day's events, but he was ready to stay for another four hours if that's what I wanted.

If I wanted.

I wished I hadn't tossed his fudge.

"Okay . . ." I whispered. "But call me once you find out anything. Please." I grabbed Yalitza's hand and held it in mine. I searched her eyes and prayed to God she knew how serious I was. My gaze landed on Ms. Marta; so many cords and beeping noises surrounding her. She would hate all of this fuss.

"Please . . . please call with any news," I pleaded.

Exhaustion hit me like a ton of bricks and wouldn't let me walk or think a minute more. My body screamed for my bed.

Alonso guided me into the house and the walk from the living room to my bedroom seemed like miles. When we got inside our room, I tripped over one of my shoes in the middle of the floor and almost toppled onto the bed.

"Fuck!" I screamed and kicked my shoe across the room.

I crouched down and flung clothes, shoes, books, and

everything in my path into a laundry basket. I pulled things from all crevices in our cramped room, and I hurled it into my closet and slammed the door shut. My chest rose up and down and my hair was stuck to my face from a cold sweat.

Alonso was across the room in a flash. He stood in front of my face until our foreheads touched. "Breathe, Josephine. Breathe." He put his hands on my chest and took his own deep breath until I followed suit. He wrapped one arm around my chest and held me as I whimpered and sobbed into his arm. "Josephine . . . Josephine . . ." He murmured. He said my name over and over with the same texture he said his morning affirmations, coached his best game, and BBQ'd his best rib. "Josephine . . . Josephine . . ."

"What's all the noise in here?" My dad knocked and pushed the door open. Clothes jammed the entrance, and he pushed the door trying to get it open. "Umph..." He pushed. "And ya'll need to clean up this room. Ya'll ain't no kids. All this mess." He looked around and frowned.

"It's two of us in this cramped space, Dad!" I shot out, annoyed. My hands shot to my face and instinctively wiped. He didn't like tears.

"Mr. Cannon, we just got back from the hospital. Ms. Marta fell and they think something's wrong," Alonso explained. He stood behind me and put his hands on my shoulders, speaking for me.

Dad stared at me and didn't even look at Alonso. "Who you talking to, girl? Don't talk to me like that. This is my house. I know you ain't got no bass in your voice in my house." Dad glared at me; his hand flat against the door holding it open.

"Huh?" I frowned. "Did you hear what he just said?"

"I heard what that boy said, and did you hear what I say?" Dad clipped his voice like he wanted me to feel every word.

Anger coursed through my body like horses out of the gates. "What do you want from me?" I shouted and took a step forward. "I go to work. We try to stay out of your way. I'm your daughter and you don't even like me. I've done everything you've asked me to do. And you don't like me. You talk to me like shit all the time and I've never done anything to you except be born! But I guess that was the problem." I slumped my head and shoulders.

I. Was. So. Tired.

Dad snarled his face and crossed his arms. "Aww don't nobody hate you, girl. You my seed and I took care of you and did the best I could. Ain't no rulebook to this. But you . . . you . . . you always need love. And hugs. Talking things out. Be wanting me to explain myself. I don't know how to do none of that stuff. Your mom was good at that. And even then. I don't know if she really was good at things, or if I was young and had nothing to compare it to at the time. Maybe I made up this fantasy of who she was in my head. And that's where you are, Josie. You live and dream in fantasy. You a Candyland, girl. I play Monopoly. Big bank always take little bank in Monopoly, girl. I done told you, you got to be stronger." Dad's voice cracked and his jaw twitched. A father in the flesh—not in spirit. Someone who thought his paycheck every two weeks and his last name proved his love. Someone who didn't know a thing about loving a daughter because he was too busy trying to survive and raise Stone Cold Steve Austin instead.

I didn't understand why the people I loved, I couldn't keep? Why the people who loved me couldn't stay? My life would have been much different if I had a mom who was here to stand in between me and Dad. She would tell him to calm down and then come to my room at night, hold me, and explain to me that dad really loves me but had a funny way of showing it. She guided us through our family squabbles. She would show us how to understand and listen to each other. Why did I have to have a dad like Cannon who chose to lead with fire, not love? He was right, I did need hugs and love. Was that too much to ask?

Alonso sat quietly on the bed, and it creaked under his weight. Our little room was bursting at the seams.

Hearing my voice so loud scared me. This was a family feud and one that was overdue. "What's wrong with dreaming? What's wrong with wanting to do something more than working in a factory doing backbreaking work? Haven't you ever wanted to do something different?" I barked in disgust. Why did I even have to explain this? Was happiness really such a farfetched idea to him?

Dad inched closer to me, and heat radiated from his body. "Yes, Josie. I wanted to do other things. But I had a child to raise, so that came first. I did what I had to do. So now *you* have to do what you have to do, too. It's how you learn. It's how you mature."

"I can mature without being miserable. I can mature without turning into you!" I balled my hand into a fist, my nails puncturing my palm. I itched to throw something, hit something.

"And what's wrong with *me*?"

"You don't *love*. You don't *like*. You have Rose and oh, what's her name? You had other ones coming and going. You don't vacation. You don't sing. You don't laugh. We've never even been to the beach together. Six Flags is right across the bridge in Jersey and we've never been. You never talked to me about college. I don't know if I would've wanted to go, but you never brought it up. Our entire life has always happened right here between these walls, and they're not big enough for my dreams anymore, Dad," I stuttered. My throat was on fire with truth that wouldn't bubble down. Wouldn't back down. It was easier to find words to describe all he wasn't to me than all he was.

"And what's your truth, Josie?" He snorted. "You about to do people's makeup and become rich and famous?" He rolled his eyes like he couldn't believe what he was hearing. He peered over my shoulder at Alonso for support. "And you're okay with these pipe dreams, Lonz?"

Alonso looked him up and down. He loathed him but tolerated him. Ran a chop shop to get away from him. "I sure am. I want her to be happy; whatever that looks like. You don't give her enough credit, Mr. Cannon. She's really talented if you stopped to look. She's going to do it anyway, so doesn't it make more sense to support her rather than tear her down? Me and her might be down and out, but we'll figure it out. I got her." Alonso clasped my hand and stood beside me. He was always on my team, even if it meant us being homeless together.

"Well, I'm glad you kids got your Bonnie and Clyde act down pact." He shook his head in disgust. "Sorry to hear about Ms. Marta. I hope she's okay." Dad hesitated in the doorway.

Nasty truths and nauseating words sat in the room thick like grits. Dad didn't answer any questions directly, and when he closed the door behind him and trotted back to his bedroom, I knew he never would. Was it possible to hate someone and love them at the same time? But what did I love about him? He didn't know a thing about me we didn't argue about, first. He liked to argue—he didn't like to love. He didn't know how to be subtle and brought a sledgehammer to every conversation. His life was filled with simple things and quiet places.

I wanted to bring the noise in every way.

I stomped across my bedroom floor and flung my door open. "Oh, and Dad. Before Mr. Childress tells you, I called out of work today!"

His mouth contorted, the hallway light illuminating his furious eyes. "You calling out the day you volunteered to work overtime? Real mature, Josie."

I sucked my teeth and slammed my door behind him.

Seconds later, the wall next to us shook as he slammed his door, too.

"Josephine, your phone is buzzing like crazy." Alonzo handed it to me.

I hadn't realized it was on vibrate. While Dad was arguing with me—Yalitza called twice. When I didn't answer, she sent me a text message.

> "It's Cancer. She has Stage 4 Stomach Cancer. They are giving her six months to live."

The phone dropped from my hand and hit the floor with a sharp thump. I fell onto the bed, crumpled into Alonso's arms, and wailed.

Maybe I wouldn't be going to work the rest of the week.

I was so tired.

CHAPTER 17

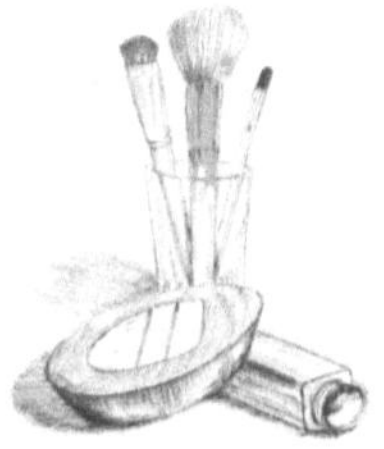

"So, do you think you're going to work today? Or you're still sad?" My dad stared at me.

It was 8 a.m. My head was resting on the kitchen table in front of a mushy bowl of cereal I couldn't bring myself to eat.

"Dad, please. I'm not in the mood right now." I rubbed my eyes.

Rose shot glances at me and dad, catching the tail end of something icy but not knowing where the coldness came from. *Or maybe she knew.* Maybe he told her he was sick of me and silently hated the fact I had called out of work the past two days. Everyday a Cannon shadow loomed in front of my bedroom door; I could see his paused feet from the crack under the door. He could not fathom what could be so bad it made someone not go to work.

They called them sick days, but they didn't want you to actually be sick and use 'em. My body wasn't physically sick, but thoughts of Ms. Marta made my stomach churn and want to crawl into a ball.

She was coming home today.

Yalitza and the doctors read all the reports and it was as grim as grim could be. Something deadly and despicable was moving through her body, giving her only weeks or months to live. When she finally woke up and heard the news, Ms. Marta refused any chemotherapy or radiation treatments. She said she wanted to go home and damn near ripped the cords from her veins trying to get out the bed.

"Mr. Childress pulled me to the side, talking about is Josephine okay? You got the white man calling me to his office to ask about you? I didn't know what to say. Girl got me lying to the boss, talking about she sick. And don't get me started on Amna. I don't know what she said to him, but he can't stand her," Dad gargled out a hearty laugh at his comical, Amna.

I banged on the table ready to fight.

Dad secured both of us jobs—and I was grateful for it. But when Amna quit her job, she got a laugh out of Dad and he thought she was a hoot. When I took two days off because my life was falling apart, I got ripped to shreds and left wondering how a man who was supposed to love me talked to me like a stranger on the street.

"Why are you always on me about everything?" I shot out. My lips were dry, and I licked them, waging war.

Dad stopped in his tracks. "Girl, ain't nobody on you about nothing. You're too emotional. Everything ain't about you all the time. You want the world to be easy. To just stop because you're not feeling good. We got to suck it up and do what we need to do." Dad pumped his fist. I'm sure he meant that as some sort of pep rally speech, but it made me want to pump my fist straight into his face.

"Honey, leave her alone. She's got a lot on her mind and you know Mr. Childress ain't mean nothing by it." Rose patted

Dad on the back. Dad was ground meat—just like the rest of us —but Mr. Childress had him doing his dirty work believing he was filet mignon.

His nostrils flared as he stared at me, waiting for a response. Any response so he could pounce back.

"Ughhh!" I grabbed my sling purse, bubble coat, and stormed out of the kitchen, disgusted. The front door slammed behind me.

Only three things were on my agenda today, and none of them involved chicken.

Stomping down the street, I observed the neighborhood where my whole life took place. The same people who had also been here their whole lives were getting the mail and sweeping their little plot of grass surrounded by concrete.

To calm my nerves, I stopped in the drugstore, and bought a few more lip shades and lip liners that were recommended by some big influencers on YouTube. They would add perfectly to my kit.

I walked about six blocks and two streets over until the gym came into view. When I peered through the door Alonso was right there—right where he was supposed to be. Curtis was nowhere in sight.

A sloppy smile spread across his face when he spotted me and ran over to open the door.

"Hey baby." He grabbed my behind and kissed me on the lips.

It was later in the afternoon and his basketball students behind him covered their mouths and giggled at the public display of affection.

"Alright ya'll. We have about an hour left. Let's make it count. Start the drill and run it from the top just like we prac-

ticed," Alonso commanded. The middle school students grumbled and jogged back to the court.

"You okay? Didn't know you were popping up on me
today." He smiled. His teeth were so perfectly straight and
gleaning against his school-issued track suit. Alonso started
working with his big client in Jersey, but he still made time and
ran the after-school basketball program. Plus, they both gave
him a hefty starting bonus. Regular deposits to our joint
savings account were happening and if we kept this up, we
could be moved out of my dad's house in just a few months. I
prayed this was enough to keep him away from Curtis and the
chop shop.

"I had to get out of the house. Dad was on my nerves again.
I went and bought some new makeup and then came here."

"What did he say this time?" Alonso frowned.

"Enough about him. Did you talk to Curtis?"

Alonso turned away from me and watched the boys
huffing and puffing up and down the court.

"You talked to him, right? He knows that you're not in this
long-term . . . right?"

"Yes, Josephine. But it's not that easy to just get out. I took
an oath. That's family."

"And sometimes it's family who will run you into the
ground. Dad is already on my ass. We can't have him find out
about this, too. You promised you would be out of the game." I
squeezed his arm. "Look how well things are going for you." I
gazed out at the kids all running plays that he taught them. He
stayed up for hours at night with a dry erase board and marker
figuring out ways to make their team stronger. He did it
because he loved it. How much longer would we spend talking
about Curtis? I met the man twice and what little I knew about

him and had witnessed, I didn't like. Alonso was not like them. He wasn't better than them, but he was better than ***them***.

He nodded. "I hear you. I'm trying here, Josephine. I'm trying."

For the next few minutes, I sat in the bleachers and checked my Instagram messages from people inquiring about my services. Amna made me a price listing and a little homemade logo. I was getting good at sending it through direct messages and responding to people within at least twenty-four hours. For the first time in a few days, a smile snuck on my face. I was good at this.

Alonso was also good at this. He pulled some players to the side and spoke to them with so much love. He listened and corrected. He taught and understood. He left them with quotes and different things to ponder. He got on the court with them and physically showed them drills. My gangbanging, coach, extraordinaire. He was everything he needed at that age in his life. No one could reinvent themselves like him.

When they finally ended practice and left the gym, I ran up behind Alonso and kissed his cheek. "That was amazing. You are amazing." I breathed into his ear.

His lip curled into a little smile. "Come on, girl. Always trying to talk sweet to me after you cuss me out and threaten to leave me. Let's go see Ms. Marta."

He made me seethe with anger, and with one smile, ice melted my twisted and curved, Philly pretzel of a heart with forgiveness. Love always brought me back to him, even when I didn't understand.

I curled my fingers into his as he pulled me ahead.

Ms. Marta's apartment was filled with machines and a large hospice hospital bed beeping from all ends. She was laying in the living room in the makeshift bed, asleep. I had just seen her days earlier, but today she looked like she was fading away. Like her body was giving out on her and had decided it was time. Yalitza signed paper after paper as medical staff that looked no older than me, handed her pink, yellow, and blue forms. Overwhelm lived on her face and she looked as tired as I felt as she thanked them for setting everything up.

"Is there anything we can do?" I asked Yalitza. I pushed Ms. Marta's flan cake forward. I was up last night making it, and it damn sure didn't taste like hers, but it was a good start.

"Can you please sort through her medicine and put them into a pill container? There's so many of them. I have to call the home health aide and see what hours she can come. I have to call the insurance; something about a pre-authorization, I have to call the life insurance company. . . you know . . . just in case." Yalitza's eyes drooped.

"We'll take care of it." Alonso nodded. "We'll also clean up and get dinner started."

"You don't have to do that." Yalitza shook her head.

"It's no trouble, and I'm a good cook." Alonso didn't wait for Yalitza to respond and darted to Ms. Marta's kitchen.

"She'll need a pre-authorization, and they're a bitch to get on the phone. I called a few times for her last year, and it took hours. And I know where all of her insurance paperwork is. She showed me just in case . . . something happened . . ."

"Thank you. I didn't know if I could do this on my own." Yalitza's eyes filled with tears.

I hoped she didn't feel like I was overstepping, but I was here every day, anyway. Pulling on some gloves for the next few hours, I cleaned the bathroom, vacuumed and moved all of Ms. Marta's favorite things into the living room. When I passed her bedroom, Yalitza had fallen asleep on top of the bed with her cell phone in her hand and paperwork strewn around her. She was snoring lightly. I pulled a throw blanket from the closet and draped it across her. I closed the blinds to block out some of the sun and gently closed the door behind me.

I pulled off the gloves and plopped down on the couch next to the hospital bed.

"Here, come get something to eat." Alonso stirred a large pot in the kitchen. He sat a steaming bowl of chicken soup at the table and I gobbled it up.

"I'm going to run to the shop. I'll be back in a few hours," he added. He said it softly like he was waiting for my reaction.

A tired soul consumed me. "Okay. See you later," I said blankly. I slurped broth from the spoon. My belly was too hungry to fight with him.

Alonso stared at me, waiting for a different reaction. He was used to me yelling. He was used to me getting upset. When I looked over at Ms. Marta stirring and starting to wake in her bed, I didn't want to be upset or yell.

I just wanted her to be okay.

Alonso cleaned the dishes, kissed me on my forehead, and tip-toed out of the apartment.

No sooner that he left, Ms. Marta nudged me. "You made that flan?" Her voice was raspy from being asleep off and on. She had lost weight in just a few days and her eyes were puffy.

"I did." I nodded. "You want to try it?"

Ms. Marta giggled and it seemed to take all her strength. "You ain't use the vanilla extract we got from the market. I can smell that imitation stuff from here."

"You know what? I couldn't find the vanilla we bought when we went to the market."

"You lost it? You know that stuff is expensive! Come straight from the islands."

I couldn't tell Ms. Marta that she was carrying the bag when she fell, and it disappeared in all the hoopla. Imitation vanilla it was. "Do you want to try it or not, old lady?"

Ms. Marta's eyes lit up and her lip curled into a smirk. She was as fiery as I was and loved fussing. "No, I don't want none of that dollar store flan. Save it for Yalitza, though, she can't cook either. She'll think it's restaurant quality."

Ms. Marta and I giggled.

"I was sleeping, but I heard you and Alonso. What's that boy doing that you don't like?"

"How do you know I don't like it?" I avoided her eyes and picked at the couch.

Ms. Marta rolled her eyes. "This my house and I know everything that goes on. I know you better than you know yourself. So, what that boy done did?"

I sighed and explained the issues with Curtis and the chop shop.

"Do your daddy know about this?" Ms. Marta whispered, and her droopy eye peered around like he could hear us.

I shook my head. "He knows about the Young Lords. But not about the chop shop."

"Good. The Cannon is made of stone and the only people he cares about is Benjamins and Grants. Don't play with him, Josephine. You make sure Alonso gets in and gets out."

I nodded, knowing all too well this couldn't end with Cannon finding out.

"And Josephine." Ms. Marta tried to sit up in her bed. "I know you love him, but don't forget you can't change no man. So, if need be, you change your man. Always choose you."

"How are you feeling? Do you need anything?" I batted my eyes, trying to change the subject.

Ms. Marta started coughing and choking at the same time. "You can leave the flan and make me a bowl of that soup you were slurping down. You know, Alonso missed his calling. That boy can cook his behind off. And if you can't get through to him, call that boy's mama."

I scrunched my nose. "You know, they moved to Delaware. They hardly talk."

"I know that, but if you can't get through to him, a man will always listen to his mama. At least if he got some respect for her. She needs to know her son is making friends with a demon."

"A demon?"

"Chilleee, a demon." Ms. Marta hissed and her blood pressure monitor beeped. We both jumped in place.

"Are you okay?"

"Oh, I'm fine. All this talk about the demons got my pressure up. Now tell me more about these people paying you to paint their faces. Ohhh you're about to really make a name for yourself! I don't know why we ain't think of this before, it was right in front of our faces! See? Everything happen when it's supposed to." She whooped and clapped her hands.

A smile spread across my face just as light from the sun beamed through, illuminating Ms. Marta's face. I talked and talked and talked. I told her about Amna spearheading this whole thing and how I worried at first but now felt good about it. It was a different feeling when you knew you were supposed to do something; you felt it in your gut. My belly sent me one puzzle piece and I was in search of the rest. I didn't see the puzzle, but I knew it was there.

"So, are you going to leave that chicken job?" Ms. Marta raised an eyebrow.

I sighed. "I *have* to go in tomorrow. Yes, I'm going to eventually quit." Butterflies swirled in my stomach saying the words out loud.

Ms. Marta clapped her hands together and shrieked. "What's your dreams? If you could have anything you want, what would your life be like?" Ms. Marta's eyes glistened.

I leaned my head back on the couch and sighed. "I don't know. My worst fear has always been never leaving the city and following in my dad's footsteps. I don't know how to dream. I do know I want to see the world. I want to work in fashion shows and maybe be a makeup artist for famous people!"

"Start dreaming. Start planning. Start imagining yourself as all the things you never thought you could be. You have to make room for the things you say you want. You never know when it's your time. So be that person—today. You got what it takes, Josephine. Don't count yourself out."

"I won't. Not anymore."

Not anymore.

CHAPTER 18

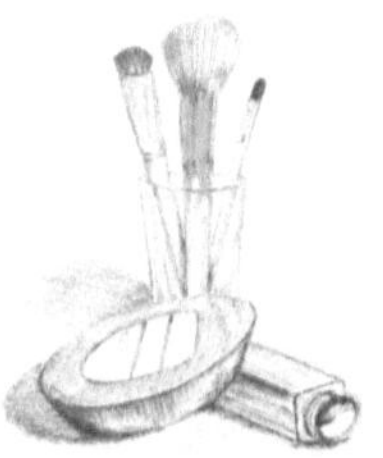

Crumpling the pink paper in my fist, I flung it into my locker.

"Please come see me first thing this morning." Signed, Mr. Childress.

Day one back to work.

I zipped my hazmat suit, pulled my gloves over my hands, and mask over my nose. I slammed my locker shut and trotted to the floor. He would have to catch up to me before I voluntarily went to his office.

A dull ache radiated through my thumb and pointer finger from cutting the chicken quarters into wing pieces. Even though it was a few days since any chicken touched my hands —pain remembered the closer I got to the floor.

"Josephine Scott, please report to Mr. Childress' office," someone called my name over the loudspeaker.

My head shot around. "Did they just call me?" I confirmed to the lady next to me. We worked together side by side and I barely knew her or anyone else around here. No one was as fun as Amna.

She nodded with wide eyes. Whenever someone was called to the office, they usually returned with an attitude, if they returned at all.

A few minutes later, I was sitting in Mr. Childress' office very much feeling every bit of the principal's office. He had pictures of his kids and their travels scattered throughout the space. Everything from the metal desk and hard chairs, white speckled drop ceiling, and loud radiator on the wall—looked like it could rival prison. Who would want to stay and stare at these four walls for hours on end, years at a time?

"Ms. Scott." He leaned back in his chair and crossed one leg over his knee. "I thought during orientation we were clear about the work culture of this plant. We do not encourage the use of sick time early into your probation, although it is permitted. If you are trying to climb up in the ranks like your father, then I suggest you get more serious about your work habits." He rubbed his chin. "Take this as constructive criticism but don't forget, we are an at-will company, which means we can let anyone go for any reason. Now, I'll keep this little conversation off the record; I won't even put it in your file." He nodded and smiled like he was waiting for me to thank him any minute now.

I blinked.

I wasn't anything like my father nor would I be climbing any ranks. I saw what Amna saw when she stormed out of here. This was supposed to be stability. Consistency. And to some— it was. I was consistently bored. Mentally tired. Turned off.

This wasn't a place that cared about me or Ms. Marta. Hell, they didn't even care about my dad like he thought. They didn't care about the bruises on my skin or forcing yourself to watch a clock, just for thirty minutes of peace to yourself at lunch. When I stared at him and thought about all the things they *didn't* do, a small voice in me said, *'it's time.'*

"Mr. Childress, thank you for the opportunity. For some people, this is enough, but for me, it's not. I hate this fucking job, and I don't care who knows it. Consider this my last day." I rose to my feet. The chair made a loud scraping noise when I pushed back. Pulling the hazmat suit from my body, and yanking my gloves and mask off, I disrobed right there, shedding the layers of anyone's expectations of me except mine. This was not the place for me—I was a big fish.

Mr. Childress' mouth fell open in surprise. "Are you sure you want to do that? You're more than halfway through your probation period. Your benefits and insurance will kick in soon. Think about what you're really saying, Josephine. A lot of you young kids like to come up in here and turn your nose up at honest work and then come crawling back when you see how much the real-world costs."

"I've already thought about it. Actually, I've thought about nothing else. To stay here will cost me even more."

"Humph." Mr. Childress put his finger up to say one more thing, but I closed the door softly behind me, leaving him alone in his office.

I took the long way home. I trotted through Target like I did months ago. Worry swelled in my belly. It was a gremlin's voice deep inside me that was dying to be heard. My next steps weren't clear, and that voice wanted me to be afraid.

I was. I so was.

I wanted something different for my life and me doing the same things I've been doing were getting me the same results. I browsed through the racks and stopped and stared at the brightly lit makeup display. So many colors and smiling faces on the models' photos. *One day. . . one day . . .*

When I got home, Dad and Alonso were in the kitchen sitting at the table.

They were *never* sitting together unless something was wrong.

"What's wrong? Is it Ms. Marta?" I tossed my keys on the front table.

Alonso avoided my eyes.

"Mr. Childress called. He said you quit your job today."

I swallowed. That fat bastard. "Yes, I did. Before you yell, I have a plan. I'm going to do makeup. Full-time." I nodded. My voice cracked as the words sounded funny out loud. They sounded like Bambi trying to stand for the first time.

Dad clasped his hands together. "I don't understand you and this makeup thing. I went out of my way and got you a job. A good job! And you and your little friend quit. You young kids have no respect. What makes you think you can paint people's faces full-time? What kind of life is that?" he asked, looking confused. The more baffled he looked, the more cobwebs in my mind melted away my fears. I was headed to a place where he couldn't go. Somewhere he would never understand. A life he couldn't fathom.

"Mr. Cannon, I stay quiet around here out of respect for both of you. You let me live in your house and that was big of you. But I think we need to let Josephine figure this out. She's not . . . not . . . like you. She needs to fly."

Dad leaned forward and gave a death stare to Alonso. They were sitting across from each other at the table squaring off with me creating the top of a triangle between them. It was funny whenever something happened in our house that needed to be discussed, we all met at the dinner table. Some might call that a family, but there was no love here.

"So, you're in on this beauty brigade, too, huh?"

"I'm going to make this work, Dad. You have to trust me." I crossed my arms. My heart was beating out of my chest as the gremlin's voice asked me who I thought I was, churned in my belly. It made me weak in the knees, and not in a good way.

"Well, I need you both out of here in one month, Josephine. I'm tired of talking and trying to help you be responsible. You know if your mom was here, she would talk some sense into you."

"Yeah, but she's not here," I interrupted. "And no one ever told me about her. What she was like. If I was like her," I uttered, feeling flatter than a pancake. "So, I have to be who I know how to be. Me."

Dad leapt to his feet and looked me up and down like he was seeing me for the first time. His mouth parted and whatever words he wanted to say sat between his lips, refusing to be seen or heard. He clamped his mouth shut. Disappointment lingered on his face and he didn't even try to hide it. "You have her fire," he mumbled and walked out of the room. The apartment shook when he slammed his bedroom door.

"So, what's next?" Alonso stood in front of me, pressing me against the sink.

"Can I use your computer? And I need you to take some pictures of me."

"Ohhh pictures?" He raised an eyebrow.

"Not like that!"

Back in our room, I searched the internet. When I was walking into Target after leaving the chicken coop, I saw a HELP WANTED sign for a day spa. I scoured through the job openings until I found what I was looking for: *Makeup Artist.* They required a short application and a few photos from my catalogue of work. I would hardly call the few pictures I had a catalogue, but it was a start. With one month until I was potentially homeless—the clock started *now*.

"Do we have anything to prop up the camera? I need you to take pictures of my makeup today. And I'm going to upload some pictures Amna took from my last event." I plopped down at my princess vanity. I checked out Alonso from the reflection in my mirror. "Alonso, be honest. Do you think my look is. . . a little homemade?"

Alonso tilted his head and studied my face. "Not at all. I don't even know where you got that word from because it ain't got nothing to do with your face. You got that ratchet and righteous look going. It's quite sexy." He licked his lips and brushed his fingers across my neck.

"Shut up, I'm serious!" I flung one of my eyeshadow brushes at him while I touched up my face.

He ducked, and the brush ricocheted off his affirmation board on the wall. The board promptly fell and slammed to the floor as we erupted in giggles.

I uploaded the pictures and answered all the questions on the application. There were so many of them, but I typed anyway, determined to finish it tonight. When I finally hit submit, relief washed over me. This job was mine. I knew it and felt it. I smiled to myself and closed Alonso's laptop.

He was stripping down to his boxers. He pulled the covers back and slid into the bed. I removed my clothing and snuggled in next to him in my T-shirt and panties. He smelled so good.

"Thank you for standing up for me tonight. With my dad, and all." I kissed his ear.

"It's me and you, girl. It's always us. We don't stay down for too long."

I closed my eyes, inhaling him. Some girls had a *man* but

didn't have a *partner.* Some men put you under pressure—like my dad. Some men alleviated it—like Alonso. My Lonz.

And he could lay me down and screw the Mario coins out of me any day.

When our family started in West Philadelphia decades ago, they started from ground zero. They created a story that was passed down through generations and repeated over and over. A story of survival and hard work. But I was the crack—the spark. If I could create even just one more crack in our foundation until it fell apart then I would. I had to for them. For Mom. For me. It would be me to change what has been in order to create what's possible. Keep putting cracks in a shaky foundation until it falls apart. One step at a time.

If this was my rock bottom then I had nowhere to go but up.

CHAPTER 19

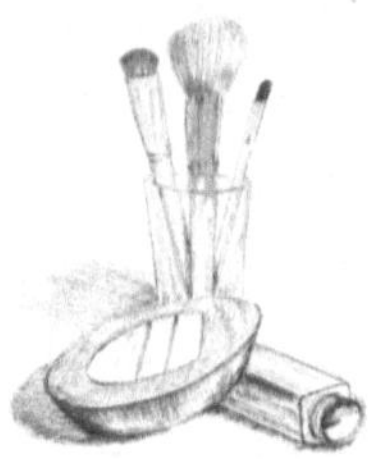

Amna's foot bounced as she squirmed and scooted around. "I'm ready for my close up," she said with a grin.

Another interview. The day spa was actually the closest interview I'd ever had to my house. I passed it many times riding to the market with Ms. Marta but paid no attention to it until now. Not until we were both ready for each other.

"You have about twenty minutes to complete your best natural face." Karissa checked her watch. She was the owner. A leggy Black girl with a long weave hanging down to her mid back and bright red lipstick. I thought the lipstick clashed against her sepia toned skin and she would fare much better with a soft pink lip. But hey, maybe that's why I was here, to learn a thing or two.

With Amna as my happy, obliging model subject, my hands got to work, knowing what needed to be done. I brought my kit from home, and had it set up in less than thirty minutes, just like the lengthy directions from Karissa stated.

A few of Christeen's friends, and even some of their friends, reached out. I did each of their makeup flawlessly, but it was always a bitch to lug this stuff to and from my next client. With the shop being so close to home, staying in one place with regular clients excited me. And Dad thought I wouldn't lay down roots somewhere. *Ha!* They would come to me. The thought alone made me dance in place next to Amna in the seat.

Makeup didn't feel like something I had to do. The *'had to do'* stuff woke me up mean and nasty at Alonso. The things I *wanted* to do, though . . . the things I wanted to do made me dance in the morning making him toast, two scrambled eggs, and grits, Jilly from Philly style.

My entire kit laid across me on the table. I dabbed some foundation onto my hands to match Amna's skin tone, just like I did with everyone else. Karissa walked back and forth checking out my progress. I almost chuckled at how easy this was going to be. Besides my own face—Amna's was the only one I knew up, down, in, and out. Underneath that tough, Aquarius exterior was dramatic cheekbones, sweeping bushy eyebrows, deep set cat eyes, and fleshy mounds of beautifully, curved lips for days. For the next twenty minutes, I swept the liner across Amna's eyes and laid her lashes down to perfection; not a wisp in sight. She blot her thick lips when I creased the gloss across her mouth and batted her eyes, adjusting to her new long, full lashes.

If I did say so myself—I beat her face down to the ground. It was easy, though. Amna already had the canvas, I just added to my best friend's art.

Karissa stood around me and examined every side of Amna's face. She said nothing. There were no other nail technicians or makeup artists in the spa, so either she gave everyone the day off, or she needed me. I was cool with either. I just needed the opportunity.

"Okay, time is up." Karissa's heels clicked around the tiled space. Each nail desk sat pink throne chairs and granite countertop nail stations. A chandelier shined over us, and my stomach growled at the snack bar behind Karissa. In the corner sat a small bar and I heard it brewing coffee that sounded and smelled delicious. A small tv sat perched in the corner of the room on low playing *The Tamron Hall Show*. There were small candles throughout the space placed out of harm's way, but creating a soft glow in the room's corner. Each station and piece were chosen for a specific space in the room. It was warm and inviting. *Now this is a place I can work every day.*

"What do you think?" Amna batted her eyes at Karissa.

Clearing my throat, I choked away my nervous cough and leaned against the makeup table station. Was this station going to be mine? *Mine . . .* What a thought.

Me and Amna blinked, waiting for Karissa's response.

A few seconds later, she broke into a smile. "Looks like we found ourselves a new makeup girl."

"Ahhhh!!" Amna screamed before I did.

Karissa jumped and gave her a bewildered look.

"You won't regret it, Ms. Lady, I promise you. My girl is the bomb.com. She about to hook your shit ***uupp***!" Amna grinned and babbled.

"That sounds amazing. Thank you for the opportunity," I sputtered.

I'm a makeup girl.

When I was a kid, Dad used to bring women to our house, and I would sit alone in my room. I would imagine what it was like to have siblings. To have someone who genuinely wanted to know about my day. Giggles and laughs at the breakfast table.

One of Dad's women must've sensed my loneliness because one day she gave me an old, Avon makeup kit. I was pretty sure it was even used; it couldn't have been new. The palettes were so old, and definitely not made with the shades and tones of a Black girl in mind. Some of the makeup was so dry it crumbled between my fingers. I mixed it with a little bit of water and a dab of dad's shea butter from his medicine cabinet. I made it work. When she placed it in my hands, magic happened. A world opened up to me that I understood immediately and intricately. A world that left words behind and spoke to me through colors and shades. I could be exactly who I wanted to be and could make myself over time and time again. Maybe that's part of what life was about. People screamed find your purpose. But what if you were not meant to find your purpose? Maybe your purpose was to live. Have great sex. Eat amazing food. Spend time with people you loved. Maybe your purpose was someone giving you hope—and you giving it right back to them when they needed it most. Maybe purpose meant standing in your truth. Or perhaps, it was knowing this is what *could* happen when you let magic lead the way.

"There are a few new hire forms I need you to complete. I will send them to you electronically for your e-signature. Can you be here Monday at 10 a.m.?" Karissa shouted over her shoulders as she removed the *Help Wanted* sign from her storefront window.

"I sure can!" I gushed, trying not to jump up and down.

"Good." Karissa crossed her arms. She wore a navy-blue business suit and the fiercest strappy stilettos that sat right above her ankle. She was all business and about her shit. I could dig it. "We'll split everything 60/40, plus $100 booth rent due monthly. I have a few clients that have been asking about makeup services already, so they should be booking appointments soon. If you would like to advertise your services through our business social media page, you are welcome to do so."

I barely listened as I shook my head yes to Karissa. *I'm a makeup girl.*

When Amna and I burst out of the shop, we squealed like little schoolgirls and skipped all the way down the street.

"This is so good for you! I wish something just landed in my lap like it always does for you. Ugh, you're so lucky, bitch! Let's grab lunch!" She pulled my hand until I stopped and looked up. We were smack dab in front of our favorite diner. I looked at Amna and grinned as we ducked inside.

Minutes later, I had to poke my head over a stack of pancakes to see Amna across the table.

"What are you going to do with your millions when they start rolling in after you become a makeup artist to the stars?" Amna flailed her head back and fanned her face with all the dramatics.

I giggled.

"I guess it's time to start looking for apartments since my dad finally gave us our walking papers." I pondered and stuffed my mouth with cheese eggs.

Amna frowned. "You gotta think bigger than that. You talking about rent? Tuh!" Amna sucked her teeth. "You're up to 2,000 followers and people are beating up your inbox for makeup appointments. This is your thing, Josephine."

I blushed and sipped my apple juice.

"What are you afraid of?" Amna peered at me with curious eyes.

I looked out the window at a group of men getting out of a

service vehicle in overalls. "I don't know," I mumbled and dropped my shoulders. "Dreaming is new to me. I live in the real world, and now I have all these other thoughts about what I think I can do."

"What *I know I can do*," Amna corrected.

"But it's scary. It seems like everyone around me has the same problems. Money. Work. Relationships. But they seem to just deal and accept it as normal. I sometimes feel like I'm the odd one out for wanting something different, you know? Like, who do I think I am?" My cheeks flushed.

"You've been preparing for this forever, Josephine. You've been honing your craft like a motherfucker. If you've been consistently afraid of the forest all of your life and now you've said what the hell, I'm going into the forest—ain't you still going to be scared? But you go in anyway. You go in with that fear. Life is fucked up like that. Situations don't get easier to lift, you get stronger. You've been putting your happiness on the backburner for way too long. All of Alonso's quotes won't help if you keep living your life for everyone else." Amna's eyes were wide.

"Okay, Oprah." I giggled and checked the bill. "And what about you? Have you found another job? What's next for, Ms. Amna the Great? I know your mom came down hard on you about losing the chicken coop job." I held back a snort.

Amna leaned back in her booth. Her braids were fuzzy at the top and she scratched her head. "My parents definitely chewed my head off over that job. But I don't give a chicken shit about it. Pun *intended*." She giggled. "But . . . umm . . . I wanted to talk to you about that. Funny that you brought it up." She took a big gulp of her water. "My brother invited me to move to Hawaii, and I'm going to go."

"What?" I raised my voice and gripped the table.

"There's nothing here for me, Josephine. I need something different."

"Different like what? I'm here!" My bottom lip quivered, and I willed myself not to cry right there, seated next to the bundt cakes. "You just found him and you're already planning to move?" Amna helped me see me. I needed her here. A huge lump formed in my throat.

"I don't know, Josephine. Different like sunshine. I want to put my toes in the sand. Have you ever been to the beach? Ever? I haven't. I want to experience that. I want to go somewhere and take deep breaths and wake up with the sun and go to sleep with the moon. I want a life I've never experienced before, and I'm willing to shake up everything to try it out. I need to see if something is there for me, too, like we know it's here for you. I'm an adopted kid, Josie. I'm never afraid to start over."

I swallowed away my lump and listened to my best-friend.

"You work to pay for a house that you don't even spend time in because you're working to pay for it. And then you retire at some godforsaken age and *then* you live your life? After all that? No, Josephine. I want to live it now. I *need* to live it now."

I wondered if Dad thought about it that way. He grew up in Philadelphia and had never ventured out. He mentioned going to the Jersey Shore once when he was a kid, but it was a fleeting conversation and one he thought was only reserved for white people and luxuries.

And Alonso. How did he want to live? What went beyond moving out of my dad's house for us?

My phone rang, interrupting my thoughts. I smiled when I saw Ms. Marta's name. "Hey, young lady," I answered with a smile that she couldn't see but I'm sure, felt.

"Hey yourself. I just called to see if you shut your mouth for a half-a-second and landed that job?" Ms. Marta joked.

She seemed to have a burst of feisty energy every few days, and she was bursting at the seams today.

"I did!" I hissed into the phone.

"And I knew you would, my girl! Wait til I tell Yalitza you're a big-time makeup artist now. Maybe you can give her some tips so she can find herself a nice man. She got a pretty face, but I wish she would do something about that eyebrow and at least make two of them," she whispered. I heard a muffled noise and Yalitza's voice in the background fussing with Ms. Marta.

"Ms. Marta, I'll come see you when I leave here. I'm out to lunch with Amna. Do you need anything while I'm out?"

"Tell my girl I said hello. I haven't seen her pretty face in a while. Did you tell her I have the cancer?"

My stomach sank. "Yes, she knows you have the cancer," I repeated. "She's moving to Hawaii with her brother," I said, making eye contact with Amna waiting for Ms. Marta to squawk.

"When?"

"*When?*" I mouthed to Amna.

"Maybe a few months." Amna had a sheepish smile.

The line was quiet for a second. "I should still be around by then. Good for her. Tell her to come see me before one of us goes." Ms. Marta's somber voice breathed with more sadness than I had words for. "Tell her Ms. Marta said to see the world, date all the men, and make her some money. And you, too."

"I will, Ms. Marta." I nodded. Her wishes for us sounded more like prayers sent right up the mainline.

I hung up with Ms. Marta and glanced at Amna, my best friend— and besides Alonso, my only friend. My Black hippie at heart. I clasped her hands from across the table, and let the salty tears pool in my eye. "I'm happy for you, Amna. Really, I am. I know you need more, too. Life ain't been easy here. I'm just going to miss you, that's all." I wiped my eyes with a napkin.

Amna's face crept into a relieved smile. "I'm going to miss you, too, girl. But more reason for you to come visit me in Hawaii." She rubbed the tops of my fingers. "You will be fine. I know you. You have to know it, too. There's no better time than now for the both of us," she said in a hushed tone.

"A few months is so soon, though."

"My parents have been great and they've given me a life filled with love, but I need to see what else is out there for me. Get to know my birth family. I don't want to waste time and have anyone talk me out of this."

I wanted to beg her to stay. I wanted to tell her that birth families weren't all they were cracked up to be. I still didn't know dad and he didn't care to know me. But I kept quiet and smiled for my friend.

After Amna and I left the diner, I headed home to get dinner started for Alonso and Dad before going to Ms. Marta's. I wasn't hungry but the men still had to eat. The apartment was quiet. I kicked off my shoes and grabbed Alonso's laptop. I looked over at his board of quotes and today he wrote, *I keep my mind focused on what I desire. I walk into situations designed to serve me.*

Humph. He was on the money today.

I logged into my email account and, sure enough, Karissa sent a bunch of documents for me to fill out. I blew through them, filling in all of my information and barely reading. I hit accept on all the documents: W-9, demographic sheet, references, non-compete clause attesting to no outside employment (whatever that meant), and tentative work schedule. I approved everything and sent it back to Karissa within minutes. I closed the laptop and held it to my chest. I was focused on what I desired, and I loved that for me.

The front door shot open and slammed. Steps barged to my room and Alonso burst through the door with a ripped shirt collar and eyes ablaze.

"What happened to you?" I jumped up from the bed and tossed the laptop beside me. I stepped in front of Alonso and placed my hands to his collar, but he shoved my fingers away.

He paced. He growled. He screamed as angry tears welled in his eyes. He raged and with one swift motion, flipped the bed—leaving the box spring in place and tossing the mattress. Sheets and pillows hit the floor along with his quote board.

"What happened?" I screeched.

CHAPTER 20

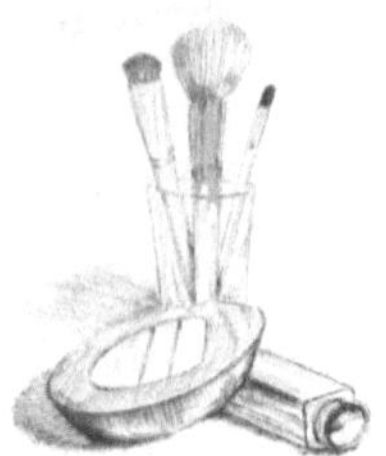

Alonso beat the floors down, scurrying back and forth; Invisible steam escaped from his ears. "One of the car owners came looking for their ride. We barely got out of there alive."

"One of the owners?" I crossed my arms in confusion. My heart pounded from what I didn't understand yet. When it finally hit me, my eyes widened.

"One of the car owners?" I repeated.

"Yeah." Alonso dropped his head and leaned against the wall.

"What car, Alonso?" I questioned. My fists clenched, waiting for answers that were starting to make sense.

Alonso slid down the wall and cradled his head in his hands.

"Curtis had us move some cars and break them down. Just a few Kias. It's easy once you get a little system going. One of the owners . . . well—you know. He caught us in the act and came at us with a pipe. He got a few hits off." Alonso sighed and rubbed his chin.

"Alonso, baby we can't be doing this. Fuck Curtis! He ain't your friend or your brother. I don't know what this hold is he has over you." I kneeled in front of Alonso and placed both hands on his knees until we were eye level. This had to end, we had too many things going well for us for Curtis and his bullshit brigade to ruin our plans.

I paddled to the bathroom, grabbed a washcloth and ran it under the hot water. I silently thanked God my dad wasn't here.

I held the washcloth over Alonso's face and let warm water trickle down his temples. His frown lines relaxed, and a heavy sigh escaped his body.

"Lonz..." My voice was barely above a whisper. Sometimes I came in too hot, and he was the one who calmed me down. Sometimes I opened my mouth, and my dad came out. I didn't always know when or how to control it and had to choose my words carefully. "Baby. How do the Young Lords and Curtis make you feel? Explain it to me. I'm trying to understand, but I don't get it." I leaned over his knees and hovered in his face. "Help me understand." I kissed his forehead, eyelids, lashes, and cheeks.

Alonso paused and closed his eyes. He hesitated, his conscience warring with his loyalty to a gang that had ensnared him. He said, "Your dad ain't shit—but he's here. I have no one. And when I had no one, I was *already* thinking about what I would need to do to get by. My family left. Straight up, moved away and didn't even think twice about me. My mom said I was older and could make my own decisions, but I wasn't grown. Everybody got mama issues, Josie. Everybody. When you feel like the odd duck in your family and you get a taste of real love, you don't let it go." Alonso gripped my waist and maneuvered me into his lap on the floor.

I straddled him, wrapping my legs around his midsection.

"Josephine, I don't know what I'm doing anymore. I want to coach kids and this can't be part of that life. But Curtis is family, too. He helped me and held me down, even before my family left. Did I ever tell you my mom kicked me out of the house when I was fourteen? She was dating some man at the time, and he said he didn't like the way I looked at him. Next thing I knew, she was reminding me that I was a man and could make my own decisions. Told me I could leave if I wanted. I didn't want to, though. Where would I go? That was the first time she pushed me out of her life and made it seem like I had a choice in the matter. When I left that night with no options in sight, I hit Germantown Ave and ran into Curtis. He offered me $200 to run a package uptown for him. He asked a bunch of questions, wanted to know who my people were and where I was staying. After I did it, he let me stay on his couch for months. He saved me."

I clenched my arms tighter around his neck. Alonso hid it better than I did. His anger with his mom was barely there but always simmering below the surface for making him become a man before he was ready. Mine boiled over like a hot pot of thick grits on the stove.

Alonso talking continued, "Curtis told me straight up he was in the game. He was about that life, knew nothing else, and didn't want to know anything else. And for me, at that time, it was okay. I needed money, and he had work. It's not like how people portray it to be on tv. We all became family. My brothers."

Alonso's life before me didn't sound any better than how I felt about our life now, but somehow—it was. "What happens now?" I rested my head on his shoulder and pressed us deeper against the wall.

"I know this doesn't look good but trust me. I don't want this life any more than you do. We have about three weeks until we're out of the house to make this happen. Did you put in those apartment applications?" Alonso whispered into my ear and tightened his grip around my waist. My dad's deadline loomed in front of us like a lit-up neon sign, always on both of our minds.

"Yes. Fingers crossed we get our first place." I stroked his face.

His anger, his confusion, his pain. I wanted to be his sponge and absorb all the worry he carried that he only told me about when the chips were down.

Alonso and I sat quietly listening to each other breathe. He never loosened his grip and even though my back was hurting, we held each other. Soon, his heart rate evened, and he was softly snoring on my shoulder. I untangled myself from him and walked him to the bed. In silence, we removed his shoes and I pulled the blankets back and tucked him in. His quote board was tossed to the side, and I picked it up and placed it on top of Alonso's mounds of sneaker boxes.

Creeping out of the room, I slipped quietly into my house shoes and sat outside on the porch even though it was freezing. I fumbled with my cell phone in my pocket and searched through my contacts until I landed on a name and number I had only called one time before on his birthday. She said they were too busy to come back to Philly for the party I threw for him. A few of his Young Lords members came—but not his mom.

"Ms. Gloria? Hi, it's Josephine," I said, sucking in the cold March air.

"Oh, hey, Josephine. Is Lonz, okay? I can't talk long, I'm at work on break," she rushed. I heard beeping sounds in her background.

"Yeah . . . yeah . . . I'll be quick. I know you're busy. Something is going on with Lonz. He really misses you and his family. I was hoping . . . I don't know. Can you call him? Check on him?"

"What that boy done got himself into now?" she rumbled into the phone. She sighed like she was exasperated and I hadn't even said anything yet.

"He's just having some issues with work, and I think he could use some talks with you."

"If Lonz wants to move to Delaware with us, he can. We ain't got no extra room, and he would have to share a room with his younger brother. But whatever trouble he got hisself into, you tell him don't bring that riff raff down here."

A shiver ran through my body as Ms. Marta's back door, directly across from our back door, came into my sight lines. Home is where the heart is—and Alonso's home was not in Delaware. "He doesn't want to move, Ms. Gloria. Actually, he doesn't even know that I've called. It's just . . ."

"Josephine, just have my son call me. The phone works both ways and he can call sometimes, too. It ain't just us over here who don't pick up the phone. Listen, I have to go," she said and hung up before I could say another word.

I wouldn't be calling her again.

With my head hung low, I paddled a few feet to Ms. Marta's house. Alonso was desperately looking for a family, and although he found pieces of it in me and his Young Lords, the family he was given thought it was too much to even call him. He was out of sight, out of mind for them. And for a man who was literally left in Philadelphia while they moved down I-95, why would he call them? Why would he reach out when he already felt abandoned? How was it possible that I lived with my dad and he barely cared about me, and Alonso's family left him and didn't care either? Was it too much for us have consistent people and feel like someone was proud?

Alonso kissed me and told me to trust him. Just *trust* he was going to figure this out. Should I go hard on him? Kick him out and tell him I won't stand for this? Or should I be his ride or die?

But I don't want to ride or die.

I want to live, and love, and laugh. Just like all the stupid wall signs said.

I wiped my face and took a few deep breaths before entering Ms. Marta's house.

She was in the living room, standing next to her hospital bed. She had a weak smile on her face, but it was a smile nonetheless, and it made me smile.

When I walked closer, her smile fell. "What's wrong?"

My chest heaved, and the tears spilled. I tried to be strong, but this was too much. We had no one. Me and Alonso had no one.

I sat on Ms. Marta's hospital bed in the living room and deflated. I told her about Alonso and the phone call with his mom. She motioned for me to get into the hospital bed, and she covered me with her blanket. I rested my head on her pillows and wiped my face, tucking myself deeper into the bed and even deeper into my confusion. Ms. Marta seemed to have a burst of energy and Reggaeton music bounced around the walls in her apartment.

"This is a tough one, Josephine. All mamas ain't mamas and all daddies ain't daddies. You and Alonso are going to have to create something that is only for you two." Ms. Marta's chest rattled as she coughed. She grabbed her handkerchief beside the bed and spit mucus while spitting the game of life to me. She pressed out words and it sounded hollow inside. "You have to take care of you in every state. Don't dull it with any nonsense from anyone else." She leaned in and pointed a finger in my face. "You take care of him, and he takes care of you."

"But I'm trying to do that, Ms. Marta." I rubbed my eyes and blew out hot air.

"I know'd you are, girl. I'm not saying that you ain't. You can hate something and still know that you deserve better. You and Alonso got a lot going on right now, but you gotta see that you still deserve better than this. Him, too. You support him as best as you can but take care of yourself, too. If all you did was make it through the day today, that's a win."

Ms. Marta handed me a bottle of water from her small folding table beside the bed. It was full of medications and instructions for medications. I noticed one of her medication bottles was empty. "Do you need this refilled?" I shook the bottle.

"I don't care nothing about these medications. If it's my time to go, then it's my time. Besides, they got me all consti-pated and one thing I do not like is being backed up. I only take them to keep you and Yalitza off my back. So, matter of fact, I sure do need them refilled. Do you mind?"

"Of course not." I wiped my face. "Where is Yalitza?" I gulped a swig of water. I felt my body relaxing under Ms. Marta's words.

On cue—Yalitza walked through the door lugging grocery bags. She grunted and kicked the door closed behind her and stared at us from the hallway with a frown. "Ummmm, Ma?

Why is Josephine laying in your bed? And why are you serving her water like you're her nurse or something?"

Ms. Marta and I glanced at each other, realizing our role reversals and smirked.

"Oh nothing, girl. Come on in here with them groceries. Josephine is about to run to the store and pick up my medicine."

"Oh crap! I knew I forgot something." Yalitza's face reddened. "Do you mind, Josephine?"

My coat was already on and tears dried and forgotten. Ms. Marta needed me. "I'll be back soon, it's no problem." I matched Ms. Marta and Yalitza with the fakest smile I could muster.

A few minutes later, I was crossing the street and hustling to the drugstore. The sun was already down, and the moon was full and suspended in a hazy, white glow, illuminating secrets. Rounding the corner, I saw him parked in an all-black Kia.

Curtis. In a *Kia*.

I ducked inside the drugstore, tucking myself behind the makeup shelf. He couldn't see me, but I could see him.

Even though it was dark, his face was clear as day through the broken driver's side glass. He must've punched it out just moments earlier. His jaw was tight and eyes hardened. He was on a mission. Curtis was a man who had my man suffocating in his fake concern. I wondered if Curtis' descent into darkness was about survival, like Alonso's was? Was every decision he made born out of poverty? Or choice?

I stared at him through the window with so many questions. Curtis slammed on the gas and his face curled into a twisted smile. The stolen vehicle's tires screeched against the asphalt, leaving behind trails of burnt rubber. He tore through the city's streets in a frenzied blur with lights and sirens echoing in the distance.

The car was the target, but the real prize to be claimed was Curtis' need for power. He could dominate *them* if he wanted. He couldn't have me and mine.

CHAPTER 21

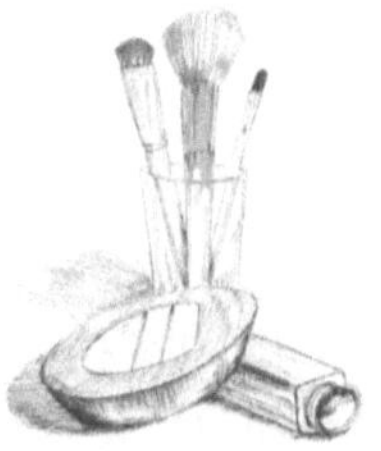

My first client at the day spa was a teenager getting ready for her sweet sixteen. She wanted a full glam look, and with permission from her mom, opted for glitter rhinestones and bold eye makeup. Setting spray hissed onto the girl's face when I spun her around in the chair to stare in the mirror.

"What do you think?" I waited.

She looked striking and way more than sixteen years old.

"Looks amazing!" the girl mumbled. She seemed astounded by her own beauty and stared in the mirror in shock.

"You already had a beautiful canvas. We just added a few strokes," I said, giving her one last spritz to the face to hold the makeup in place.

"What's your social media? I'm going to tag you and tell all my friends!" The girl grabbed her phone. We exchanged information and within minutes of her tagging me on social media, two new messages appeared in my inbox from others requesting my services.

My services. Can you believe it? Karissa had a newsletter list a mile long for past spa clients, and when she emailed them and introduced me as the newly hired makeup girl, clients were plentiful. My calendar was booked with at least three people per day—every day.

Even in my excitement, thoughts about Alonso had me in a chokehold and wouldn't let me get a wink of sleep last night. This morning, I rolled over and slung my arm over his belly just like I usually do.

Only my arm went limp. He wasn't there.

On the short walk to the spa this morning, I passed three different murals, all depicting their version of brotherly love. I worried about him then, too. Was that him and Curtis? Some backward ass version of love I didn't understand, but Alonso did? A man thing?

I didn't tell him I saw Curtis dodging the police through West Philly in a stolen vehicle.

"You need to tell him, Josie," Ms. Marta fussed when we talked about it. *"Don't let his secrets silence you."*

The ladies in the salon listened to a lot of podcasts, and there was one episode when they discussed forms of love. They said the highest form of love was consideration. It stopped me in my tracks and my ears piqued cleaning up my makeup station. Did Alonso consider me when he stole cars and ran the streets with Curtis?

He did. He so did. But then again—he didn't.

Love lived all over me for Alonso, but his words and his actions weren't matching up when it came to Curtis. Some things I had to sit on and just let cook a bit longer.

Alonso was across town meeting with Curtis as we spoke. Curtis demanded that all Young Lords come together for a meeting and figure out what went wrong in their last heist.

Alonso was also telling him he wanted out of the game. For good.

When my client exited the shop, I grabbed the broom, popped in my earbuds, and hit one number—Alonso. What would Curtis say when Alonso told him he would be out of the game soon enough? Alonso had something worth more than gold waiting for him at home. Did Curtis know what that felt like?

He answered on the first ring.

"Hey, Lonz, babe. How did it go with Curtis?"

Alonso breathed into the phone. He gave a nervous laugh and spoke to someone in the background before I heard him close a door and everything got quiet.

"I'm in the back office. I talked to him. He wants me to reimburse him for the car parts that we weren't able to sell since the owner recovered the car. Plus, he's charging interest now that the cops are watching him."

"What? He can't do that!" I yelled, pounding the broom into the floor with all my might.

Karissa shot a look at me from the register where she was checking out a client.

"We have to fight this. Fight him. He's running an illegal auto-body shop and yet, he's charging you for getting robbed?" I kept my voice down in the shop at the last part and checked to see if anyone heard me.

"I know, Josephine, I know. I'm trying to think of something. We'll talk more when I get home," he mumbled into the phone. He sounded so unlike himself. Caught between two worlds that required him to pick a side. It was getting easier for him to pick the wrong one.

"Okay, I love y—"

I didn't finish my sentence before he hung up and the line

went dead. Curtis was bad news from the beginning. Alonso might've considered him family, but everyone knew it was always family who did you worse than anyone else.

I emptied the used makeup into the wastebin and took the bag out of the can. Karissa had a contract with some of the big-name makeup brands, and I didn't have to bring anything from my home kit; she already had the good stuff.

"Josephine, come here for a second," Karissa called me to her station. She had a full set up. Karissa could do makeup, hair, and nails. Her books were scheduled at least four months in advance, and every day she added a new aesthetic touch to the shop to make it even more cozy. Today she sat small chocolates at every table station. I swiped my finger against her station, not a spackle of dust in sight.

"You did really well for your first client," Karissa spoke and moved the furniture around a few inches. She stood back, looked at the placement of everything, and moved the furniture a few more inches to the other side. It all looked the same to me; stunning and well done.

I stood back and watched her make her passion her purpose.

"I think you went a little heavy-handed back there on the setting spray. And also, maybe she would've benefitted from more eye bling."

"You think?" I put my hands on my hip and frowned. I loaded the girl up and down with rhinestones and her bill topped $200. Her mom happily whipped out a gold card and barely looked at the bill as she signed the receipt.

Karissa paused and smiled at me. "Rule number one, when the parents come in and pay, which they usually always do, you always charge top dollar. Store policy."

"Oh . . . okay." My hands rested across her all-white leather chair. When Karissa did makeup, it was like she was an artist painting. She had a 360 stand and ring lights set up so women could take pictures of themselves when they left the shop. It was really top-notch in here, and she paid attention to every detail.

Janet, a manicurist, walked over to my station as Karissa cleaned up. "You are really talented. I saw what you did back there with that girl. She transformed once you did her up real good," Janet whispered.

"Thanks. I'm all self-taught, but I thought it went well." I smiled.

Janet said, "And don't worry about Karissa. She doesn't like anyone coming in paying less than $100 for any service. But that's what keeps us as the number one spa in the city."

"Wow. Number one?" I repeated. *I am working for the number one day-spa in Philadelphia.*

She nodded. "As long as you charge top dollar and not steal any of her clients, you'll be just fine here."

"I won't steal any of her clients. I want to develop my own clientele." There were more than enough clients to go around and besides—making money doing what I loved and learning in the process was a win-win for me. This was my first full week, but if I kept with this same schedule, I was already on track to make more money than I had at any job. With the clock ticking until the deadline Dad gave us to move out, every penny counted.

My afternoon makeup client was way pickier, she was being honored at a women's empowerment event. "I need a soft look, but with some bite. You know, like you." She closed her eyes and leaned back in the chair.

Am I soft—but with a bite?

When I finished my client's makeup, Karissa gave me a

thumbs up sign. We took a few photos of her face while she swayed back and forth on the 360 photobooth stand. I sent them to Amna and within minutes, she had them posted to my social media page. Another person messaged me to book an appointment. I already had two appointments scheduled for this weekend. My calculations showed I could make the same money at the chicken coop by doing three faces a day for $100 or more at Karissa's shop, and that didn't even include my own weekend clients. I did the math in my head and tried to contain my giddiness as I walked my last client out of the door. I was doing it! I ached to call Dad and tell him my good news, but anything resembling good fortune he had a way of making salty.

On my way home, I stopped and grabbed a warm pretzel and woofed it down before making my way to Ms. Marta's.

Her small burst of energy she exuded the day before was gone.

She walked bent over like her back was permanently at a ninety-degree angle. She coughed until phlegm shot from her throat and she was sweating.

"Ms. Marta! Sit down. What are you doing up?" I rushed to her side and guided her to the bed. She was watching her stories, and they were so loud that I grabbed the remote and turned the tv off so it stopped screaming at me.

"I had to use the bathroom. I'm okay! Stop fussing over me." She swatted my hands away. She did her best to climb into bed on her own, but her frail arms shook as she leaned over to support herself.

My shoulders felt like boulders. Weeks ago, she was heavy and happy. Now she was skinny and sick.

Ms. Marta was *sick*. I swallowed a lump in my aching

throat. No matter the good things kicking off in my life right now—Ms. Marta was sick.

"Where is Yalitza?" I looked around. Everything seemed in order. Ms. Marta's small bedside table was filling with more and more medication.

"I sent her home. She been here for days, and she got herself a family to look after. I'm okay," she said, using my forearm to hurl herself onto the bed.

"Have you eaten anything?" I opened up her cabinets and pulled out some ramen noodles. I was not a cook at all. Alonso did more of the meals in our house, but I filled the pot with water anyway and jumped back as the burner shot out from the stove.

"Girl, if you don't get away from that stove. You ain't about to cook me nothing that I would voluntarily eat. Besides, I'm not hungry." She laid in the bed with her eyes fluttering.

"You have to keep your strength up."

"Strength for what?" She gave an exasperated tone and cocked her head like I was speaking a different language.

For me, I clamped my mouth shut.

I sat down beside Ms. Marta in the chair and turned her tv stories back on. I thought they were outlandish and ridiculous, but Ms. Marta loved them.

Ms. Marta watched tv and commented while sucking on a popsicle stick. "That girl know she love that man and he love her. I don't know why she won't let him catch her. A woman needs to be caught every now and then."

I rested my head on the back of the chair. "Did you let a man catch you?"

Ms. Marta's popsicle rested in her lap. She wiped dribble from her bottom lip and turned to me and stared like she had a faraway thought that found her again.

"You know, before I met my husband, I was dating this man. We were what you kids call *'toxic'* nowadays."

"How do you know that word?" I giggled and covered my mouth.

"The kids say it enough, don't they?" Ms. Marta challenged. "Anywho, I had this man. We argued like cats and dogs and then we made up and loved on each other with the same intensity that we had just been fighting with. It was exhilarating. It was like winning the Pick 6, straight. One day, we were arguing up something fierce. I don't even remember what it was about. Probably something we both should have let go but pride wouldn't release its grip. We argued and yelled, and he stormed out of the house; or so I thought. I was sitting home eating ice-cream, talking mess about him on the phone to my girlfriend—and he popped out from under the bed and said *'how could you sit there eating ice cream not knowing if I was safe or not?'*"

"What?" I burst out laughing and my eyes were wide. "Now that is toxic!"

Ms. Marta's slim jaw cracked into a smile, and she laughed like she did weeks ago before this nightmare began. "Yeah, I said to myself. That man loves him some me." She chuckled. "So stupid. When my husband came along, it was different. We didn't have to fuss to prove our love. Our love was like one of those tug-of-war ropes. It pushed and pulled, but it never broke. It was quiet. Constant. Consistent. It calmed my young, rageful spirit. With a real man, you never have to ask, they just do. They study you and just do. I hope when I see him on the other side, he hasn't changed a bit." Ms. Marta gazed outside, and a tear slipped from her eye.

"Ms. Marta, do you think me and Alonso are toxic?"

"Now why you go and ask me that?" She fussed. "A lil bit,

child. A lil bit. But sometimes it just comes with age, you know. As you get older and more settled in the woman you want to become, the things you tolerate change."

After Ms. Marta fell asleep, I used the few ingredients she had in the fridge and did my best to throw together a chicken soup like I had seen Alonso do a few times. A half an onion left over baked chicken, a few veggies. Each stir smelled more like something. My gaze landed on a fresh lemon sitting on the table, its vibrant yellow color catching my eye. Without hesitation, I sliced into it, releasing its tangy scent into the air and squeezed it into the simmering pot. I blew on the spoon and each hot sip tasted better and better. I pulled more ingredients and added a pinch of this, a sprinkle of that. "God . . . God . . ." I whispered to myself and asked for healing. For strength. I prayed and stirred and stirred and prayed. I let the Ancestors flow through me and this pot.

Dad was in the living room watching tv when I made it home carrying the large, leftover soup. I sat it on the counter and within seconds, the scent from my deepest prayers wafted through the house and Dad was hot on my heels.

He sipped broth at the table from a humongous serving spoon. "Mmmmm." He blew on the spoon. "Who made this?"

"I did. What do you think?"

"It ain't bad." He nodded and sipped from the large serving spoon. "It ain't bad at all, Josephine.

"Here, take this one." I shared a rare smile with the Cannon and handed him a smaller spoon.

"Oh nah, girl. For good eats like this you got to whip out the big utensils. You have to devour delicious food." He sipped.

"You know." He chuckled like he remembered something. "Your mom could make a mean chicken soup herself. She used to eat it with a big spoon, too—then had me doing it," he whispered and sat still staring into the bowl, letting the memories speak through him. "Of course, at that time, we didn't have a bunch of silverware." He chuckled. "Sometimes the mixing spoon was the serving spoon, was the eating spoon." He shrugged.

"I didn't know that." My voice was barely above a whisper. New memories that weren't even mine to remember were being created. Dad doled out flashbacks of the past through his own fragmented moments of happiness that I clung to.

"You should call your grandmom; I think they had a family recipe."

"No, I mean . . . about Mom."

I tossed the pots around in the sink and started washing them. The noisy dishes broke up the awkward silent that formed between me and the Cannon.

"How is Ms. Marta doing?" Dad pensively asked from the table. He stirred the big spoon in the bowl, never touching the smaller one I sat in front of him. He was trying to make small talk like he didn't kick me out of the house. He was so hard to read, and it was exhausting trying to figure him out.

I shrugged. "Today wasn't a good day. The doctors are still saying she only has a few weeks, months at the most."

Dad stood up from the table and dropped his dirty dish into my sudsy water. "Damn shame what that cancer doing to people nowadays. You're a strong girl. That's how I raised you to be. You'll be okay. And call your grandmom." He paddled out of the kitchen back to his room. I heard a woman, who wasn't Rose, giggle and his bed creaked when he closed his door. I wanted to vomit.

He raised me to be a tough girl, alright. But I shouldn't have to be. Didn't want to be. Everything with Dad felt like competition, not collaboration. I wanted to be the bow to his arrow. But he was the type to bring a shotgun to a knife fight and didn't mind shooting against his daughter.

I cleaned up the kitchen, clicked off the lights, and shut my bedroom door behind me. Alonso piled clean clothes on my dresser for so long I wasn't sure we could technically still call them clean. We had nowhere to put them and everything in here was bursting at the seams. We should be hearing from the apartment people soon, anyway.

Gazing around my room, it was the *same*. The same room that had housed all my parental confusion. Sometimes my jail. I grabbed Alonso's laptop out of the closet, powered it on, and went straight to my social media. Who I was, where I'm from, and what I did, tapped on my forehead, dying to be heard.

I typed:

Josie's Jawns

Expert in Soft Glam—but with a bite.

I pressed save on my new *About Me* section and smiled.

CHAPTER 22

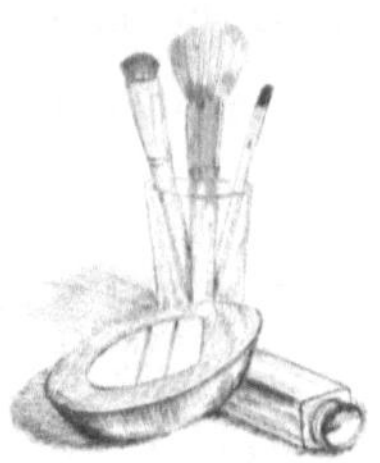

"You ready?" I crossed my legs in the waiting room chair and tugged my jacket tighter around me. My rolling cart stood next to me full with my makeup kit.

"Sure, just a few more minutes, let me give the guys some instructions." Alonso ducked behind a black curtain where the guys were in the back working on cars.

The door chimed to my left as someone walked through and prickly goosebumps sat on my forearms.

Curtis.

"Hi, Josephine, good to see you again." He towered over me as I sat in the chair gaping up at him. Perfectly white teeth and a Pinocchio nose that just wouldn't grow. He sized me up and down and took my hand and palmed the backside.

I flung my hand back in disgust. "Hi, Curtis. Me and Alonso are getting ready to leave. He just went to the back."

Curtis' slick smile made me itch all over and my butt squirmed in the seat while his eyes danced over my face. Pink cheeks, gold sepia eyeshadow, and caramel coated lip gloss had me stunning. Way too much for this ghetto, grease lightening, shit here.

"Lonz got this place running in tip top shape, huh?" Curtis glanced around and smiled, finally taking his eyes off me.

I hopped to my feet.

He wasn't going to be looking down on me like I was Little Red Riding Hood and he was the Hungry Wolf. *Where is Alonso?*

Surprise flashed to Curtis' face, and he took a step back, taking in the sight of me standing upright before him. He palmed his chin and stared at me, his rough beard begging to be released from his death grip. "You know, Lonz is my boy," he started. "My hardest worker. He's got a good head on his shoulders. I think he's management material. Long-term potential. Know what I mean, Josie?"

He liked making people feel uncomfortable and *he did. He did.* But sometimes you had to be someone else's eyes when they couldn't see.

"He is all of those things." I cleared my throat and licked my perfectly glossed lips the animal in him couldn't stop staring at.

I lived with the Cannon. Men didn't scare me.

I didn't have much experience with babies or kids in my young life, but men threw temper tantrums just like them. Sometimes, the best thing to do was to tell them how this was going to go.

"Alonso and I are moving soon anyway. And this payment plan you have him on, it's not gonna work. We don't plan on paying. Take that how you want." My heart pounded out of my chest and my underarms were wet.

He couldn't have Alonso.

Me and Curtis stood in an auto-body shop in one of the

worst parts of Philly. It was me, some cold coffee, and dozens of stolen cars chopped and screwed in the back. It was hardly a success story like Curtis believed, but we had different standards.

"You bi—"

Alonso dashed through the curtains and made his way to the front. "Let's go, Josie!" He whistled. He picked up speed when he saw Curtis.

"Curtis, I'm heading out with Josie. Everything's in the back and ready. We'll start on the second pallet tomorrow."

"My man." Curtis grabbed Alonso's hand and dapped him up. He leaned into Alonso and whispered, "and my money?"

"Oh, I'll make sure you get it, don't worry." My shoulder touched Alonso's and his body stiffened. He shot a sideway glance at me.

Curtis patted Alonso on the back and broke into another phony bologna grin like a crazed clown. "Lonz, my man. You have a good woman who holds you down. Make sure you take good care of her. People don't respect family nowadays like they used to."

"Let's go." I grabbed Alonso's arm and ushered him outside.

A few minutes later, we stomped and argued all the way down Springfield Ave, relentless, cold air whipping us in the face. Its lashings left my cheeks red and ashen. Alonso's face was grim.

"So, he expects you to pay him weekly from the stolen cars? Humph, that's not happening, and I told him that, too."

"You need to stay out of this, Josephine! I told you I would handle it my way!" Alonso genuinely looked disgusted. It was no longer cold as anger seared through me.

"You'll never move on from him if that's the case, Alonso!

He wants to keep you working for him. Keep you working *under* him. You still have the basketball kids to coach. How will you make time for both?" I hurled questions at him, daring him not to have an answer.

"I haven't coached in a while. One of Curtis' guys in California saw one of my coaching videos on YouTube and contacted me about middle school coaching position—but again, it's in California." He took over pulling my rolling cart of makeup.

I tucked my hands into my warm pocket and let him explain himself.

"I just don't have time anymore now that I'm here." Alonso slowed his walking.

My eyes dashed around the city trying to make sense of what he just said. Everyone was rushing to and from somewhere with their heads tucked and phone in hand. The cold made people mean.

I hopped the turnstile and Alonso swiped his metro card. We sat down and rode the train to the outskirts of the city where there was grass, open land, and the air was different. My head rested against the glass windows and people watched. Some waved to the mail men and carefully studied packages being delivered, others braved the cold and played basketball in their backyards. What was it like to have a backyard? A big house? Did those people still worry about money or feel like no matter how much they dug themselves out, money seemed to play cat and mouse with them like quicksand.

I turned to Alonso. "You love coaching, Lonz. Curtis helped you get that client, but you have to do your part. You must make room for your gift; for what you love. If someone all the way in California wants you, imagine who else will too, if you put more energy into doing things you want to do instead of what you think you have to do," I said softly.

"What did your board say this morning? You wrote it, so I know you know." My fingers stroked his knee.

His body went limp as we rounded a sharp corner and he sighed. *"You gotta believe in your future more than your past."*

"Exactly, Alonso. Exactly. You are better than this and you know it. We have too much going on for this to linger. You're not paying Curtis any additional money. We'll figure out something, we always do."

Alonso's jaw tightened. "I should've never let those people run up on us at the shop. It made us look weak. Now Curtis is popping up every day to check on things." Alonso frowned and looked outside.

"Made you look weak?" I raised my voice. "Did you hear what I just said? You're missing the point here."

"You think I don't know that, Josephine?" He shot up from his resting position and now he raised his voice. An older woman whipped her head around and gave us a curious look.

"I know you know. I'm just saying." I leaned in and whispered. "You have dreams, too, babe. You're always telling me to do what I love. You are a big reason why I even had the courage to step out and become a hood makeup artist."

He chuckled and I relaxed under his softened gaze. "A hood makeup artist?"

"Yeah, you know. Philly raised me, the streets paid me. Josie's Jawns." I made a muscle fist with my arms and grunted.

Alonso laughed and rested one hand on my thigh and one on my rolling cart. The train shook from left to right. "It's just tradition. This is how our set works. We move a few cars and it gets hard for a while—but that's how Curtis tests us. It's tradition."

"Tradition? What is tradition, really? It's just peer pressure from people who don't care about you, anyway. And once you pass the test, doesn't that mean you're in even deeper?"

"This won't last much longer, Josephine. I'll get back to coaching and our plans to move out." He scratched his head as the train slowed to our stop. "We should be hearing any day now about the apartment."

We bustled off the train and a blast of artic freeze assaulted us again. Spring was elusive, running away refusing to be caught. As cold as it was, I grabbed Alonso's face and talked directly at him.

Alonso's mom didn't care, she was too busy living her life. I had Alonso and he had me. But I would always stand on business about me, *first*.

"Just don't forget about you. I hear you about them being your family, but so am I. I'm your family. And this isn't good for the family. We don't have to live this struggle life if we don't want to. And I don't want to anymore. I'll always choose me if I have to. I need you to know that."

Alonso cupped my hand against his cheek and closed his eyes for a second. He looked like he was about to say something but his face tightened. "Let's get inside."

I had two makeup clients at a community center in town. I wasn't familiar with the area, so I asked Alonso to tag along. He wore his du-rag, bubble coat, and Timberland boots. He looked straight out of Philly today.

When we got inside, the room was welcoming with matching tables, chairs, and large floral centerpieces. Waiters were still setting up and tidying the decor. Just a few steps down the stairs was all the action, and my heart skipped a beat. This shit excited me to no end. Women were bustling around carrying dress bags, two hairdressers were doing their thing, and some women were even in a corner shaving their legs. "I'm gonna wait outside." Alonso frowned, looking at the women half-dressed.

"Okay, I'll be fine here." I shooed him away and began setting up my makeup station. My kit grew every month. There were some old tried and true pallets, and some new, show stopping colors. Real artistry lived in my hands and my God, strike me dead if I ever disrespected it.

I guess per Karissa, charging top dollar for extra services was the way to go. When my paycheck came through from the studio, it was massive and my eyes bugged out of my head at the number. I had never seen that amount of money and my name together on the same check—ever. I wanted to cash the whole thing, go home to my room, throw it up in the air, and wriggle in it naked.

Newfound responsibility wagged her finger at me, and said, *'now now, Josephine, simmer down.'* Instead, the money was split into thirds and put in my checking account, savings account, and paying Dad. He would be so proud, if he cared.

I did treat myself and happily took a stroll through the expensive makeup store and bought a few items that added sparkle and more shimmer to my kit. I didn't have quantity— but I had quality. I beamed and set them out amongst everything else, old and new.

I was on my way.

Two hours later, I texted Alonso that we were finished. A few spritzes of setting spray finished my last client's look and I flung the cape off her.

When Alonso knocked on the door and the girls let him in, his eyes widened. "Wow, Josephine. She's beautiful. You really outdid yourself." He pulled his phone from his pocket and snapped a few photos. "I have to send these to my mom and sister."

"You think so?" I studied my client's face and my work. She barely noticed me as she made duck faces into her phone snapping selfies.

"Absolutely, Josephine. You are so talented. You've really got something good here."

"We." I pointed a finger between the two of us. "We have something good here."

Stopping at Ms. Marta's house, I couldn't wait to show her my pictures from the day's makeup. I made $400 today and charged top dollar for the rhinestones—just like Karissa taught me. I had money left over to take Alonso out on a hot date, and still save money for our new place. I wanted to jump and click my heels together.

When I walked into the house, Ms. Marta was inching out of bed trying to slide herself off. Yalitza was bundling up her coat. "Perfect timing." She pulled her hat onto her head.

"Slow down, young lady." I chuckled to Ms. Marta and glided her off the bed.

"She just ate about an hour ago so she shouldn't be hungry. She got her medication two hours ago. She should be ready for a nap pretty soon."

"Don't be talking about me like I'm not in here. I'm not no child! Hussies!" Ms. Marta grumbled. She took all of her strength to lift herself out of her favorite chair and shook her cane at us.

She was all skin and bones—but she was still fire.

"I got it from here," I said, relieving Yalitza and shutting the door behind me.

"Ms. Marta, what are you doing out of bed?" I folded my arms and watched her struggle to stand to her feet once again.

She swatted at me with her cane. "I'm getting my joint so I can toke."

"What?"

She knocked on her kitchen cabinet with the end of her cane. "Go in there and get my joint. It ain't a lot but I don't need a lot."

"Ms. Marta, I don't think you should be doing that."

She huffed, rolled her eyes, and swatted at my behind with her cane.

"Ouch!" I yelped.

"Girl, go in that cabinet and get me what I said, now. These doctors say it's not long for me and I want to feel good."

Stroking the pain in my back from where she hit me, I frowned. She was doing her best to stand up straight and she was shaking under her own weight. Sweat was forming at her brows. My moral compass faded away, and I walked to the cabinet, searched all the way in the back until I found what she was looking for.

"Thank you, Josie." She snatched it from my grasp.

"Okay, sit here then." I fluffed the pillows behind her and pulled out the recliner.

Ms. Marta took a candle lighter and when she lit up her joint, a dank smoke wafted into the air. She leaned her head back on her chair and smiled to herself. For a moment, brief, unbridled happiness found her. What a life she had lived. Did she have any regrets? Things she still wished to accomplish? Regrets, whether loud or self-imposed, could be weights if we let them be. They were something I didn't want to carry.

"Ms. Marta, do you have any regrets in your life?"

She took a long drag of the joint and passed it to me. I inhaled a few times and snuggled into the seat beside her, kicking off my shoes.

"I probably would have spent more time with my kids." She exhaled and puffed out smoke. "I wasn't always a good mama. I did what I knew how to do. You don't really know how these things affect kids until something big happens like you're dying. Out of three children, only one comes to take care of you. You know I've only been to Yalitza's house a few times. She's never really invited me over; she always comes here. One time I had to use her printer, and she got a big ol' fast one, so I popped up to see her. I went into her bedroom and on her nightstand was a wine glass, waist beads, and one of those butt plugs, I guess you kids call them. I said, *'My! What happened here!?'* Never went back since." Ms. Marta laughed.

I puffed and pondered and pondered and puffed. I probably wouldn't go see my dad if I had to. But why? He was still my dad. I crossed my legs and wondered if he would come see about me. He never had before when it wasn't out of obligation. I didn't want anyone or anything in my life that was done out of obligation, though. I wanted love. I wanted pound cake after a Sunday dinner. I wanted homemade baked cookies during Christmas. I wanted love in the morning and then brunch later with people who made my heart smile.

"How's the Cannon?" Ms. Marta motioned for me to hand her back the joint.

How did she know I was thinking about him? I squirmed in the seat. "He's still pissed about me quitting the chicken factory. He at least gave us an extra month to find a place. The first apartment complex denied our application, said we didn't have rental history. How am I supposed to establish rental history if they won't rent to me?" I confessed, remembering the cold one sentence email the apartment complex sent me days ago. "One day he's nice, the next day he's mean. I don't know how to take him."

"You got to talk that shit back to him, Josephine. You're a sensitive one, and that's okay. Means you feel things deep. But you give it right back to him and make him see he ain't raise no punk. All the ways he tried to raise you to be strong, he did exactly that. But you also show him who you really are. Just because he don't know how to show love doesn't mean he gets to take yours."

I didn't say anything and took in Ms. Marta's words.

"Did ya'll find other places?"

"I put in two more applications, but did you know they charge a fee just to apply? It's like $50 per application. I have to pay a fee to beg them to let me live there. Sounds so American."

She curled into a relaxed lazy smile and giggled. Her eyes were red. "The world makes it hard for you to do anything nowadays. Ain't nothing easy or handed to you. Don't mind me, girl. I'm just thinking about my life. Who here and who ain't."

I thought about my mom. She was never here—but she was always here.

"I can't say that I lived a bad life." She shook her head and changed the subject. A life transition was coming, and memories begging to be remembered bubbled to the surface. "I had some rough times that taught me more about myself than any regrets ever could. You have the best experiences when you're grateful, and I'm grateful for it all. For you, too." She leaned over and patted my leg. She took one more puff and passed me the joint.

She smiled at me. Her cheeks were sunken in with a hint of

pink. Her eyes were all sparkles and she shined bright like a lighthouse in the dark. "Josephine. You hear me, good? Make sure you get yourself on an airplane. Get out of the city. Go put your feet in the sand somewhere. Take some deep breaths in a place you've never been. Just like your friend, Amna. She's on the right track. And when it's my time to go—I want you to do me up all pretty like . . . like . . . Gloria Estefan. Make me steal the show. And you know my flan recipe? I want you to try your best and make a small pie, just the way I make it. And take your time, you be rushing through everything except that makeup."

My eyes fluttered closed as relaxation coursed through my mind, body, and spirit.

"You over there sleep?" Ms. Marta shouted at me.

"No, I'm up. And you don't have to yell I'm right here."

"Good. And another thing. Make sure I have on my good bra; I want to be casket sharp. Matter fact, put two bras on me; I'm a feminist. And not a big flan pie either, just a small one. I want em' to fight for it." She nodded to herself with a half-smile.

"You remember how that girl said, *'she just ate, she shouldn't be hungry'* " Ms. Marta stood stiff and mocked Yalitza's voice.

"Yeah?"

"Well, my sixty-five-year-old stomach determined that was a lie. She is hungry and she got the munchies. And get me a piece of paper and an ink pen. I like to write while my thoughts are clear. I'm going to write these kids of mine a letter, so they know how it feel being they mama."

Ms. Marta and I both turned to each other and giggled until happy and sad tears trickled down our faces.

CHAPTER 23

The sharp knock at the door was shrill and demanded to be heard. I washed my hands with a paper towel and wiped the counter down from all the suds.

"You expecting someone?" Dad eyed me and glanced at the wall clock.

I shook my head no.

His lady friend whom I had never seen before peeked out of his bedroom with wide eyes. Anytime someone came banging on the door late at night was a horror movie for Black people.

"I got it." Dad held up his hand and motioned me back into the kitchen.

"Who is it?" Dad peered through the peephole.

"The police, Mr. Scott. Open the door!" a gruff voice shouted.

"Why? What do you want?" Dad stepped away from the door and instinctively put his hand to his waist.

"Get my gun," he mouthed to his lady friend now in the hallway.

Her face went pale and she mouthed back with a whisper, "*Where is it?*"

Of course, she didn't know where it was.

She didn't know *him*.

My shaky hands grabbed my phone on the counter to call Alonso. This couldn't be good.

"We're here about an Alonso Harold!" the police yelled on the other end.

"Alonso?" I whispered and darted for the front door.

Dad whipped his head around and stared at me with surprise. Alonso was supposed to be at the shop. Where was he?

Dad placed his palm on the door and laid his head near the peephole. "It's okay. It'll be okay." Dad nodded to me and his friend.

"I'm going to open the door now!" Dad yelled to the officers on the other side. "I'm opening it slow. Ya'll don't make no sudden moves and neither will I."

When he turned the knob and cracked the door, I spotted two officers with irritated and tight faces.

"May we come in?"

"Where's Alonso?"

"He's been detained, Miss."

The blood drained from my face.

Dad glared at me, and I felt an inch small. He opened the door wider and let the officers inside.

"Alonso listed this as his address. Were you aware that he was part of a large car theft operation?"

Dad stared at me, his eyes and anger never letting go of mine. I dropped my shoulders and looked down at my fuzzy socks.

"No, we were not aware, officer." Dad's voice was low and tense.

"A victim's vehicle was stolen and they decided to do the investigating themselves and located the car. They got into a scuffle and contacted the police."

"What can I do for you officers?" Dad breezed by everything the young, eager officer said. One thing we agreed on was knowing all your rights—you didn't give the cops the rope to hang you.

The officers glanced at each other. "Here is my card," the other one said. He looked older and sneakier. "If you think of anything we should know. Come across any cars that don't belong, give us a call."

Dad snatched the card from his hand, reading his name. "I'll be sure to do that. Detective Tom." When the officers left, Dad crumpled the card in his hand and closed the door behind him and grunted. "Humph. Tom foolery." He slowly turned to me while the air in my lungs disappeared like air being let out of tires. The cannon was ready to blow.

"I want him gone by the morning."

"No."

Dad's jaw tightened and he sucked his teeth. "No?"

"No." I crossed my arms.

"He's a hoodlum, Josie, and I knew he was. You believe in the wrong people. You can't fix him. You tried to move him in here and clean him all up but it ain't working, Josie. I've been going back and forth about whether to let you guys stay since you been doing well with this makeup thing, but nope, my first suspicion was right. He's a roughneck, and it's my fault for thinking I could help."

"And you believe in the right ones?" My truth bubbled to the surface. "I watch you come in here with different women all the time—since I was a kid! I never said nothing to you. I don't care! If someone makes you happy even for a split second and helps you be less mean, I'm all for it. But Alonso—Alonso is different. He's . . . he's . ." I stammered. "Just caught up in a bad situation. He's trying to get out of it, and you don't make things any easier."

"Easier?" He erupted. "My life was never easy. I lost my parents at a young age, too. Started working at fifteen. I went through some stuff, too, Josie. Became a daddy before I was ready, by myself. But I ain't never joined no gang or even felt the need to steal no car. I don't live with thieves."

"So because Alonso made a few mistakes, he's got to go? Who cooks around here? Who does most of the cleaning? Who is up every day with . . . with . . . positive words? Affirmations? It damn sure don't be me or you." I pointed a finger between us. His woman friend stood glued to the wall, watching a family run through twenty-five years of silence and hurt feelings.

"Don't cuss at me."

"I'm not cussing at you! I need you to understand what Alonso has been to me. You became a dad before you were ready, but you never became a dad. *My dad*." My voice cracked. "What have I done for you to never love me? I was always something you had to take care of or manage. Never love."

"Dammit, Josie! Don't you talk to me like that in my house." His face contorted and angry spit flew from his mouth. "Talking about I never loved you. You love this heat, don't you? This cable? This food? I loved you . . . No . . . I *love* you the way I know how. By giving you all this." He waved his hand around. "And ain't nothing wrong with this, but you always get the idea that it's not good enough. *I'm not good enough.*

You've never been happy—not even as a kid. You always came back from your grandmom's house with all these reasons that you've suffered. You think I'm supposed to hug and kiss you every day, but I just ain't built like that. Alonso has to leave. He can't be a roughneck living in my house; so you decide. Now you—you can stay and paint faces all day long. But he's a criminal and gots to go."

I gaped at my dad, a real-life stranger, and tears pooled in my eyes. He lived his life by his standards. He liked to work, watch tv, entertain women, and play cards on the weekends. He did what he thought dads were supposed to do and that was enough for him.

He didn't understand love—but Alonso did.

"Alonso is not leaving." I forced back the tears and tried to stand tall in front of a dragon. "You already gave us a date to move out, and that's the date we'll be leaving. Not a moment earlier."

He stared at me for what seemed like seconds. Minutes. He saw a stranger in me, too.

"You choosing him over your family?"

"If that's what you want to believe. Then yes." I puffed out my chest, but it was hollow inside. Choosing between the coldness I knew here, and the unknown coldness without Alonso was a harsh reality, but an easy choice to make. I was going where the love resides.

Dad inched in closer until we were arm's length apart. I could feel and smell his beer breath. He poked me in the chest and his lip curled up. "I knew you would be the type of woman to run behind a man."

"Cannon!" Dad's woman-friend in the back finally gasped and her hand whipped to her mouth. I could see the wetness in her eyes.

"No, baby. She need to hear it. We need to hear the truth sometimes."

My puffed out chest caved in and the floodgates opened. Within seconds, I could barely see through my own teary eyes. "Thanks, Dad," I croaked. "I'm just the woman you raised me to be." I ran to my bedroom and slammed my door shut.

Alonso's quote board slammed to the floor once again, just as my phone beeped. When I opened my emails the first sentence stared at me, right on time. *"You have been approved! Welcome to your new home!"*

CHAPTER 24

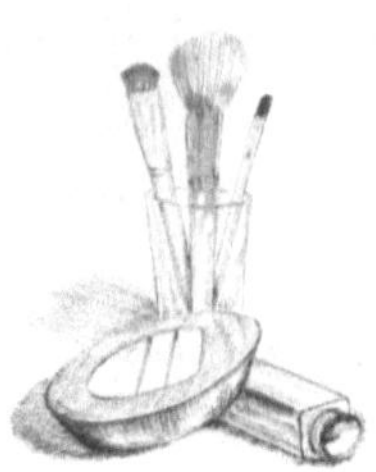

It took all night for me to get Alonso out of jail. *All night.* Every penny we saved in my personal account and our joint account went to bail money. *Bail money.* It was like we could never get ahead. *Never.*

They finally released Alonso about 5 a.m. this morning. My shaky hands shot out a quick text to Karissa informing her I had a family emergency and would be two hours late. I felt like shit. *Shit.* Another job and I was still late.

Sharp pains shot through my temples, daring me to frown. Headaches only found me when I was stressed or worried and as I pushed the front door open to the day-spa, I was all of those things.

"Morning," I mumbled, barely acknowledging the others as I strode past to my station in the spa, clutching a steaming cup of coffee and shielded behind oversized sunglasses. The scalding liquid scorched my throat, but I didn't care. It matched how I felt inside. Life was like a twisted game of Monopoly; at any moment you could lose it all and have to start over.

I didn't sign up for this shit.

While we wasted years in school memorizing useless square-roots and debating flag allegiance, nobody prepared us for the harsh reality of just how many times we would be starting over. Maybe it was something they didn't prepare you for and it was a lesson that life unfairly dealt without prejudice. No one told you what to do when you just lost it all and still had to smile and work like nothing was wrong. The apartment complex said we could drop off our security deposit and first month's rent to hold the apartment. Just twenty-four hours ago we had the money and then some. Now we just had some. And some was none.

Some was *dust*.

I stuffed Alonso at Ms. Marta's house until my shift was over. Dad wouldn't go to Ms. Marta's house anyway, and she would cover for Alonso until I got there. My shoulders dropped. Fresh blood sprang to the inside of my mouth as I chomped down on my cheek and fought back the tears. Ms. Marta and Alonso—my two people. They were both slipping fast through my fingers and it was like trying to hold onto water, each of them flowing in different directions without me.

I pulled off my coat and wrapped my work apron around my waist and back. Staring at my reflection in the mirror, round squishy bags sat under my eyes and my face held not a lick of makeup.

The other ladies in the shop gave me weak smiles and turned away, stealing glances at each other. Janet frowned and wore a worried expression.

Weird. I know they weren't acting like this because I was late.

My eyes flicked toward Karissa's office. I wanted to talk to her about taking on more clients to make up for the money I put up for Alonso's bail. "Is Karissa here?" I whispered to Janet.

Janet didn't respond but one of the girls cleared her throat. "She's in the back office. You might want to go back there and talk to her." She smirked.

Janet flashed a nasty smirk in the girl's direction and buffed out her client's fingernail even harder.

"Okay . . . thanks," I muttered and knocked on Karissa's door.

A few seconds later, I heard a muffled, "Come in."

"Hey." I closed the door behind me. "Sorry I'm late. I had to take care of something for my boyfriend. I wanted to talk to you about—"

"Josephine." Karissa raised a hand and cut me off. Her face was sharp and whatever she had to say was more important. "Do you remember your new hire paperwork?"

"Huh?" I shook my head and tried to recall clicking through the long list of emails she sent but didn't remember any outstanding documents to sign.

"Do you remember your new hire paperwork? I guess not." She finished before I could say anything. "Non-compete clause? None of this is ringing a bell?"

My breathing quickened and I wanted to douse my mouth with more hot coffee. *What is she talking about?* I shifted on one foot.

"Did I not fill it out? I must've missed it, I apologize. Do you have it? I can sign it right now. It's not a big deal." I searched her desk for the paper.

"You really don't understand what I'm saying?" Karissa leaned in her chair, back stiffer than a white girl at Odunde Festival. There wasn't a hint of shock or surprise and *that* worried me. Not too long ago, Mr. Childress had this same look with Amna. I looked around, my eyes bouncing around the room waiting for the gig to be up.

"You signed a contract to work here stating that you would not see any clients outside of this spa." Her pointer finger banged on her desk, emphasizing every point. "I see we are quite the makeup artist on social media. A few familiar faces, too—that started from here."

Ohhhh

"Karissa . . ." I took a deep breath and stammered. "Honestly, I really didn't know what that meant. You hired me . . . and . . . and . . ." I stumbled over each word figuring out what happened. I would've signed damn near anything if it meant I could do makeup. "I signed everything quickly. I barely read through it." I admitted and shifted my weight against the wall. I wanted to bang my head against it. I fucked up again. *Again. This is the shit my dad is talking about.*

Karissa tilted her head back and laughed the tackiest, most obnoxious, I'm-about-to-nail-your-ass laugh. "You think I believe that? You can't steal my clients, Josephine. You're a smart girl. I'm sure someone in your life explained how these things work."

They didn't.

I pulled the chair away from Karissa's desk, plopped down, and rested my shaky hands across from hers on the table. My fingertips were ice-cold and the seat trembled beneath me. *Think, Josephine, think.* "I didn't mean to steal any of your clients. They contacted me on Instagram and my friend, Amna, schedules the appointments for me. I mean, I'll be taking it over because she's moving to Hawaii soon, but until then, I just show up for the job."

The ramblings of a girl in the midst of a panic attack settled in. My gums flapped but who knew what words were coming out. They didn't make sense. Nothing was making sense. I gripped the sides of the seat and my chest heaved in. A small, childlike voice escaped me and it took all the energy inside to utter any words. "I can call her right now and prove it," I fumbled, pulling my phone from my apron pocket. My stomach did somersaults watching Karissa stare at me with a pitiful, older sister disappointed with her younger sister, now I have to teach you a lesson, face.

Karissa's bright red lipstick must've made her feel powerful. Or maybe the fact she built everything in here herself from the ground up, and so she wasn't afraid to make hard decisions. It was ironic. She was a blueprint I didn't think was accessible for girls like me. But today, she was smug when she rolled her eyes and sucked her teeth. "Listen, this is not going to work out. You violated the signed contract. Given the fact that you are two hours late for work anyway, maybe this isn't the place for you."

"Please, Karissa. I'm sorry. Please." I breathed, trying to keep the tears away but they spilled anyway and ran down my temples, crossed behind my ears, and tickled down my neck.

Karissa shook her head. "Please remove your apron and clear out your workspace. You can come pick up your last check when it's available."

Waves of fear shook through my body, and I heaved, feeling like I might vomit right there all over her desk. My chest was tight while gasping for air that seemed to be escaping me. I couldn't breathe, and yanked at my apron, snatching it away from my body.

"Josephine? Are you okay? Breathe. Breathe!" Karissa shouted from across the table.

Sweat trickled from my arms and my heart was beating a

mile a minute. I was dying. I had to be. I clenched my throat, wanting to claw at it.

"Breathe!" Karissa scurried from around the table. She quickly poured water into a napkin and slapped it against my forehead. The cool water trickled down my hair and cheeks, and as water fell down my shirt onto my back, my breathing returned. I loosened my grip from around my neck and soon, the tears flowed.

"Josephine, it's okay. . ." Karissa patted my back and rubbed her hands in circles.

Embarrassment shocked my body out of its death trance. She just fired me—and her sympathy wasn't needed. I flung her arms away and stood to my feet. With my body shaking like a leaf and snot sitting at my nose, I got to my station and began tossing my makeup kit back into the same box I put there not long ago.

The other ladies were silent.

Janet sat her nail polish down and walked to me. She grabbed a few of my things and gently sat them in the box, all without saying a word. My eyes were red and puffy and my body felt so heavy I was worried I could fall down right there. Even when I did right, somehow, I was still wrong.

Bursting out of the spa—box in tow, Alonso answered on the first ring. I sobbed, snotted, and coughed my way through the cruel and unusual punishment that was the past twenty-minutes and my latest job loss.

"Where are you?" he shouted into the phone.

"I just left the shop. Where are you?"

"I'm at the Museum of Art. Couldn't stay at Ms. Marta's house, she is a trip. Take the bus to Center City and meet me there."

I rode the bus the short distance and called Amna. When I

told her what happened, Amna's voice was angry and laced with profanities for Karissa. "Talk about overreacting!"

"What am I going to do?" I cried. An older woman across from me on the bus eyed me. Another person's pain was sensational.

"You can do this," Amna said, with a soft tone. "You are already doing this. Don't let Karissa stop your flow. You gotta walk into rooms like God himself sent you there, Josephine. Bet on you. Maybe this is happening for a reason. You already got the clients, maybe you can just do your own thing."

I nodded into the phone. Amna's time in Philly was winding down. She would be missed and my chest was tight thinking of how good she was at running my social media page and handling all the behind-the-scenes things. But she was right. I *could* do this. I *would* do this. My dad didn't raise no punk.

When the bus jolted to my stop, I saw him first. Alonso was perched high on the steps craning his neck down below looking for me. My eyes roamed him while he searched the many faces of people looking for me. Taking advantage of the budding weather, he wore a black tracksuit, jacket, and fresh kicks. You couldn't even tell he was in the slammer hours before.

He is so fine.

The sight of him made me break down crying again. I wanted to crawl to him, climb into his arms, and make him convince me everything would be okay and we could return to our blissful ignorance that was our life. But we weren't happy there either; we were just pretending. Not understanding what we didn't know and not utilizing what we did.

People shuffled off the bus, stopping to take pictures near the Rocky statue. When he spotted me, we both quickened our pace, me running up the steps two at a time, and him shuffling down three at a time.

We met somewhere in the middle.

The sun broke through winter clouds and shined all around him on the steps. His eyes moved slowly from my feet, my hands, until they rested on the makeup box filled with my life inside.

Real life weak in the knees was what he made me; I swear. When the time was right, I'd give this man babies. And I'd *never* leave them, in life or in death.

He'd put a basketball down for me.

But I wouldn't make him.

I'd put a makeup brush down for him—*but he wouldn't make me.*

Somewhere in the hollow parts, down deep, deep, where it rattled. He blew love into me with the flip of a switch.

My Rocky grabbed my makeup box, sat it on the ground, and snatched me into a tight hug that made me gasp for air. When doubt crept in ready to snatch away love, Alonso had none of that. He let me nurture my own garden but still fed me at the root. We were lost in a sea of arms and limbs. The wind whipped us relentlessly and froze my flowing tears and fears. He held his hood up to my face and shielded me from dozens of unsuspecting tourists seeing me break down in a city that was known for its brotherly love. I didn't have any brothers that loved me except for this one brotha' right here. People bumped us from either side and kicked at my box in their haste to move around us. I didn't care. My eyes squeezed shut as a thousand cries unleashed their levies and I buried myself into Alonso's arms for a second, minute, hour, lifetime.

CHAPTER 25

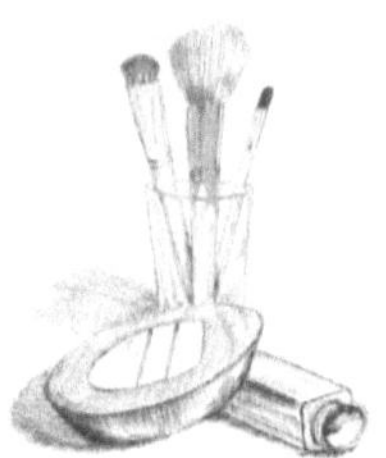

I held my calendar to my chest and took a deep breath before tapping on the door. Alonso waited for me downstairs in the hotel's restaurant. Amna and I spent hours last night going over my new booking website she built to ensure the process was easy for new clients to request an appointment. She set me up with a digital platform that accepted deposits and sent reminder texts messages and emails to all clients. With Amna leaving soon, she did all of this within just a few weeks. She drilled me, making sure I knew the ins and outs of my own business. I didn't realize how much she was taking care of behind-the-scenes, and it made me want to beg her to stay. My following on social media was growing daily and I was averaging about three emails per day with makeup requests. Every face I touched—I saved my money.

Alonso and I were back at square one with our apartment search, though.

After getting him out of jail, the apartment complex rescinded their offer when we could no longer pay the security deposit. Alonso took charge of looking for new apartments for us. I needed him to have a project, something that would occupy his mind and make him excited again.

Even though I wasn't, I felt homeless. We were living on borrowed time with someone who didn't want us there. Dad reluctantly let Alonso back in the house, but we were walking on eggshells and barely speaking since our blowup. Alonso and I tried to stay out of his way. His piss poor attitude spread through the house like a domino effect, with everyone on pins and needles waiting for him to gripe about something. There was always something.

We had no choice but to keep going. Keep moving. Every day I questioned myself, wondering if this was a precursor for the rest of my life. A life in which every decision I made felt like the wrong one, but I wouldn't know for sure until it was already messed up and I had to start over.

A gorgeous, bronzed Black girl opened the door and flashed a dazzling smile. She looked so familiar to me. Her natural, radiant beauty struck me dumb, and her dimples and white teeth said hello before she did. "Hi. I'm Josephine, from *Josie's Jawns*. I'm here for Jade and Sapphire."

The woman smiled and said, "Hi. I'm Jade, Sapphire is in the back." She opened the door further and ushered me to the hotel living room. They had the penthouse suite and it overlooked South Philadelphia. The city was busy today with bumper-to-bumper traffic and multiple sporting events. I could spot the Walt Whitman Bridge and the Eagles Stadium from here.

I got to work, setting my kit out on the long dining room table. I checked the time on my phone a few times, wondering if Alonso was okay and if Ms. Marta was feeling alright.

"So how did you find me?" I asked, mixing two different shades of foundation together to match her skin tone.

Jade with the dazzling smile closed her eyes and tilted her face forward so I could begin applying makeup. "I believe you did my cousin's face a few weeks ago for her women's empowerment event. She spoke so highly of you."

Jade's phone rang three times back-to-back, and each time she barked out orders and crossed things off a long to-do list she held in her lap.

Another woman I presumed to be Sapphire, paddled into the room barefoot from the bedroom. She wore a silk robe and her long, flowing, silk press cascaded down her back. She wiggled her fingers in my direction and waved. "I'm next?"

"You are." I nodded, trying my best to smile and be present in the moment. So many things were on my mind. I took a deep breath and brought my focus back to Jade.

Studying her bone structure, cheeks, and pouty lips, I knew a pop of red with a bold smoky eye would bring her look together. My hands excitedly moved around my kit, searching for the colors and shades I needed to bring my vision to life.

Jade's phone rang once more, and I had to take a step back from applying her lash so she could take the call. She hung up and shouted, "We landed the BET account!" to Sapphire.

Sapphire slid out of the room and danced in place in the foyer of the penthouse. "And I knew we would!" she shouted.

Jade and I giggled as Sapphire shimmied and wiggled in excitement.

"What do you guys do if you don't mind me asking?"

Jade closed her eyes and stood still so I could apply her lash. "We have some properties that we manage, but we also curate a food and wine blog. BET just picked us up for a syndicated cooking show in California."

I didn't know the ins and outs of blogging, but I said, "Oh, cool! How do you guys like it?"

Jade held up her to-do list in her hands. "As you can see, we are swamped. What Cardi B say? *'I be in and out them banks so much, I know they tired of me!'*"

Sapphire gave a raspy laugh from the other room that made me snort.

I cleared my throat, tuned in. "Was it hard? Starting your business? Getting everything off the ground? Are you ever scared?" My fears lingered in the air as nervous questions poured out of me. As much as Amna helped, these were questions I had to ask someone who had been there and done that.

Jade opened one eye and stared at me. "Success leaves clues. You have to be open to the work and a little luck."

"Luck?" I slid some glue onto the other lash and got ready to reapply.

"Yes, luck. You have to believe in yourself and know that you can do it, but you also have to leave space for the magic to happen. When something is for you, like, really for you, nothing will stand in the way and it'll seem easy. Things will start falling to the wayside that weren't meant for you or your journey. You may think you're losing out, and the whole time you're being redirected back to what you're supposed to be doing anyway. That's the hardest part. Believing in yourself when the world tells you to be regular. You almost have to be delusional."

Sapphire waltzed into the room with a freshly scrubbed face. "Jade is right. And sometimes, you have to move on. If you've lived in a place all your life, maybe you've hit your glass ceiling here. You might need a new one."

"Are you from here?" Sapphire plopped onto the couch and tucked her feet.

"Born and raised." I swept liner under Jade's eye embarrassed by the fact that I had never even been out of the state.

"I grew up in a little town in Mississippi. It wasn't a bad place. My mama and daddy still live there. Some of my siblings, too. But I knew there was more for me to see and do. Home is where the heart is, but you can make home wherever you are, too."

As Jade and Sapphire switched seats and I began working on Sapphire's face, I thought about every job I lost the last few years. I thought about Karissa and her Santa Claus, or whatever it was called. I wanted to punch her in the face, but I also admired her and what she had built for herself. It wasn't her fault—it wasn't anyone's fault. Maybe these things were being stripped away so I could make room for what I was supposed to be doing. I didn't have all the pieces lined up, but they were there and ready for formation. Could I be the type of girl who packed up everything and moved away? The thought calmed me in places that needed warmth and excited me like a new idea ready to take shape. Maybe . . . just maybe . . .

After I packed up my kit, Josephine and Sapphire circled me, both of them shooting knowing eyes at each other. "You're really good at what you do. Really good. Your makeup technique is flawless, and trust me, I've had my fair share of makeup artists." Jade nodded. "I'm going to post your information on my social media page. Once I do that, I need you to believe in yourself and prepare for what's about to happen. Do you understand?"

"I understand."

"Oh, and if you're ever in California, look us up."

Jade and Sapphire paid me almost $500 for two hours of work, and they didn't get a *lick* of rhinestones.

A few minutes later, Alonso and I were woofing down pancakes in the hotel's restaurant as I excitedly told him about my morning.

"Lonz. . ." I said, pausing to sip my orange juice. The words sat excitedly in my throat, but I was nervous to say them out loud. The thought was new to me, and I hadn't even tried it on for size yet, let alone telling Alonso.

He looked up at me expectantly between bites of food.

"Have you ever thought about . . . us moving?"

Alonso leaned back in his chair. "Ain't that what we're trying to do?"

"No, I mean moving, moving. Like out of the state or something."

Alonso sat back in his chair; a dribble of sweet pancake syrup sat on his lip. "Where would we go?"

"I don't know. I haven't really thought about it too much. But now I am."

Alonso scratched his chin and looked out the window. People were walking fast trying to get out of the damning cold. Or maybe trying to get out of Philly. "I wouldn't mind living somewhere a little warm. Where's all this coming from?"

I gave Alonso a brief recap of my conversation with Jade and Sapphire. When I checked my phone to show him a picture of her, I noticed I had dozens of new followers and messages. Jade had over 200,000 followers on her social media page. She tagged me in a post and people were blowing up my inbox with appointment requests already.

"If we're honest here. Really honest, Alonso, are you happy?"

"*Are you happy?*" he retorted without answering the question.

I dropped my shoulders and circled a spoon into an empty coffee cup. "No."

"Me either," he muttered.

Truth sat between us as thick as cold grits on the table.

"I want something different for us. Philly is home and will always be home, but maybe we can make a new home and life . . . somewhere else. Dad says we have to leave, anyway. And maybe that's exactly what we need to do. Move away—out of the city."

Alonso was quiet as he people watched and avoided my eyes. I could see the wheels turning in his head. "You know I would have to come back in a few months for these car theft charges. My first court hearing is in the fall. And I still owe Curtis a bit of money."

"It's your first offense. We'll get the best lawyer that basketball and makeup money can buy. And we'll pay off Curtis however we have to. We'll figure it out."

"I thought you said we weren't paying Curtis?" Alonso's eyes darkened and he shifted in the booth.

"Fuck Curtis." I sucked my teeth. I never wanted to beat up a man so badly in my life, but I knew that wouldn't end well. "I still don't think we should but if we have to pay to finally be free of all of this. Then maybe we should."

Alonso's shoulders fell and he gripped the sides of the table. "I wouldn't mind a day without Curtis. Or your dad."

I placed my hand over top of his. "I wouldn't mind a day without my dad and Curtis, either."

"I don't want to be connected to Curtis like this. Him and the guys. They're my brothers, my family. But this life ain't for me. Maybe a move wouldn't be the worst thing," he said with a spark of excitement gleaning in his eyes as he allowed himself to dream.

I nodded. "I need something different, too. I'm making money, but I can do better." I bit my croissant and let the warm buttery taste melt into the parts of me that had been bitter for too long.

"What about Ms. Marta?"

I grabbed my phone shooting her a quick text message. I would talk to her shortly about my latest, greatest idea. This one made my heart swell, and I couldn't wait to tell her more and we troubleshoot things together. Although she was sicker and weaker than ever before, she would be excited for me.

Convincing Alonso was easier than I thought, and with him and I on the same page we prepared for what was about to happen. Right now, all of my makeup clients were in the Philadelphia area. If I could make it here, I could make it anywhere. Wasn't that what Jade said, anyway? Bet on yourself? I just had to believe. Alonso had to believe in himself, too. Ms. Marta would help me sort this out and think things through.

"Maybe we can nail down a date after she . . . after she . . ."

It was Alonso's turn to reach across the table and grab my hand. "Whatever happens with her, you will be okay. We will be okay."

I couldn't imagine a life without Ms. Marta. I couldn't imagine a life without Amna. But here I was—imagining both. And worse, both were quickly becoming a reality. When I did makeup, each face was a blank canvas, and if I had to tell the story of their life using shades, colors, and palettes, what story would I tell? What story would I want to be told about my life? What would their features, imperfections, and beauty allow me to share? It felt great to be loved for something I was good at, but Ms. Marta loved me simply for being me.

I wanted to live out loud every day of the week. A big life with big moments, big fun, big money, and lots of love. These days I had less and less to give, and the walls of our small bedroom were closing in on me. Perhaps there was some place in the world where people felt like they had space to grow and change. Did those people live in Philadelphia or did they have to move away? What did my best self look like? I stared out of the window, imagining me as her. What did she talk like, walk like? What did she see and feel? How did she act? How did she manage money, and handle the roadblocks life threw at her? My dad wouldn't understand, and at this point, I didn't care. I was searching for, *her*.

Something was changing in our house. Homes were usually filled with love and laughter, but that was never in our house until Alonso and I filled the barren space. A coldness lived there, and it was getting more frigid by the day. Spring was rounding the corner in our little slice of life, but a constant desperation festered and lived in my home with Dad. Me and Alonso would create a space for us– filled with love, fresh croissants, affirmations, and space for his sneakers, my makeup, and lots of happiness.

Dad never experienced love. Maybe he did with Mom, but what good was it doing him to hold onto memories of love with her, rather than allow himself to experience it again and again? Or even show it to me? He never experienced what I struggled to give to another man because I had never seen it for myself. Even if I crashed and burned after it was all said and done—I wanted to *feel*, to live.

I checked my phone again, waiting for Ms. Marta's response. She usually kept her phone right up under her and answered within minutes.

Nothing yet.

Ms. Marta would understand. She would be proud.

CHAPTER 26

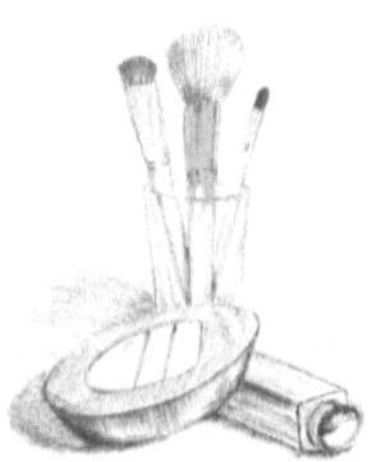

lonso stuffed his clothes back into the drawers. They were neatly folded but littered the floor of our tiny room. Didn't take much for that, though. Dust flew around us and settled into hundred-year-old cracks and crevices of an unhumble abode. I swept and felt sunlight warm my arms peeking through the blinds. This spring would bring something new and I welcomed the big thaw. We were cleaning up and then going to check on Ms. Marta. Rose was doing her job keeping Dad occupied and out of our faces as we planned our new life.

A sharp knock at the door jarred us out of brooms and trash bags.

I froze and glanced at Alonso with a scowl. Every knock these days seemed to be followed with something ominous. My ears rang and my heart plummeted to the floor where love should never be.

Ms. Marta always said bad news came in threes.

Her. My job. The apartment. Amna leaving. Curtis . . . Well, that's more than three.

Alonso and I waited.

Dad opened the door and Yalitza pandered on the other side with a swollen, red face.

"Josephine," she croaked, looking past Dad. "She's gone. She's gone," Yalitza cried and fell into the wall.

"Wait a minute now, wait a minute." Dad pulled up Yalitza as she immediately crashed into his arms and wailed and wailed and wailed. Her whole body convulsed into his arms.

Never one for high emotions or theatrics— Dad froze. Unsure. Confused. "There, there. There, there." He awkwardly patted Yalitza's back and guided her to the couch to sit down.

Air caught in my throat. My brain said gasp. *Take a breath, bitch!* Just open your mouth. But I couldn't. I couldn't breathe. The same feeling reared its ugly head from when Karissa fired me, but this time it was back with vengeance. Within seconds, I would be dead. No one could live without oxygen and right now, my body couldn't breathe. *I can't breathe.* I clutched my neck and clawed at my throat. This was it—this was the big one. I was dying and I felt it through my body, beckoning me, calling me to join my mother. Ms. Marta. Give up this maddening, cruel world and let the lack of oxygen take me out right here and now.

My knees buckled and body crumpled. All the lights on my dashboard went out. Before I hit the ground in the living room of our make-believe family home, Alonso caught me.

"I got you. I got you," he whispered in my ear and carried me to the couch.

Tucking my legs around myself, I curled into a ball and waited for death to come for me. My chest constricted and stomach knotted.

Ms. Marta. My Ms. Marta. She was *gone*.

"What happened?" Dad questioned.

Yalitza was shaking like a leaf and her phone ringing off the hook. The word was spreading. People wanted to know if it was true. Was it? This couldn't be happening. It was too soon. They said she still had . . . I licked my chapped lips and counted back when this all started. Now. The time they gave was now . . .

Yalitza didn't answer Dad. She snotted and sneezed as she wiped her nose with the back of her hands.

"Hello?" she answered the phone. I heard hurried voices on the other end. "I don't know," Yalitza replied robotically. She stared off into space. "I went to relieve the night nurse. She was fine then. I checked her vitals and gave her the pain meds. She kept saying she had made it, she made it. I didn't know what she meant." Yalitza's head dropped into her hands. "I thought it was the pain meds working."

Dad kneeled beside Yalitza and continued rubbing her back and helping her gather her words on the phone. He did what I had never seen him do before. Comfort someone with emotion—not logic.

Bile rose up in my already aching throat. Stumbling to my feet, I raced to the bathroom and emptied the contents of my stomach into the bowl. She was losing weight, but she was in good spirits. I should've called her again. I should've texted her again, but I was too busy making plans with Alonso. I didn't even get a chance to talk to her about the move. I needed her guidance . . . her opinion. Her approval.

I needed *her*.

I tumbled into the corner of the bathroom where the tears began to flow and rocked back and forth. A strange sound escaped me. The vibration from my chest tremored. My pulse was fast. But it couldn't be me making those wailing noises. No—that couldn't be me.

Alonso stormed toward me from the living room, lifted me off the bathroom floor, and flung me over his shoulder. He kicked clothes and shoes out of the way and pushed his way into our room and gently laid me on the bed. He tucked me into the blankets like a burrito, and I could barely move. I buried myself deep into the blankets, tucked my chin in my arms, and wished I was anywhere but here.

Hours later, it was dark from our blackout curtains and a chilly draft blasted its way through our old windows. I reached over to Alonso's side of the bed and it was empty. My head pounded and although I didn't feel hungry—my grumbling belly said otherwise. Pots banged and a shrill scream came from the blender in the kitchen. Muffled, worried voices tempered the walls.

When I sat up in the bed, my body felt like it had been hit by a truck. I wanted to go back to sleep and wake up when this nightmare was over. I knew it was coming but still . . . Dammit, man. Schlepping in the direction of the noise, I held the wall for support and my dark eyes adjusted to the light of what I was seeing.

"You have to dredge it in the cornmeal first."

"Well, I use flour."

"Cornmeal is better. And grab the cast iron skillet. It fries up better that way."

"What you know about a cast iron skillet, boy?"

"I did learn a little something something from my mom." Alonso chuckled.

"When is the last time you talked to your mom, Lonz?"

He paused. "I haven't reached out in a while. A long while."

"Alonso missed his calling. The way these potatoes taste should be in one of those cooking shows," Amna's voice rang through. Her mouth sounded full of something that also had the house smelling delicious. I stood against the hallway wall in shock and watched Alonzo grab the skillet from under the sink where he always kept it.

Dad scurried around the kitchen, flour all over his hands and wrists, and one long streak across his forehead.

Amna had Alonzo's laptop open at the table and she was eating fried fish and typing away.

The floor creaked beneath me, and their eyes shot up in surprise at my presence.

"Hey, baby." Alonso grabbed me by the arm and pulled me into him. "We thought we'd make you some breakfast," he said and stole a glance at Dad.

"Breakfast?" I questioned. The clock on the microwave said it was 4:00 a.m.

Dad grabbed a paper towel and wiped his hands. Flour littered his black eyebrows and hair. "Well, you know. We were up." He shrugged. "How are you feeling? You know what? I'll make some coffee! How you like it?"

"More cream than coffee, please."

"Just like your mama." He hesitated like he was remembering.

Amna pulled back a seat at the kitchen table and I plopped down next to her and sulked.

"This all my fault."

"Oh no"

"But it's not."

"Don't talk like that."

They all sang out. I know it wasn't my fault, but that's how it felt.

"Everyone I love, I lose." I clasped my hands together and laid my head on the table.

The table was quiet as everyone pondered their own losses. The fish sizzled and popped in the pan.

"Josephine. You ain't lose everybody. You got us." Dad pointed a spatula at himself, Alonso, and Amna.

"Us. When did we turn into an us?" I cowered. Exhaustion was winning and I didn't feel like faking it.

Dad pulled up a chair and sat next to me, sandwiching me in between him and Amna. "I been listening to this uhhh . . . podcast."

"Poooddcasstt?" Me, Amna, and Alonso repeated in shock.

He cleared his throat. "Uhh yeah. Something Rose put me onto. Anyway, girl. It said if all you did was . . .Hold on, hold on . . . Let me get it right," he mumbled to himself and used his fingers to think. "Okay, I got it. Our hardest moments are the bridges to our peace. This is hard now, but you will get through it. We'll help you." Dad shared a glance at Alonso and Amna. He grabbed my hand under the table, and Amna grabbed my other hand and they nodded their heads in my direction. We sat at the table like we were in an important meeting, and before long the fire alarms began to ring, jolting us back to life.

"See, boy! I told you the fire was up too high! Talking about he can cook. Yea, he's about to cook me right into the poor house!" Dad fussed and jumped to his feet.

"You were supposed to be watching it!" Alonso shot back.

Amna's computer dinged next to me, and her fingers were moving fast as she typed and coughed from the fried fish smoke.

"What are you doing here? You're supposed to be packing to leave?"

Amna bumped her shoulder into mine. "You think I would leave you like this? Hawaii will always be there. We have bigger fish to fry. No pun intended," she giggled. She turned the computer toward me. She kept scrolling and scrolling and I saw dozens of makeup requests.

"What's all this?" My eyes were wide.

That post from Jade and Sapphire had thousands of like and hundreds of comments.

"Welcome to the big leagues, best friend. You're viral." Amna's face lit up.

"Wha-what?" I sputtered.

"You're blowing up, girl. Just like I knew you would!" Her face beamed like a proud parent. Amna saw me in ways I had yet to see myself. She was lightyears ahead of me about me.

"Amna, I can't do that right now. I . . I . . . I have to bury Ms. Marta. I have to . . ." *Grieve. I have to grieve.* I pushed the words from my brain.

"I know that, girl. I got you. No one was looking for an upcoming appointment, and so I scheduled everything for at least a month out. I set your appointment schedule to require a deposit, and you already have half of their full fees banked. Girl, you're sitting on a couple stacks *right now*, just in deposits." Amna bounced in her seat.

"I don't have the energy. I don't want to. Who do I think I am?" a weak voice escaped me. Dad was holding a plate lined with paper towels and Alonso was scooping hot fish onto the plate. They shared glances with each other but stayed quiet as Amna laid into me.

"You don't have to get right to work, Josephine. But you will get your ass up and get moving. You have something special here, and it's real, raw talent."

I collapsed into the seat and turned away from Amna. The weight of a woman Amna saw me as, and the woman I felt myself to be were two different people.

She pulled my arm back and made me face her. "Life is fucked up sometimes. It can be happy, sad, up, down. It can be a maze. But it's amazing, Josephine. You are amazing. Ms. Marta would not want you holding yourself back like this."

"You weren't fired because of some bullshit clause; you were fired because you've got magic, and she was intimidated! This was supposed to happen! You got the lemons, let's make the lemonade." Amna grabbed my hands and squeezed. One lone tear washed down my face. "What did I tell you, Josephine? It's time, Josephine. It's time for you to walk into rooms like God sent you there," she shouted. "Now you say it, too! Alonso? Mr. Cannon? Ya'll say it, too! Walk in the room like God sent you there." She stood up and clamored. We all repeated the words, even Dad. I said the words over and over in my head and out loud.

You gotta walk in the room like God sent you there. He sent me there. It was my time. Ms. Marta knew it, too; she told me so.

I knew about loss. Knew about being motherless. But my mom had already passed when I was born, so I didn't really *know* about loss. Not like this. This felt much worse. Was love worse when you knew it and then lost it? Or when you knew it was there but never got to fully experience it before it was taken away?

I was a West Philly chick and Josie's Jawns was my baby.

There were a lot of spaces I shied away from. I was quiet and grateful to be in the room. Taking up space didn't come easy for me, and it wasn't a feeling I was comfortable with. But just because it was uncomfortable didn't mean it wasn't for me. In fact, as I looked at Amna, maybe the point was to lean into that discomfort. Ms. Marta would agree—I knew she would.

Taking a deep breath, I stole glances at Dad, Alonso, and finally Amna. I cracked a small smile. A smile felt wrong sitting on my face knowing Ms. Marta was gone—but it felt right. The people I loved the most were in this room. They all loved me the best way they knew how. Some, in ways that I didn't understand and maybe never would. But God was in this room, too. Right here, right now, and that deserved a smile.

"Okay," I murmured.

"Okay." Amna shook her head and clasped her hands together. "That's all you're getting from me. Then I'm going to Hawaii."

"Okay," Dad and Alonso said at the same time. They glanced at each other in surprise.

With a sigh, I scooted from the table. "I'm going to call Yalitza and see if she needs anything." I nodded at the three of them.

"Yessir!" Dad yelled and slapped his hands together. He and Alonso two-stepped in the kitchen while a second batch of fish popped behind them. Alonso was blowing on a hot piece of fish and stuffing his mouth. "And you don't have to do a thing right now, Josie. I'll call Yalitza."

"I'm going to get some t-shirts made, and I already ordered a few business cards, so you'll have those ready," Amna said, squirting ketchup onto fried potatoes.

"Amna, I think you may have found your calling, too," Dad admitted.

"What's that?" She crinkled her forehead and paused.

"Business management. You got the juice." He winked.

Amna's chocolate cheeks turned red, and she lowered her eyes. She pondered his words and her shoulders jumped. "Humph," she grunted and continued typing at the keyboard.

"Are we going to eat or what? This is the best fish I've ever cooked if I do say so myself." Dad gave a smug grin.

"You cooked?" Alonso crossed his arms.

I snorted and dipped out of the room. Tears that were always threatening to fall escaped down my cheeks. The wall behind the kitchen was out of view, and held my fears as I leaned against it, closed my eyes, and exhaled.

"I've seen her all done up before, playing in that makeup. But is she really *that* good?" Dad whispered. I heard the skepticism in his voice.

"She is. She really is Mr. Cannon." Amna replied.

"Real shit, Mr. Cannon. Josie's got something good. She makes it her own." Alonso agreed.

I trotted back to my room to throw back our curtains and let the light in.

CHAPTER 27

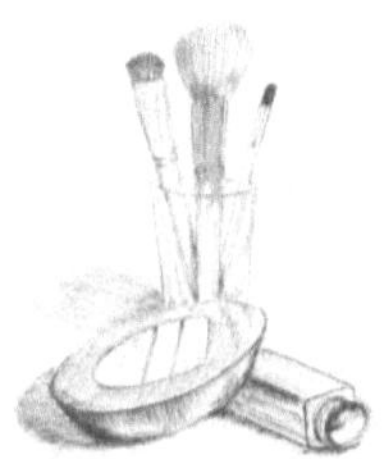

He slipped out of the house for the second night in a row. Probably fucking around with Curtis. I pretended to be asleep as he gently shut the door behind him. His linger smelled of burnt tires and fresh lies. I poked my head outside and saw Ms. Marta's back kitchen light on. Muscle memory commenced and my heart skipped a beat thinking she was up cooking and dancing. I furrowed deep into my blankets and tucked myself in when I remembered it was just Yalitza and her brothers preparing for a funeral and cleaning out a home they only visited out of obligation. A home I knew my way around with my eyes closed. A newly installed semi-permanent scowl sat on my face when I thought about the mom they took for granted. Ms. Marta never said she was the best, but dammit she was *there*; and that was more than some of us had. My phone buzzed and a text message from Yalitza interrupted my pity party.

It read:

> We found a will. Did you know she updated it within the past six months? It says it must be read in the presence of her children—you included. Give me a call when you get a chance.

My phone made a thud when I slung it against the wall and stomped to the kitchen. I stole a swig of juice right from the container. Gulping it down and wiping my mouth with the back of my hand, I tried washing away the resentment, but it wouldn't or couldn't shake me loose.

There was all types of rain in this cloud.

Alonso's laptop glared at me. I hadn't picked it up since Ms. Marta passed. I hadn't left this room except to use the restroom and eat bits of food. Alonso's two-night disappearance was even more pronounced when these four walls were my self-imposed prison.

I gave the laptop one last evil eye before snatching it into my hands. Upon logging into my accounts, five more makeup requests and one interview request stared back at me. Amna, my hood manager, was already in various stages of responding to their messages and collecting deposit payments. Sure enough, everyone was scheduled for at least the next two-three weeks out.

I hope time was on my side.

I responded to a few messages, texted Yalitza back, and shot Amna a thumbs up text. Three hours of me staring at a computer had me seeing red. Where the fuck was Alonso? I checked his location on my phone and realized it was off.

That was it.

I hopped up, plucked my sneakers from under the bed, and slid into them without socks. I found my favorite sports bra and lifted the girls into its protection. If my fist ran into Alonso on my way out, well I wanted to make sure he tasted my knuckle sandwich especially for him.

The front door opened and closed. I tip-toed toward the wall. I felt his familiar taps rapping down the hallway. I yanked the door open and swung on him.

"Where the fuck have you been?"

Alonso ducked and batted my hands down. "At a meeting! Damn, girl!"

"You left last night and again this night. You cheating on me?"

Alonso's eyes widened. "Ain't nobody cheating on you. You give me enough grief."

"A meeting? Do you think I was born yesterday? Where were you?" I pulled him in and shut the door behind me. Dad was a hard sleeper and out like a light, but if my fist really did connect with Alonso's face, I didn't want it to wake Dad.

Alonso paced the floor. "Well. . ." His lips curled into a nervous smile. "I have good and bad news. Which do you want first?"

My head pounded. I spent too much time policing Alonso. Grief had taken over my body and refused to release its grip. I was so tired. "Give me the bad news first."

"Curtis has this grand plan to hit the arena next week during the Sixers game. He . . . uh . . . wants us prepared. All hands on deck."

My eyes bugged from my head. "You and your gang friends are planning to steal cars from the most guarded—heavily populated—cameras perched up everywhere—spot in the city? Right after you've *already* been arrested for it?"

Alonso ran his hands through his hair and paced, thinking about his words. "Yes, Josephine. Yes."

"Alonso. What are you thinking? You're considering this? Every time we have a conversation about this, you talk all this shit and it seems like we're on the same page, but then you get out in the streets and do the exact opposite of what we discussed. Which one is it? Is it us, meaning me and you?" I pointed a finger between us. "Or is it you and them?"

Alonso grabbed my hips and jerked me into him. "It's you, it's always you. But in order for me to get to you—I have to let go of them. And I let go of them by doing this one last job."

"We're supposed to be moving. We have to bury Ms. Marta soon. You're a coach and the kids love you. This can't be your weekend life, Alonso. You have to let this go now. Let it go or let me go." I collapsed onto our bed and rocked in place. Was I going crazy? Losing my mind? My all-star team was fouling out of the game.

"That's the good news I wanted to tell you if you be quiet for a second." Alonso shuffled in place and rubbed the back of his head. "Curtis came through. Again. Remember that client I had a few months ago? The Sixers power forward's kid? Well, he told another teammate, who told someone, who told someone. I got a phone call from the NBA Youth Development Specialist Team. They want to bring me on as a consultant and help coach some of their youth summer leagues."

"Alonso . . ." I groaned. "You can't rob the Sixers parking lot, and then go work for the NBA. Make it make sense!"

Alonso grabbed a pillow and plopped down in front of me. He brushed a curl out of my face and wiped sweat from my nose. My usual pulled back low ponytail was in crinkled loose ringlets shooting up from all sides of my head. It was unruly, unjust, and unavailable for the bullshit. "Can't you be happy for me? I'm moving us along. This is going to help us even more!"

I dropped my head and plopped down on the bed. His words and delusion were too much to break down. "You keep finding ways to entangle yourself even more with Curtis. Don't you want more? It's always *something*. I'm tired of putting our life on hold for Curtis! Who is he? Who is he?" I asserted. Curtis had my man in a chokehold and I needed him back.

Alonso was quiet.

"I have an idea . . ." I hesitated. "You're not going to like it. But it's the best I can come up with. You know, under the circumstances."

"What's that, Josephine?" He blew into his hands.

"Curtis will only stop when he is stopped. He's got all of West Philly on lock. How about we go to the cops and tell them what Curtis is planning, and then we'll leave town?" Every word was filled with doubt and deception. It went down bitter, but in the end had the potential to turn sweet, if he allowed it.

"Snitch? I ain't no snitch." Alonso swayed back and cocked his head at me.

"Dammit, Alonso! Do you have a better idea?" A handful of his t-shirt twisted between my fingers and closed the space between us.

He smacked them away. "Get your hands off me, woman."

"Then that's it. You've made your choice."

"Do you ever be quiet? Even for just one second to let someone else think?"

"Well?"

Alonso took a deep breath and the weight of a twenty

something, misguided, underemployed, Black man in America took shape. "You're right. Something has to be done. But I don't think that's the way to go about it. I have another meeting with the NBA youth team soon. There's too many variables, too many what ifs." Alonso spread his legs on either side of me and scooted in closer for a kiss. Our foreheads touched.

"Alonso. . ." I wiped a tear from my face and gazed into his eyes. The same eyes who saw a diamond in the rough when the world saw a roughneck. The same eyes who fried fish with the cornmeal—not the flour. And the love I would walk *away* from if I had to. With tears streaming down my face—I would.

He forgot pressure made diamonds.

"I want nothing more, than you. Me and you. But one thing about it, and two things for sure. If you go to that stadium and steal cars with Curtis, you'll have this little room all to yourself because I will leave. On my own. I will leave."

I squeezed his hand and stared into his eyes. I bored into them, wanting to see the depths of his soul and the truth behind his eyes. Did he feel me? Understand what I was saying? It took me this long to find myself. To believe in myself. But if he was stuck in the sunken place and refused to see the forest from the trees, where did that leave me? Me without Alonso wasn't a thought that I was ready to fathom. It was one of those hard pills to swallow and it tasted disgusting in my mouth. Too often we leaned on our friends and family for love. Advice. And nothing was wrong with that, but for a girl who had minimal friends and family to lean on—my bottom-line decisions lied with me and had to be my own. Sometimes I made good decisions and sometimes they were so-so. But they were mine. And even though I felt like shit and every part of me wanted to curl up and cry, my decision would always be to move forward.

With or without him.

Taps at the door interrupted our impasse. The door creaked open. "Ya'll okay? Josie?" Dad eyes lowered between me and Alonso. He had worked overtime and was still in his uniform when he passed out on his bed.

"We're fine, Dad," I said. My eyes never left Alonso.

CHAPTER 28

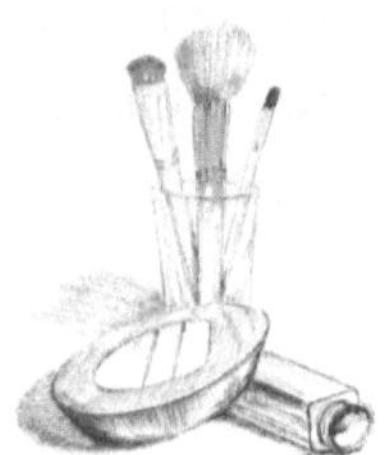

It took them weeks to come up with the money to bury Ms. Marta. The room that now housed her body the night before her funeral was freezing. No windows and definitely no light made its way down here. I shivered and crept up to her body. Yalitza's hand grazed my back. "Do you think you'll be able to do this?"

No. No . . . I don't want to do this, I thought. This would forever go down as the worst Saturday in history. But doing Ms. Marta's makeup for her funeral would be an honor.

The funeral home issued latex gloves cinched my hands, and I inched closer to check out her skin. Thin and rubbery. Months ago, it was thick and oily. Checking my kit, I grabbed a few different foundation shades and mixed them together. I did a patch test against her skin to make sure we had the perfect shade. I needed my girl to steal the show. Using nude shades with a pop of sparkle, I highlighted her eyes, which always sparkled when she talked about things she loved. When she gushed about food or found something really funny. Sunspots on her face were visible through the foundation, and I kept them like that. She didn't need to be fully covered. Her sunspots were like rings around a tree and told tales of a full life lived and many stories to tell.

Pulling my curling iron out of my bag, I twisted and coiled her curls into perfect silver ringlets. I sprayed a pop of perfume to her neck, painted her fingernails white, and finally lotioned her hands and massaged into the cracks of her fingers.

Stepping back, I glanced at her one last time. If it wasn't for Yalitza, I would've collapsed right into the seat behind her. No one told you when you lost someone, a bone-rattling tiredness followed and haunted you. Your body felt heavy and every thought, every unanswered question, every everything, felt like bricks weighing you down; a constant reminder you were alone. Alone again. My Marta Ruiz. I wondered what it would've been like to do my birth mom's makeup. Would she teach me makeup tricks only women knew? Did she have dreams? Goals? Did she want to get out and see the world? Be something different than she already was? Did she have a woman in her life who challenged her to be better and loved her through all of her mistakes?

I didn't. Then I did. And now I don't. Again.

Angry tears ran down my face fast and furious. I leaned over Ms. Marta's body and my chest rattled over her hollow shell, and I prayed to God that she would wake up one last time. Just one minute, one second, I could have with her again. She still smelled like herself, but the smell was fading away. She got further and further away from where she was and closer to her final destination, somewhere in a heaven where I wasn't.

"It's okay. It's okay." Yalitza tugged at my shoulders and pulled me off Ms. Marta.

"Mr. Scott?" Yalitza called out over her shoulder.

Dad half-knocked and rushed through the door with

Alonso hot on his heels. Alonso pulled me into his arms, up from Ms. Marta's body and squeezed until I could barely breathe. My face was sweaty, and I was breathing through my mouth trying to catch my breath. Dad gave Yalitza a quick hug and hopped around the table where Ms. Marta's body laid. He packed up my makeup kit and tossed items back into my bag.

"You did a real nice job here, Josie. Real nice job." Dad nodded in my direction, looking over Ms. Marta's body with soft eyes. He held fingernail polish in his hands.

"Thanks, Dad," I wheezed.

After the funeral, I pushed soggy fruit, and a jiggly piece of flan around on my plate. Yalitza's younger sister made it. It was good, but nothing was better than the original. I could taste one difference, though. It didn't have real vanilla. I guess that was the point. You took the scraps that you had, and you made your version of something.

A store-bought cheese and pepperoni tray sat on the food table untouched, antagonizing me. Fury welled up and I stormed across the room, grabbed the flimsy pre-packaged tray of plastic, cheap ass cheese, and tossed it in the trash, leaving a few people gasping. Ms. Marta would have a fit if she knew they were serving her favorite foods but bottom of the barrel quality. Hearing her voice fussing in my head over cheese selections made me chuckle as I plopped back down in my seat.

"The girl throwing away perfectly good food and over here laughing about it. What's wrong with her, God?" Dad sat down beside me. He looked handsome in his navy-blue suit. His beard was filling out with salt and pepper specks and a round belly pudge through his jacket. It was the first time in years I had seen him dressed up. It was always weddings and funerals.

"Was just thinking about Ms. Marta. What she would think of this funeral." I leaned against the wall.

"You know, your mom had a funny bone, too. She would turn everything into a joke. Everything was something to laugh about. You get that from her. Not me, though."

My eyes widened hearing his admission. "Get what from her? I'm not funny."

He cocked his head and stared. "You over here stomping around, flipping food tables, and giggling at a funeral. Something has to be funny. Or you crazy."

"I'm not crazy." I chuckled and then blurted, "Did you love her?"

He held his breath like he wasn't expecting the question. Just as fast, he blew out air like he had been waiting with an answer all my life. "Ain't found nobody like her since. Believe me—I've tried."

"Why are you so hard on me? Do I remind you of her?"

Dad inhaled another deep breath, not knowing what to do with my questions. But I needed to know why me just existing seemed to make his life hard.

"I don't know how to be one of those nice guys. Your mom had the fire. She had the passion. She wanted to go everywhere and see everything. I wanted to stay home, work, and save. Seemed sensible enough to me. I ain't never wanted to be more than what I was and do anything other than what I already do. If she was still alive, I think we could have complemented each other. She would have made me go places I never dreamed about going, and I would have tried to get her to stop feeding those damn cats by the back door."

Alonso was sitting on the couch across from me lightly snoring. People milled around us in a sea of funeral black, everyone in different stages of grief. They shared weak smiles and pushed around mediocre food on their plates. Dad and I leaned into each other until our knees touched.

"I understand what Ms. Marta meant to you, Josie. She was your mama, too. These past few months . . ." He sucked in a breath and exhaled. "These past few months watching her slip away and you grieve her has been hard. When I took off work, Mr. Childress asked me if I was sick. *I said, naw, man! I gots to be there for my Josie.*' I ain't never really been. Not in the way she needed."

"You took off work? For me?" I sat up straight in the chair.

He grinned and puffed his chest. "I did."

I leaned my head on his shoulder and rested it there. His arm was around me and I felt his heart beating. Within a few seconds, his heartbeat matched mine until I couldn't tell which was which.

"You know, Josie. You did real good with her makeup. The way you do that eye stuff, it's nice. Oh, and I been thinking." Dad turned toward me and peered around to see if anyone might be listening. He sat up straight like he had something important on his mind. "That girl at the day spa firing you, I don't even think none of that 'clause' shit is enforceable noway. You can't keep someone in the dark when the light is right in front of them. You know before I worked at the chicken coop, I worked as a delivery truck driver for about a year. Horrible shit. Terrible job. In and out of the truck in all types of weather. Didn't matter if it was a blizzard or 100 degrees outside, you still had to drive. Just terrible. Anyway, they fired me over some bullshit." Dad wagged his finger and smirked. "But they ain't take me off the employment list for months, and after it was all said and done, them not taking me off the list put me in the ballpark for unemployment benefits. I stayed on unemployment for a few months, you know, to get my mind together. But I knew I would eventually get something. And I did. I got me this chicken coop job. You see how it all worked out? You just got to believe in yourself, Josie."

As the Cannon himself explained why I needed to be more confident, he transformed right before my eyes. He was younger Cannon, before we put **'the'** in front of his name. He was a dreamer, a provider, protector. A thinker. He didn't settle for the chicken coop; he flourished there in his version of stability.

"I didn't know you worked anywhere before the chicken coop."

"There's a lot you don't know." Dad smiled and glimpses of hope settled into his dimples.

Alonso stirred in front of me and when he peeked open his sleepy eyes, he saw Dad and I leaning on each other.

"What's going on?" He cleared his throat.

"Nothing." I lifted my head from Dad's. I gazed around the room at all the people mourning Ms. Marta. I had a piece of her that would live in me forever, and that was something I would mourn and celebrate.

"I'm ready to go," I announced.

CHAPTER 29

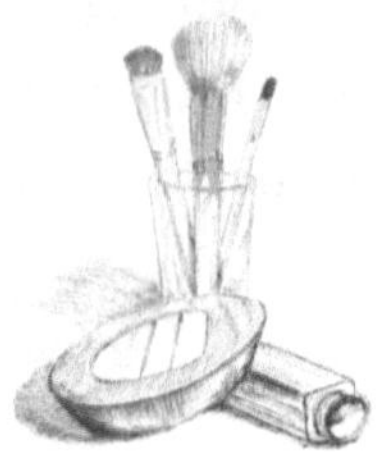

"I'll only be a second," I said to Dad and Alonso.

"Don't worry we'll wait." Dad threw the car in park. The three of us were out running errands when Karissa called and said I could pick up my last check.

I pushed the chimed door open to the day spa. Janet and the other ladies were cleaning up their spaces and getting ready to close for the day. I said hello to Janet and rolled my eyes at the rest of them. "Is Karissa in?" I leaned over the checkout counter.

"I'm here." She breezed into the room. She wore blue jeans, a long white kimono, and yellow kitten heels. She was breathtaking and every bit of a businesswoman. "How have you been?" She searched me up and down.

"I'm fine," I said cooly.

"I have your check, and there's a few things you left behind that we packed up for you."

The front door chimed again and four women loudly talking, burst through. "Are ya'll still open?" one of them shot out.

"I'm sorry, we are not," Karissa replied, checking the time.

"Please, miss lady, we're supposed to go to a birthday party tonight, and our hair and makeup girl backed out at the last minute. We need someone right now."

"I'm sorry, we're closed. We don't have the manpower to handle everyone, plus we don't have a makeup person currently."

"We have Josephine." Janet shrugged and glanced between me and Karissa.

The woman turned and looked me up and down. "Are you Josephine? Pleasseee, Josephine, we'll pay extra. It's an emergency."

Karissa and I looked at each other. Her favorite words, *pay extra,* were uttered, and one thing about it—Karissa didn't turn down extra money.

"Uhh . . . Are you comfortable using my kit?" Karissa questioned.

"Yup." I grabbed an apron Janet tossed to me and suited up for the game I was always prepared for—even on my worst day.

"Janet, you and the ladies take these two beauties right here and start on their hair. Josephine and I will work on makeup and then we'll switch out when we're done."

"I'm ready!" I shouted. "Just one second!" I scurried to the running car and told Alonso and Dad what was going down.

"We'll come back in two hours. Give you some time to do what you need to do." Dad nodded.

"You two behave now." I shot glances between them. It dawned on me this was our first-time riding in the car—the three of us. And now—the two of them.

"Awww, girl, get out of here and go make up them faces and get that money." Dad waved me away.

For the next two hours, me and the girls at the day spa took turns slaying the women. We did full glam makeup with heavy smoky eyes. We did extra rhinestones and sparkles. Janet and the girls whipped their hair into sleek ponytails and swooped bangs, even adding rhinestones into their hair at the insistence of Karissa.

After we sent them for a spin on the 360-camera stool to get a few shots, Karissa swiped their credit cards for thousands of dollars. I saw her eyes sparkling and mouth salivating from my former/new workstation. We made in two hours what Karissa would normally make in one full day.

"What luck this ended up being! You guys were right here, and we didn't have to go far. I think you did even better than my regular hair and makeup team." The girls clamored from the mirrored glam station staring at their hair and makeup.

I was running on fumes these days and they believed our meeting to be good luck. Talk about two sides of the same coin.

When the ladies left, Karissa and I fell into her office. She handed me a water bottle. I took large gulps and caught my breath.

She leaned back in her chair and stretched. "We killed it out there."

"We did." I nodded. I reluctantly came in to pick up my last check and left with that and a couple hundred dollars bulging in my pocket. We did *damn* good.

"Josephine . . ." Karissa started. She cleared her throat and kicked off her heels underneath her glass desk. "I have to admit, when I saw your social media page with all of your followers, I was jealous. It's hard running a business, let alone a women-led Black owned business. I thought you were trying to steal my clients."

"Karissa, I would never purposely do that. I respect every-thing you've built here." I swept my hands around. Her place was the flyest spa in Center City owned by a Black woman. I didn't want her piece of the pie; I was still learning to bake.

She nodded like she finally understood and was putting the pieces together in her mind.

"I see that now. There's more than enough work for all of us. Sometimes it just drops into your lap, like today."

"So, we're cool?" I extended a hand.

Karissa rubbed her feet together. She peeked at me. "I was thinking. Actually, before this even kicked off, I wanted to talk to you when you came in today. I'd like you to come back. You can have your same workstation and rate. You can see clients outside of here, I just ask that you build your own clientele and do it on your own time."

I cupped my hands in my lap and I let out a long sigh. Last month when she fired me, I would have come running back. All I wanted was to make my own way, doing what I loved to do. I just wanted a seat at the table. To be a part of the conversation. This winter was the coldest ever and through that, I learned to keep my heart warm. Stand in the sun. My hardest moments became my biggest teachers. Spring had sprung, and I was now in a new season that still required me to stand on my own.

With a deep exhale, I said, "Thanks, Karissa . . . But I think I'm going to pass."

Karissa's mouth dropped open in surprise. "What are you going to do?"

Philadelphia was too small for me these days. It didn't fit right anymore and everywhere I turned, signs told me it was time for a change. I had all the puzzle pieces, but the puzzle didn't make sense quite yet. Not like it did for Dad. With each decision I made, the picture came into focus.

"I don't know just yet. But I'm going to live and live well."

Karissa stopped rubbing her feet. She leaned back in her chair and gave a proud smile.

I grinned back.

fter Dad and Alonso picked me up, we headed home. A small, glass bottle caught my eye on the kitchen table and drew me closer like a magnet. It hadn't been there when we left this morning, and it sat in the middle, beckoning me closer like it had waited for me all day. When I picked it up, I smiled and held the bottle of fresh vanilla to my chest.

"Hey you . . ." I beamed.

She was there. She was here. She was always with me.

CHAPTER 30

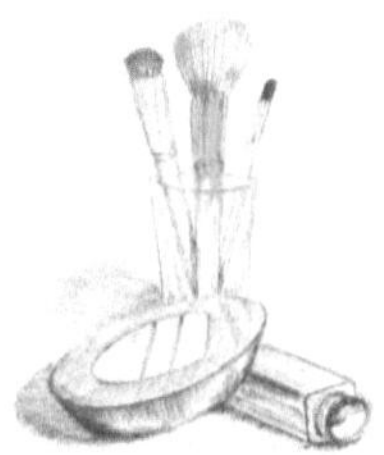

Sunlight swept across my face and nestled me awake. When I opened my eyes, Alonso was sitting on the bed staring at me. My hair fell out of my bonnet and I peeked at him through fallen bangs over my forehead.

"What?" My raspy morning voice meaner than I meant.

Alonso gazed out the tiny window. His eyes landed back on me, and his face was still.

"Let's do it," he whispered.

"Do what?"

"Go to the police about Curtis."

I shot up in bed and gaped at him. It had been weeks since I brought it up and we hadn't talked about it since. "What brought this on?"

Alonso's head dropped and with that, let me see him. His body showed a tiredness his words would never admit. "There ain't no other way. Curtis ain't gon' let me and none of the guys go voluntarily. And after I thought about it, you're right. Curtis wants us to hit the most visible spots in the city. It's suicide. But if I bow out and refuse to do it . . ."

I closed my eyes, knowing what the alternative could look like. Too many people in our neck of the woods were either going to extremes to prove they were down or being picked off and sent back to their families in body bags for refusing to be.

"There are no good options here," I lamented and pulled the blankets back from my body. I snuggled closer to him, wrapping my arms around his waist, and hugging him from behind.

"We'll tell them what you know, and then we'll leave."

"Just like that?"

"Just like that," I repeated.

Curiosity got the best of me, and I cocked an eye at him. "Will you be implicating yourself in anything? You know . . . serious?"

Alonso froze. His eyes darted around the room and landed on his basketball in the corner of the closet, signed by all of his mentees.

"I've been thinking about that, too. And I'm not sure. I mean, I know on SVU they cut deals and shit. Maybe they can do that?"

I squeezed him around his waist. "This ain't SVU! This is real life, Alonso. Other than the car theft charges we already know about, would they have anything else to charge you with? Just how much shit have you done with Curtis?" I frowned and shot questions at him, leaving no space for answers. I hoped there weren't any.

Alonso was silent. His inability to fully pick up the truth and move it down the field to the end zone was nonexistent. When it came to telling the full truth, the whole truth, and nothing but the truth, he always threw a flag on the play. "We can't let none of that stop us." He changed the subject. "We're going to leave here. Soon. We'll go to the station, I'll give up

Curtis and the stadium job, and nothing more. They have to take care of the rest."

"Do you think this could work?" I ran my fingers along his bumpy back and clutched him tighter.

He nodded. "I just have to figure out what to say, and how to say it, so as not to incriminate myself. You know, like SVU," he giggled.

I smiled and gave him a tiny pinch to the waist.

He flipped me over on the bed and pinned me down, planting wet, morning breath kisses all over my face.

"Ewww get off!" I coughed.

He laughed. "Did you think you were going to get rid of me, woman? Me and you are stuck together like Ms. Marta and compression socks."

A hoarse laughed escaped me followed by tears. Waffling between laughter and sorrow, even the mention of her name made my spirit sad.

"I'm so sorry. Too soon?" Alonso stopped kissing me and searched my eyes.

"It's okay. I'm fine. Everything makes me think of her," I admitted and wiped my face.

I smelled sausage wafting from the kitchen followed by the sharp shrill of the fire alarm. My stomach growled while Alonso was lying on it.

"Let's go see which lady of the month is burning the house down." Alonso lifted off me.

As me and Alonso made our way to the kitchen, Dad hopped around with a fly swatter.

"Done flew your ass in the wrong house, hoe!" he bellowed and squashed a fly on the trashcan lid.

"What are you doing, Mr. Cannon?" Alonso grinned.

These days he loved to see Dad surly and cussing as opposed to his usual silent treatment or disdain.

I plopped at the table and watched Dad and Alonso interact. They had done more talking in the past few weeks than the entire time the three of us lived together. What different people we were then. Hell, what different people we were yesterday. That's what grief did to you. Made you lose track of sense and time. Every moment felt like you were waiting for another shoe to drop. All the moments felt the same.

"What are you doing today?" I pulled my sweater around my body.

Dad scooped eggs onto three plates. "Work. What about you guys?"

"I have to meet Yalitza downtown. She wants to read Ms. Marta's will together."

"I thought you guys were supposed to do that weeks ago?"

"The kids couldn't settle on a date to read it together. Yalitza says there's a lot of hurt feelings."

Dad stiffened. "Why? Does she have millions stashed somewhere?"

I chuckled and scarfed down a sausage and scoop of eggs. "It's probably nothing. Ms. Marta never mentioned being loaded." *Besides,* I thought. *Her presence was worth more than anything I could have, anyway.*

"I have to check on one of my mentees, but after that I can meet you in the city?" Alonso stuffed his face.

"Do what you need to do, I'll be fine." I leaned in and kissed his cheek.

It felt good to choose someone who chose you.

I took a long elevator up to the eighteenth floor. I saw the Philadelphia Skyline and the Ben Franklin Bridge from this standpoint. The people looked like dots from up here, and I wondered if they were curious about me, like I was about them. What made them happy? What made them tick?

The directions Yalitza gave me were precise. I made a left and headed down a long hallway until I hit the last office on the right. Yalitza, her younger sister, two brothers, and the attorney anxiously waited with pained looks on their faces. Yalitza was already crying.

"Hey, Josephine," she greeted me. We embraced for a long time, and I saw her brothers give each other a look.

"Thank you all for meeting. I'm so sorry for the loss of your mother. She was a remarkable woman, and I am grateful to have known her," the lawyer said. He looked young and had some pep in his step. I chuckled to myself. Ms. Marta always seemed to attract a younger crowd.

"Thank you. But she was *our* mother," the younger sister corrected and pointed to her siblings, making sure to ice me out.

She couldn't rattle me. Being iced out of families wasn't nothin' new over here.

I crossed my legs under the table so I wouldn't accidentally kick anyone in the face.

"Very well, Ms. Ruiz." The lawyer cleared his throat and continued. "I have asked you all here specifically because Ms. Marta updated her will a few months ago before she got sick. If there are no objections, I will begin the reading of the will and discuss disbursement procedures."

The siblings at the table nodded and didn't look my way.

As the lawyer read Ms. Marta's last will and testament, I glanced around and studied her children. They all looked so much like her, even the boys. What kind of relationship did she have with them that made them not want to see her? Or be around her? How did life seem to get harder as people got older, and it ended up fracturing the most important, sacred relationships with their parents? Did I want kids? Never really thought about it before. I mean, I took my birth control faithfully every day, I wasn't a dummy. But did people voluntarily *plan* to have children and bring them into this unyielding world of everyday giving away pieces of yourself until there was nothing left to give? If kids were a part of my future, nothing, and I mean nothing, would keep me from them.

"Ms. Josephine?" the lawyer called out.

I uncrossed my legs and sat up. My face was hot at being caught daydreaming.

"Ms. Marta left you this envelope. She said that she wants it read out loud, in front of everyone."

"Uh . . . Okay. . ." I licked my lips.

What do this woman have up her sleeve?

Ms. Marta's kids huffed and checked the times on their watches. They made out well in the will and she left them everything she had, yet they still couldn't give me five minutes to hear her last words.

Unsealing the envelope, I pulled it open and caught a whiff of Ms. Marta. The smell made me sway in my seat and close my eyes as thoughts of her swarmed me.

I read out loud.

My dearest Josephine,

If you're reading this letter, it means I have passed on. I don't want you to be upset because I know you will be. And don't go thinking you could have done anything different because sometimes these things just happen. I guess it was my time and that ain't nobody fault but mine.

I won't make this too long because my stories is about to come on. But I want you to be nicer to the Cannon. He don't always know how to say what he feels. Hell, he probably don't even know what he feels, so he surely can't explain it. You keep going anyway. You keep living your life anyway, despite what he or anyone else thinks or says. Progression will make stagnant people uncomfortable. You could be the nicest person in the world (that ain't you, you can be a mean something) but if you are progressing, you will have enemies. Sometimes those enemies be your own family. With every level of elevation, there will be opposition. You fly regardless. Sometimes you will have to let go of the same person many different times to do what's best for you. One step at a time. It's tiny little steps, and you in the thick of it, baby.

I want you to know how grateful I am for you. You came into my life when I was mad at the world. Mad I was not a better mom to my kids. Mad they wouldn't talk to me. I was just mad. But you came along and wanted to make flan, and take trips to the market. And talk, talk, talk, talk. You wanted to talk. You wanted to be loved on. It swelled my heart up something good to hear your steps rushing up the staircase when you had something exciting to share, and even the slow jingle of your keys when you were upset. You allowed me to see you, and I thank you for breathing life back into me at a time when I was holding my breath. Thank you for allowing me to be love, again. To be love, Josie.

Now Ms. Marta ain't have too much, but I been saving, and I took out a small life insurance policy on myself a few years ago. I wanted to tell you, but I didn't want you to try to talk me out of anything. I want you to have something tangible, something real to help you on your journey. Oh, and what a journey I know it will be. Live your life, my beautiful girl. You and Alonso take good care of each other. Laugh. Travel. Eat good foods.

Move away from here. Live your dreams and know that they're just as important and real as anything else. Don't let anyone box you in or tell you what you can or can't do. People try to talk you out of happiness, so they can pull you back down to their misery. Don't be a miserable woman. I was one too long and wasted too much time. Never tell people what you are doing until it's done. And most of all, be brave. Be so brave, Josephine Scott.

Love always,
Ms. Marta

I stopped reading out loud. A check fell out of an envelope made out to me from an insurance company. When I saw all the zeros, my eyes bugged out of my head.

$200,000.

Tears streamed down my face, and I let them fall. I didn't wipe my cheeks but folded up the letter and stared at everyone in the room with their own wet eyes. She had left them all money, a house, clothes, jewelry, and other family heirlooms; but she left me her money *and* love.

The lawyer glanced around the room and gave a nervous cough. "Well, I guess that just about does it. Ms. Josephine, please sign right here for me, and you are free to go."

I rode the train home in a daze. The city whizzed by me, and the sleek, high-rise buildings disappeared and row homes, empty grocery-store carts, and insufficient funds returned. *But not for me though*, I leaned against the window and smiled to myself.

When I got off at my stop, I ran into the corner store and bought a bag of cat food. It was bulky lugging it home and I kicked the front door closed. Carrying the bag into the kitchen, I grabbed one of our bowls out of the cabinet and poured cat food into the bowl.

I sat it outside of our back door and waited for a chocolate cat to find its way home while I plotted to find myself some bigger spoons.

CHAPTER 31

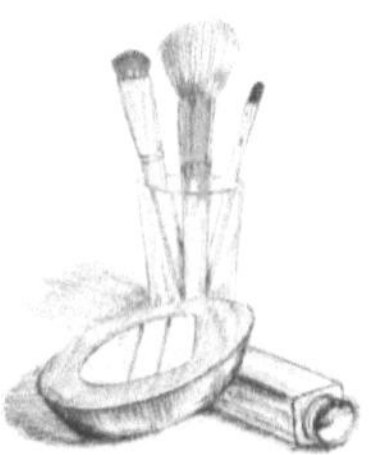

Alonso was on the other side of our room putting on a third t-shirt and pulling up his second pair of boxer's drawers.

"Why so many?" I eyed his extra attire.

"Just in case they take me to jail, I'll have extra clothes."

I gasped. "You think they would take you to jail after giving up Curtis?"

He paused and stared at me. "I know how this works. There are things I'm just as involved in as Curtis. I have to be prepared."

"Okay, Mr. SVU," I reminded him. I flopped on the bed and became hot suddenly all over.

The police precinct was just a few blocks away, and we were preparing to tell them what we knew about Curtis. Our eyes burned from staying up all night practicing what to say and how to keep Alonso's name out of certain conversations.

A knock on the front door interrupted my thoughts and Alonso and I frowned at each other.

I heard Rose answer the front door and voices got louder,

demanding to be heard. We rushed out of the room, and I saw Drew, one of Curtis' henchmen arguing with Dad.

Dad's work uniform was still on and his shirt was unbuttoned at the collar. He was rolling up his sleeves and preparing for a fight that wasn't his but showed up to his door, anyway.

"I don't have nothing to say to you, I'm here for Lonz." Drew took a step into the house.

"Rose and Josie, go in the room." Dad inched closer, daring him to take more steps. His hand was on his waist, twitching for something that wasn't there, but Drew didn't know that.

Drew lifted his shirt, and he brandished something shiny and black that *was* there.

"No. We're not going in the room. We're staying right here." I nodded at Dad and Alonso. Whatever went down in this house—it went down with all of us, or none of us.

"Drew, what's all this about?" I crossed my arms.

Drew was tall and fair-skinned. His cheeks were pink, and his hands were covered with a big Young Lords tattoo. Drew had a big heart. He was the person you sent in because he had nothing to lose.

"I'm here about this snitch ass!" Drew pointed at Alonso.

I squinted at Drew. "Alonso ain't no snitch."

"Sure ain't!" Alonso stepped farther into the living room.

So did Drew.

"Then tell me why Curtis just got picked up by the police? He's being questioned right now about the shop and the game. Only a few people knew about that job, so the process of elimination leads us here. I knew you wasn't about this life. You always thought you were better than everyone. *'I mentor the kids. I'm a coach.'* and all that shit you be talking about. Don't nobody care about who you think you are. You're the same as us." Drew's hand was still at his waist, but now me, Rose, Alonso, and Dad circled him, ready to pounce.

I searched around the room looking for something to bust Drew over the head with. He wasn't about to come up in here talking about Alonso. Not when it was me who had to convince him to do what needed to be done, anyway. And who snitched on Curtis? When I eyed the old lamp on the coffee table, Dad spotted it at the same time and shook his head no. My fingers itched for it.

"Drew, I didn't snitch on anyone, and no one else knew about the job." Alonso closed the gap between him and Drew. They faced each other; a man hellbent on changing his life, and another man determined to remind him where he came from. "And I don't think I'm better than anyone. I'm no better, but we are not the same."

Drew pulled the gun from his waist band and pressed it to Alonso's head. "Say that shit again." Drew's nostrils flared. "Why is Curtis locked up then? How they know about the drop before we even got there, then?"

"It was me."

Curious eyes turned to Dad. Rose scurried to Dad's side and stood in front of him, blocking him from anything Drew was thinking about doing.

"I turned him in, not Lonz. Somebody had to do it. You young boys is all punks, and its time."

"So, it was you, old man?" Drew smirked. "You really don't know who you're dealing with here and it's a shame Alonso didn't warn you." He stuffed his gun back into his pants.

"You got your girl's daddy fighting your battles?"

"He didn't know nothing about this so you can cut that out right now. Ya'll think people run scared when you menace to society boys flash around your piece? You think you run this city? You think what you're doing makes you strong? It makes you weak. Alonso ain't no better than ya'll, but like he said, he ain't the same. I did what had to be done to protect my family and untangle us all from this web. Drew, I know your Ma and Auntie and them. You better than this too, son."

We filled the room with fear and spilled secrets. Alonso's head was high and regardless of the words spewed at him, I couldn't be prouder. He was willing to implicate himself and tell on someone who literally sent a man here to end his life. And he did it all because I had threatened to leave him. I never knew a love that feared losing me.

Drew and Dad stared at each other, both looking ready to attack. Our semi-circle surrounding Drew was tight, and we stood shoulder to shoulder. He frowned at each of us before stepping back. "This ain't over, old man. You and me are going to move furniture, real soon."

"You know where to find me." Dad flexed his fingers and his eye twitched.

Drew sneered and retreated out of the front door.

Rose closed and locked it behind her, her chest rising and falling. "What are we going to do? What did you tell? You a snitch, Cannon? What did he mean move furniture?" She shot out questions at rapid speed.

Dad galloped to the front door, held up a finger to Rose, and listened for any signs of life on the other side. Satisfied he heard none, he sat down on the couch and ran a hand through his balding head. His hands shook and when he saw that I saw, he clasped them together.

"I overheard you guys talking the other night. You were going to turn in Curtis at the station. I beat you to the punch."

"What did you tell them?" Alonso inched forward.

"Just what I heard. That Curtis was planning to hit the stadium and jack some cars."

"Then why did they arrest him?" I questioned and took a pensive seat next to Dad.

He shrugged. "He's the head of a major gang Josie, and already on probation. He had lots of enemies. I guess this was just the straw that broke the camel's back."

"Why would you do that, though?" Alonso glowered. He wasn't used to anyone doing anything decent for him. At least not without him owing them later.

"I did it for her." Dad pointed at me. "You come in here with black eyes filled with worry. I see you're not happy. I see myself in you, Alonso. Doing what you have to do to get along. You turning in Curtis would have been suicide for you, and you know it. And I know Josie probably talked you into that. It wasn't a bad idea, but it couldn't be you that did it. I'm older and I have nothing to lose. Not like you two do. It had to be me."

Silence filled the room. Rose was rocking back and forth in the armchair, her body tight with concern. Snitching on a major figure in the gang world meant you would be looking over your shoulder for a long time. Legal justice was swift and underway with Curtis in custody. But for how long? Street justice was much sweeter. Dad knew the consequences of being labeled a snitch, and effectively labeled everyone in the house one by default. Snitches got stitches, and he decided to fall on his own sword for us.

For me.

I loathed his cold demeanor any other time, but today when I stared at him and the growing crow's feet around his eyes and drooping shoulders from years of backbreaking work, it hit me that everything he did was always for me. Love wasn't said, it was shown. He was a single father, trying to raise a woman. He had only ever seen strong Black women, and he decided that was what I needed to be to survive in this world.

"What are we going to do?" I murmured.

Just as fast as it felt like Alonso and I had plans, they were pulled out from under us. Again.

Dad turned to me and for the first time in my entire life, I saw tears in his eyes. "Like I said, I heard you guys talking. Thin walls." He raised his eyebrows and shrugged. "Philadelphia might not be the safest place for you anymore. Go somewhere else and dream. Have big, big dreams. Find better for yourself. Hell, create better for yourself. I'm sorry for holding you back and standing in your way, Josephine. You've done enough watering. It's time to become the garden."

"Excuse me!" Rose jumped up and darted down the hallway. Dad and I locked eyes and my entire twenty-five years with him replayed like a movie in my brain, each moment filled with protection I couldn't see before.

Alonso cupped his hands under his chin and wore a faraway face I only saw when he was thinking about his mother.

When Rose returned, she had a map of the United States tucked under her arms. She rolled it onto the living room table. "Josie, Alonso. After your dad told me about your big move, I bought you this map so you can start tracking all of your upcoming adventures."

"How do you know it'll be an adventure?"

"Didn't Dorothy have adventures when she left Kansas?"

"Yeah, but all she wanted was to go home."

Rose put her hand on her hip and smiled. "True. But she found herself a new home, too."

I glanced at the map. Alonso leaned forward, checking out the color-coded legend.

 He nodded.

Dad nodded and gave a thumbs up.

Rose gave two thumbs up.

No words were needed.

Alonso and I held up our pointer fingers. On the count of three, we squeezed our eyes shut and pointed to a random spot on the map. I felt Alonso's finger close to mine, and when I snapped my eyes open, Alonso and I picked the same place. It had, in one way or another, been inviting us all along.

California love.

CHAPTER 32

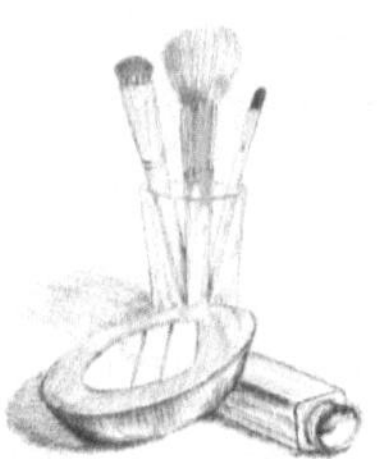

To get something you've never had, you have to do something you've never done.

Alonso's quote board was back on the wall and this one was the best yet.

He was sitting on top of his luggage pressing it down trying to fit another pair of sneakers inside.

"Your bag is going to be overweight on the plane, crazy." I laughed at his reflection in the mirror. I slapped the last lash onto my right eye and I used a handheld fan to dry it in place.

He wiped his forehead. "I can't leave any of my kicks. It would be like leaving your makeup."

"Hardly the same."

"Semantics." He beamed. I saw the doubt hiding behind his smiles and running laps in his thoughts. Still, we moved forward.

"And why are you packing right now anyway? We're not leaving for another week?"

"I don't know," Alonso admitted. "I'm just excited, I guess."

Snapping a few pictures of my makeup, when I turned around, Alonso was staring at our room. I followed his gaze and my eyes fell on our tiny bed. The bars on the windows that tried to protect us from the outside but ended up giving me something else.

False comfortability.

My eyes landed on my princess makeup vanity that had been with me through tears. Confusion. Loneliness. Prayers. And now death. Alonso's shoe boxes lined every inch of the floor to the ceiling in our closet. Clothes baskets were scattered throughout the room, and the hardwood floor sank in the middle from years of a heavy life. It was never big enough and always crowded me and my thoughts. Alonso surveyed the room and put together his own goodbye to a home that he never chose but welcomed. It was there for us when we didn't know any better but now that we did, we were forced to uproot. Grow. It had to be now.

I don't know what would've happened if Drew didn't come to our home. I don't know what would've happened if Dad never overheard us talking that night. Would I be packing up and going to California by myself? Would I even still be going to California? There were a thousand scenarios that could have been, but this is where we were and how it happened. We were almost snitches, running away on that midnight train to Georgia. Except it was a plane to California. And yet, excitement shot through me and begged me to embrace it.

"What are you thinking about?" Alonso slid his arms around my waist and kissed my nose.

"This is it. My entire life has been in this room. We've gone through so much. Right here."

Alonso rested his chin under my head and I heard his heart beating.

"Everything we do from this point on is in the pursuit of our dreams. I don't know what's going to happen, but I know I want to experience it with you. My dream begins and ends with you."

I pulled him in tighter. "Your haircut looks good."

A grin shot to his face. "I watched some YouTube videos. They said the California boys wear it real low."

"Oh, is that right?" I pinched him in the stomach.

A few seconds passed. "This is my first time on a plane," he whispered.

"Me too," I confessed.

"Well, they got hella traffic, so I'm sure there's plenty of cars that need fixing. I know the inside of an engine better than anyone else. Sheitt, I can disassemble one in minutes."

"Yeah, that's exactly how we got into this mess," I joked.

He hit me with a pillow. "Seriously. When we get out there, I'm gonna be on my shit. I have another interview with the youth development team and when I told them I was moving they said that wouldn't be a problem and they had even more leagues on the west coast. I was even thinking about maybe officially going back to school for Automotive Tech or something. And they're crazy about makeup out there, so you're gonna be booked and busy. We can do this. We're gonna make it."

We scoured the internet and searched dozens of pictures before we found a reasonable studio apartment in Los Angeles. We used some of the money from Ms. Marta and paid a hefty deposit for a full six months. We didn't want to have to worry about rent for a while. Alonso had some money saved and we paid the retainer fee for an attorney who confirmed Alonso could leave the state with his pending charges. He felt good about Alonso's case since it was his first offense.

I felt good. Like I could breathe.

"We're gonna make it," I repeated and said a silent prayer for him, us, and Ms. Marta. She had changed me in life and in death. She gave me a head start. Considered me.

We were on our way.

A light knock at the door untangled me and Alonso.

Amna burst through. "Hey, what ya'll doing all hugged up? Nasties."

Alonso chuckled and grabbed some of the laundry baskets." You ladies have fun. I'm going to the laundromat."

"You are late as usual. I already finished my makeup so we can't shoot the video."

Amna sat on my bed and rummaged through her bag. Her hair was cut into a jagged bob and some of the pieces were dyed honey blonde. "I have good news. I was late because I was able to reschedule all of your Philly makeup appointments to one weekend a month. So, you'll have to fly back at least once a month until you build your LA clientele. You'll be bi-coastal for a while. Oh, and I wanted to bring these." Amna pulled a black and white t-shirt from her bag. When I held it up, the weight of what I was about to do hit me in the chest. The long-sleeved t-shirt said, *"Josie's Jawns."*

"You got these?" I sucked in a sharp breath.

"Yeah. I figured for your high-profile clients you can give them a t-shirt and then post it to social media. We can make this like, your logo, or something."

"My logo, huh?" I plopped in front of her and studied the shirt. "I'm going to miss you. My best friend and business manager. Thank you for . . . for . . . waiting. Not leaving when Ms. Marta . . ."

A tear dropped from Amna's face. "I don't always under-stand my emotions. I just feel things and sometimes have to go. Have to follow my heart. I feel it right in my gut and it won't leave me alone until I listen. Your friendship has always been a gut feeling to me, Josephine. And I'm lucky to have a best friend like you. Thank you for showing me I can have it all. I can have great friends and family. I don't have to choose." Amna wiped her face with her sleeve and giggled. "Who thought after it was all said and done, we would be leaving Philly at the same time?"

"I know. You held me up. You loved me to life. Thanks for being my best friend." Tears welled in my eyes. Amna and I went through so much together, and the thought of her so far away was scary.

"Hey, at least we're heading in the same direction. California and Hawaii aren't that far apart. Not like Philly and Hawaii." She shuddered.

"One of the main things I'm going to miss about you is how you inspire me. You challenge me. You say things noncha-lantly—but they're so on point with what I'm thinking or feeling before even I know. I guess that's how sisters do. We know each other better than we know ourselves. You go to Hawaii and let yourself love your family. You waited a long, long, time for them." I hugged the t-shirt to my chest and dabbed at my eyes.

"Sisters." Amna chuckled, and her eyes were red and puffy.

"Me and you have to make time for each other. We have to pick up the phone. Even when we don't feel like talking. Even when things get hard. We have to keep showing up for each other. Deal?"

"Deal." She nodded and held out her pinkie finger.

"Oh . . . and since we're laying down the rules to this friendship. I need to ask you a serious question."

Amna frowned. "What?"

"You've added a lot of value to my business. I'm grateful for your friendship and business savvy. I would like to officially hire you as *Josie's Jawns* business manager. It's a fully virtual position, obviously. You can handle social media, book appointments, and anything else you can think of like this." I palmed the t-shirt. "I don't have a ton of money, but with the help of Ms. Marta, I think we can come up with something decent for a salary."

Amna's face lit up as she processed what I was saying. "Are you sure? You trust me with this?"

"Trust you? Come on, girl. Like I said, we keep showing up for each other. Me and you."

Amna and I embraced. Our wet faces dampened my shirt, and I didn't even care that I just did my makeup. When my phone dinged, I pulled away from Amna.

"Oh shit . . ." I breathed.

"What?"

"Jade and Sapphire. Their page just DM'd me. Says they're going to be in Los Angeles next month and want to book me for an awards show. Says she'll fly me out."

"Does she know that you're moving?"

"No!" I shouted.

"This is huge, Josephine! "It's really meant to be then. She wants to fly you out to a place you were planning on moving to anyway! That's how it goes, girl. When you choose yourself, the universe chooses you, too!"

"The universe?" I chuckled.

"Yea, girl. The universe. I been reading up on some stuff. It's fucking fate!"

Fucking fate.

CHAPTER 33

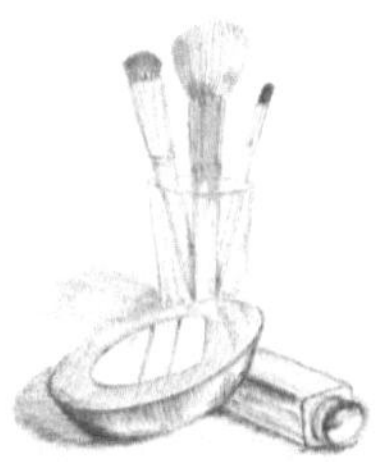

What's it called when you have the munchies, but for a person?

That's how I felt about *him*.

With every quote on the wall, he affirmed me. He handled me. He was patient. He calmed my thoughts and brought them back to stillness.

I sniffed the last of our clean clothes and tucked them away into our suitcases. We didn't even have suitcases when we started our adventure—Rose gave me hers.

When I flipped the inside of the next suitcase open, a few loose-leaf papers fluttered out.

Reading the white lined pages in her silky cursive handwriting, I heard her voice for the first time. It was sweet, low, sultry.

Chicken stock

Butter

Celery, thyme, carrots

Mom's voice was like a hummingbird on its best day.

Her chicken soup recipe.

A connection stronger than any birth or death filled me to

the brim and I didn't want it to escape. The words flowed through me and put me back together. Where there used to be black and white inside of an empty shell now shined with color.

I read through all the ingredients and realized we had everything on the list. It was only a few short hours before we left, and if I started right now . . .

The ancestors themselves compelled me, and minutes later, I stood at the stove for the last time, stirring chicken soup and hearing Mom's voice.

The aroma of the simmering chicken soup wafted through the air, and with it, a few tears fell. Each chop of the knife carried with it memories of times spent in this kitchen, cooking alongside Dad.

"God..." I whispered to myself; the name escaped my lips in hushed prayer. I added a pinch of this, a sprinkle of that and allowed my namesake, Josephine, to be my compass, but it already coursed through my blood. A presence enveloped me as if the ancestors themselves were guiding my hands.

This pot was for the Cannon and it would always bind us.

Rose would be taking care of him now—if he let her. She was a quiet woman. A patient woman. If I stayed in Philly, I would be swallowed up and disillusioned by life and love. These days it was like it wasn't cool to say you wanted to be loved without looking desperate. This was the part of my story where I got the money and the man. And I craved him. I had a taste of motherly love with Ms. Marta, and now even a whiff of fatherly love from Dad. Me and Amna were locked in and that left, Alonso Monty Harold.

I like to call a titan by his full name.

I kind of wanted to cook for him. Kind of wanted to kiss his neck.

He was a man who spoke his love of me out loud. I never had to guess. Never had to wonder. It was always there, ready to protect me.

Who wouldn't crave that?

You ever bought something on Amazon, and when you scroll down the page you hit the *'maybe you'll like this?'* section? He was like that. He anticipated my needs. He learned me in a way that synced his algorithm with mine.

We were going on our biggest adventure yet. Leading an expedition of love, all the way across the country to some foreign land we had only dreamed about on tv. Now that things seemed to be happening at warp's speed, I understood why I had to wait for it.

You're allowed to wake up one day and decide to change who you are. You could dress different, talk different, walk different, act different. You don't have to stay the way people see you or what they have decided is their safe space for you. I learned that the slow way—at a snail's pace. But dammit—I learned it and I was here. And Alonso was right there with me.

None of my fears could go where I was headed. Playing it safe was no longer an option for me. The world was a better place because I was in it, and when I let my strengths lead the way—magic happened.

With Alonso by my side, we would be ready together. I didn't have a nonchalant man. I had one who was obsessed with me, willing to change for me, and that was how I wanted him.

Whatever we built—we would protect. Me and him. Sometimes he was the soft and I was the bite. Sometimes I was the soft and he was the bite. We were straight outta Philly, ready to be transplanted to a new place because of love and fear. Wasn't that what made people act anyway? When staying the same hurt more than changing?

I prayed he made me a better woman. I prayed I made him a better man. I prayed he trusted me with this vision. I prayed I am who I say I am. Who I now believe myself to be. I love me —I love my mistakes. I don't want to be anyone but me. And I don't want to be *her* without Alonso.

I prayed. I prayed for us. I prayed.

"Josie, you almost packed up? Do you have everything? ID's? Medications? Do you take medication for anything? You on that birth control? I guess it's too late to ask those things. Do you need some money for snacks on the plane?" Dad lingered in the living room and nervously shot out questions. "What's all this?" He eyed the pot simmering on the stove.

"Just made you some soup, because I love you. That's all." I zipped up the last suitcase and drug it to the front door. I gazed at the rest of the suitcases by the doors. Our entire new life fit into five suitcases. We bought a full set at Marshall's. Two for him. Two for me. And one filled with makeup.

"Yes, we're all packed up. Yes, I have our ID's. No, I don't take medication for anything. Yes, I take birth control. No, I don't need money for the plane, but if you're offering snack money, I'll take it." I stood in front of him, held out my hand, and chuckled.

He dug into his pockets and pulled out a wad of cash. He peeled me off two twenties and stuffed it into my hands. "You take care of yourself, Josephine Scott. And . . . I love you . . . I love you, too."

I don't remember the last time I did this, but I inched closer to my dad, flung my arms around his bulging waist, and pulled him into a hug.

"Whooahh." He stumbled back, squeezing me into a tight embrace. His back was hot to the touch, and I heard a sniffle.

"Philadelphia is always home, you hear me? This door is always open for you. You go out there and make something of yourself. You go and do it real, real big, Josie." His body shuddered. "And you make sure you eat breakfast. It's the most important meal of the day, you know. If you're gonna be painting up them faces you need your strength." He wiped his eyes and I swear, I swear, I swear I saw a tear.

"I know, Dad. Two scrambled eggs, and two silver dollar pancakes," we said at the same time.

"And don't be putting your hands on Alonso. That boy loves you, but you can't beat no man, Josie."

I wiped my face on his shirt collar. "And you be careful, okay. Be on the lookout for Drew and Curtis and . . . and . . ."

"I'm not worried about them. I did what I had to do and I know how to take care of myself if that time comes. Imma get me one of those *Ring* cameras, put 'em up outside. Watch everything going on around here." He pointed back and forth. "I went to Best Buy and the man was showing it to me. I think it's simple enough, even I could do it." He gave a sheepish smile. "Besides, Rose will help me."

"Dad . . . you do right by Rose. Please. I like her. And I think she really likes me, too," I admitted.

Dad nodded. "She's rooting for you something serious, Thelma and Louise asses."

My hand snapped to my mouth as I muffled back a chuckle.

"Me and Rose been talking about some things, anyway. I'm thinking about letting her make an honest man out of me. Move me out to Jersey and take me away from all this." He rubbed his stomach and gave an embarrassed smile.

I raised an eyebrow. "And what about the other ones?"

He looked around the room. "You see anybody else here? They heard me talk. Now they watch me walk."

We giggled together again, and I couldn't remember ever having a conversation this long with my dad. *He's funny.* I wiped his wet eyes with a napkin sitting on the table.

"I didn't get a chance to tell you the good news." His brown cheeks reddened.

"Good news?"

"Mr. Childress offered me a new position. Plant manager of the conveyor belts."

My eyes flung open in surprise as Dad's mouth fell into a smug grin.

"Cannon, the Cannon, a plant manager?!" My heart swelled with pride. If this made him happy—it was good enough for me.

Dad grinned and then quickly frowned. "Cannon, the Cannon?"

"You take care of yourself, Dad." I grabbed his hands and skirted over his comment.

"And California is open for visits, too, you know."

"I know, Josie. I know."

"Listen. I know you just handed me snack money, but I have something for you, too." I ran back to our now cleared out room, found what I was looking for, and ran back.

I handed my dad a check for $10,000.

"No, I can't take this." Dad shoved it back in my direction.

"Dad, stop. You've done a lot for me. Who else lets their daughter's teenage boyfriend move in? I know things haven't always been easy for us, but I appreciate you. Take it." I shoved it back.

We stared at each other for seconds. I never realized just

how much his face resembled mine. He grabbed my hands and held them to his chest. He took the check and stuffed it into his pocket.

After Alonso and I packed the last of our belongings, I trekked to the drugstore, knowing what I needed to do. The building loomed in front of me like it remembered our last encounter. My bank account was healthy. I walked in with my head high and traipsed down the aisles, placing a few things in my cart without looking at the prices. I needed it all, anyway. I studied social media and made a list of popular colors and palettes. Even though it would be a bitch to transport to California, at least I would be ready to hit the ground running when we got there.

A young, Black girl stood off to the side. She palmed a few eyeshadow pods and reveled at the lipstick shades, just like I did many times in the past when it was still a dream.

"See anything you like?" I asked.

"Everything is so beautiful. I love makeup," she uttered. Her face was beat to the Gods—freckles not covered. I swept her up and down admiring her artistry.

"I love makeup, too. If you ever want to learn how to do some of these looks, hit me up." I balanced the handcart on my forearms and rummaged through my pockets until I found my business card.

"Josie's Jawns," she read. "I'll do that!" She jumped up and down and grinned.

I went to the checkout counter and the woman scanned my items. I whipped out a card and some cash, too. "I'd like to pay for my stuff with my card. But here's a fifty-dollar bill. There's a girl back by the makeup. When I leave, please give her this money and tell her to get whatever she wants."

The girl at the counter beamed. "How nice of you. I will make sure she gets it."

Glancing over my shoulder, it dawned on me this may be my last time here. If it was, I wanted her to have what Ms. Marta had given me.

Hope.

CHAPTER 34

I knelt down and brushed a few leaves away from her head marker. "We're heading out," I said. The warm earth crunched under my feet. Her plot was still settling, and the dirt was squishy. Flowers were trying to bloom for spring, and their buds were perched, ready to peek through any day now.

It looked strange without a headstone, but a beautiful, grand piece would adorn her resting place when it was ready. I would make sure of that.

"I wanted to say thank you. Again. I'll love you forever, Mama Marta." She ministered to me, prayed over me, and simply believed in me. I had friendships, old and young that transcended time. I had people who loved me and would fry fish at 4:00 a.m. when times were hard.

I had love.

A tear slipped down my face, but I wasn't sad. I was hopeful. Open. Honest. Free.

Ready.

Big Josephine. She was the ghost that chased me. She was me. All this time I worried and whimpered about a mom I never met when I should have been making the most of my time with the one I had here. The one who had to have been sent by Big Josephine, to care for her most precious work when she couldn't. And when it was time for me to stand on my own, God took her back. It warmed my heart thinking of Mom and Ms. Marta giggling and cooking with real vanilla somewhere up there.

The black t-shirt I carried warmed my hands, and I placed it down on her marker. Brushing my fingers against my lips, I stood up and headed back to the car, leaving a *Josie's Jawns* t-shirt to keep her warm.

"What did she say?" Alonso asked inside the taxi.

"She said, mind your business, nosey." I shot him eyes and smirked.

Alonso grinned and swatted at my knee.

"To the airport?" the taxi driver asked.

Alonso and I beamed at each other. "To the airport," we said in unison.

Two long streets in both directions filled with people on each side guided our way. The weather was changing and the sun shined high in the sky. People were out like it was a blazing, summer day ripping down 52nd and Market St in the heart of West Philly. I wondered what a Los Angeles summer day looked like. I would experience it soon enough.

One thing was for sure. There would be no more bars in the windows for me or Alonso. No more beds that blocked the windows. My life wasn't a prison—and I wanted nothing in the way that obliterated my sunlight.

That was on everything.

Stopped at a light, my head flung behind me. We passed the

day spa. Karissa was probably in there right now, training a new makeup girl, and making her sign non-compete clause paperwork without really explaining it. The new girl would learn just like I did.

But it wasn't about her or Karissa. It was always about me.

In some ways, I saw myself still as that little girl with the princess bedroom furniture. I waited at the top of the tower for a mom to come and save me.

No one came.

But in the process of making friends with the aloneness, clarity came instead. And she bust me upside the head and rapped to me. And she said, *save yourself. Bet on yourself. Love yourself.*

I wondered what Los Angeles tasted like? Would it be sweet, light, and fun? Or would it be spicy, bold, and thick?

My gut told me it was all of those things. Because I was all of those things. When I kept my mind focused on what I desired, I walked into situations designed to serve me.

We blew through a yellow light and hustled down the street, passing the market. My heart jumped and I swore I could smell fresh vanilla and chocolate-chip cookies from right here in the taxi. The smell punched me in the belly and slammed me back to memories in Ms. Marta's kitchen— cooking, talking, sharing, laughing.

Grief was a process. One I didn't have a map for. But it was always there, daring me to let it go. Just when I thought it had, a smell made me revisit its door.

Like he knew what I was thinking . . . feeling . . . Alonso's fingers brushed against my back. He pulled me into him and kissed my forehead. He saw me. He saw me in ways that consistently proved to me that I hadn't been seen by anyone *but* him. If I could wish one thing, for every girl in the world, it would be to experience a man who would slay a dragon for them *and* bend the knee.

We were gonna make it—him and I.

I wore no makeup today. No foundation. No lashes. Hardly no gloss on these lips. Nada, nothing. Wrapping my arms around his waist, I wanted to just be me. The real me for as long as it was possible. It was a feeling I wanted to experience more of. The more makeup I applied and faces I beat—the realer I became. The new me was new to me.

It was time for a makeover—and it was me all along—making me over.

"We have to still be us. Just you and me. From West Philly," I whispered into his ear.

We passed the school that he used to coach, and his eyes lit up. "We will."

"How do you know?"

"We talked about this. We keep choosing each other. No matter what."

I exhaled under his plans for us.

"I see you all fresh-faced and ready to take on the world." He smirked.

A jab to the gut forced a cough out of him. "Shut up!" I giggled.

Philly did what it did best and we were jostled around and detoured for road construction. The taxi took us the long way around the city to avoid the swells of people, places, and things. I didn't care, I got to see *her*, one last time.

We passed the art museum and Rocky steps. We rode through China Town and got stuck in traffic around the convention center. We had to ride around LOVE Park and City Hall. My city. Our city. We were West Philadelphia—born and raised. Where dreams and nightmares were made.

I inhaled Alonso's neck and closed my eyes. Whatever followed, we would handle—together. We were in search of bigger spoons. That was on my momma. On my hood.

Fortune favors the brave, and I planned to be the bravest.

The End

JOIN THE NAYNATION!

Stay up to date with Janay!

Join her NayNation email list to grab some freebies and never
miss a new release.

Sign up:
https://www.naywrites.com/newsletter-sign-up

DISCUSSION QUESTIONS

1. How would you describe Josie's relationship with her dad?
2. Ms. Marta was both Josie's god-mother and best friend. What do you think she represented to Josie?
3. Josie steals to advance her career. Do you believe this was justified?
4. Josie and Alonso had a toxic relationship. What do you think they meant to each other?
5. Amna was the backbone of Josie's business. Have you ever had someone support you like that?
6. Josie is a skilled makeup artist, but she doesn't recognize her talent right away. When do you think she finally began taking herself seriously?

ABOUT THE AUTHOR

Janay Harden, LCSW, known as "The StoryTelling Therapist," is a millennial mental health therapist. As the CEO of *Restoring Your Destiny Counseling & Consulting* in New Jersey, she brings over a decade of experience working with teens, families, and schools. Her approach blends individual counseling, group therapy, and dynamic mental health workshops.

Janay is also an award-winning author, seamlessly weaving her expertise into fiction books. Her stories explore the complexities of love, friendship, and family, particularly through the lens of melanated characters, inviting readers to engage in thought-provoking journeys of healing and expression.

For more information visit:
www.janayharden.com
www.naywrites.com

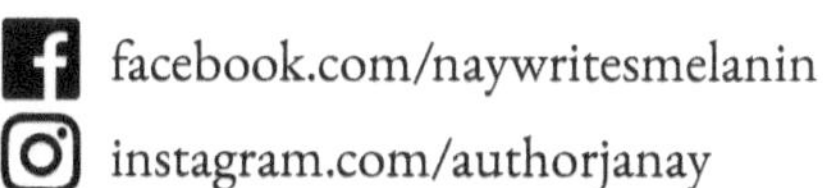

ALSO BY JANAY HARDEN

- Hey, Brown Girl
- Forty-two Minutes (Book 1 of the Indigo Lewis Series)
- Someone More Like Myself (Book 2 of the Indigo Lewis Series)
- Locked In (Book 3 of the Indigo Lewis Series)
- April Showers